UNRAVELED

Also By Claire Olivia Golden

The Books of Feylinn
Unraveled

The Goose Creek Cycle
The Lost Girl of Goose Creek
The Girl in the Northwest Tower

Content Warning

This book contains mental health prejudice,
anxiety, OCD, depression, suicide (off-page),
mention of domestic abuse, and possibly more.

FEYLINN
N
W   E
S
Lenia Mountains
Basil's Tower
Windermere Castle
Northpass
Pearlpond
Aethelney River
Briarwood Forest
The Well

UNRAVELED

CLAIRE OLIVIA GOLDEN

ISBN: 979-8-88785-046-7 (Paperback)
ISBN: 979-8-88785-047-4 (Hardcover)

Library of Congress Control Number: 2025934225

Any references to historical events, real people, or real places are used fictitiously. Names, characters, and places are products of the author's imagination.

Map and chapter art by Audrey Golden.
Cover design by Ivy @BeautifulBookCovers.
Interior book design by Allison Chernutan.
Edited by Carol Kudeviz.

Printed in the United States of America.

Second printing edition 2025.

emily@fracturedmirrorpublishing.com
Fractured Mirror Publishing
Knoxville, Tennessee

www.fracturedmirrorpublishing.com

To Audrey

"Magic is always pushing and drawing
and making things out of nothing.
Everything is made out of magic, leaves
and trees, flowers and birds, badgers and
foxes and squirrels and people. So it must
be all around us."

- Frances Hodgson Burnett,
The Secret Garden

Chapter 1
Auri

"If you think that faeries don't exist, the noise of our world has filled your ears for too long. Magic is everywhere. You just have to listen for it."

- *The Modern Manual of Faeries by Eleanor Bishop*

IT WAS NEARING CLOSING TIME AT YARN EMPORIUM, AND I didn't expect to get any more customers. Usually traffic died down after five o'clock, so I viewed those hours as a chance to wind down, relax, and make myself a cup of herbal tea.

I was sitting behind the counter, completely absorbed in a fantasy novel as thick as the Bible, my feet propped on the lower rungs of the stool I was perched atop, when the door bells jingled. I looked up to see a red-haired lady swaddled in a thick, woolen coat. She walked as if she expected the floor to rise up and eat her, stepping gingerly and looking furtively around. I closed my book to show her that she had my full attention, but she didn't even glance my way.

That was fine. Plenty of people just came in to browse— even if it was a little late. I took a sip from my mug and quickly put the cup down; it was still scalding hot. I glanced at my watch. It was 5:56 PM—I was almost done. Ani, my coworker, left early to pick up her son from school, so that left me to close up the store. I hoped the lady would be gone before then; it was always awkward when I had to politely ask customers to leave.

I casually glanced over to see where she was, but I didn't spot her. An alarm bell went off in my head. Genevieve, the owner and the person who had done my training, demanded that I keep tabs on the customers at all times. "This is a quality establishment," she would say, "and you never know when shoplifters will come."

Picturing Genevieve's displeased face was enough to make me stand up and go in search of the lady.

Yarn Emporium used to be a furniture store, and after it closed down, Genevieve bought it and gave it a complete renovation. With its whitewashed walls, beachy wood floors, and floor-to-ceiling yarns, it was any knitter or crocheter's dream. The day I discovered the shop, it felt like I had stumbled upon a secret oasis. I used to spend hours browsing through the stacks of yarn, striking up conversations with the other shoppers, and befriending the employees. After a while, I was such a fixture in the shop that Genevieve offered me a job. The Yarn Emporium staff felt like family, and I wouldn't disappoint them by letting a shoplifter take off with any precious yarn.

I rounded the corner into our "Projects" section. I had come up with this idea myself about six months ago, and Genevieve had implemented it almost immediately.

Customers could bring their half-finished projects, with the pattern and enough yarn to finish them, and leave them on a table. They were free for anyone who wanted them. At first, people were a little doubtful about its success, but it actually made the local newspaper and we'd been getting more business ever since. I had found some projects from there myself, including the ugliest Christmas sweater known to humankind, which I planned to give to my brother for his birthday this December.

The red-haired lady was taking something out of her bag and examining it. From this angle, I couldn't quite see what it was.

"Excuse me," I said, "can I help you with anything?"

She whipped around, clutching the item to her chest. A ball of pink yarn dropped to the floor and rolled under the table. With a start of recognition, I realized I knew her: she was one of our regulars and a student at the weekly crochet class I taught. *Eleanor*, I thought, but I couldn't remember her last name. She always came in with her granddaughter, who was around my age. But Eleanor showed no sign of wanting to make friendly conversation. She looked like a woman on a mission with the firm press of her lips in a line. And I had interrupted her doing…whatever it was she was doing.

"Sorry to startle you," I said, wondering at her odd behavior. I bent down to retrieve the ball of yarn, but Eleanor crouched and scooped it up before I could touch it. *Okay then.* I stood up, bumping my head on the underside of the table.

"I see you've found our Projects section," I remarked, trying to prompt her into talking.

She nodded and began searching through the pile of projects, knocking a sweater, a scarf, and a stuffed owl to the ground. I discreetly picked them up, unsure if she would object, but she ignored me as I replaced them on the table.

"Um." *Was there protocol for a situation like this?* "May I help you with anything?"

She met my eyes. "Yes, I believe so."

I nervously tucked a strand of hair behind my ear, although it was too short to stay contained there and immediately popped out to tickle my cheek again. She continued, "I want to donate a project."

Now we were getting somewhere. "Great!" I said. "Is it this pink thing?" A bit of lace poked out from under the woman's arms.

"Yes," she said, holding it up for me to see. It looked like a shawl, and my brain instantly started analyzing how it was made, like it did whenever I spotted handmade goods. It was a traditional triangle shawl with a lacy stitch pattern, made from the top down. With triangle shawls that started from the bottom up, you could stop whenever you declared it was the right size, but from the top down you had to keep going until it was finished unless you wanted a trapezoid instead of a triangle. I didn't make many shawls myself, but this one was exquisite. The picture on the pattern package showed a stitch pattern of clusters twining their way along the fabric and a lacy flower fringe along the sides. It looked like a field of flowers.

"It's beautiful!" I gently brushed the lace with my hand. "So to donate, you just have to leave it on this table, and someone will come and pick it up if they want it."

"I don't have to pay?"

"No." I folded the wrap and set it on the table, a ball of yarn trailing behind it. "You have the pattern here and we need the rest of the yarn."

"I have it right here." She produced a transparent plastic bag through which I could see a couple more balls of that pink yarn.

I took it from her. "Okay, excellent. Can I add your name to our Project Donor Hall of Fame?" Genevieve said people would be more likely to donate things if they got some credit for it, so we had a bulletin board above the project table. So far it had about fifty names, including my own, hidden away in the corner: Auri Davis. True to form, people were happier to give away projects when they discovered they would receive some recognition.

"No." Eleanor backed away and quickly made a break for the door. I followed her and got to the door first, blocking her path.

"That's okay, I won't put your name down," I said, "but can you tell me why you seem so distressed?" Genevieve would chew me out if she knew I was interrogating customers, but I had to ask.

"The shawl," said Eleanor. "It's the shawl." She looked past me, not seeming aware of her surroundings. "It's taking over my life. I can't get it out of my head—I need to get rid of it." Her eyes cleared and focused on my face. "I'm sorry, what am I saying?"

"Just talking about the shawl," I said, uneasy.

"Yes, the shawl. Well, I hope it finds a happy home."

I gave her the obligatory donation receipt, writing the date at the top. After she took it in her trembling fingers, she pushed me out of the way and made a beeline for the door, the bells jingling as she left.

I stared after her for a couple minutes, but then I snapped out of my trance. My watch said 6:05 PM so I flipped the sign to "Closed" and started locking up the store. But as I tidied the shelves and swept yarn scraps into the dustpan, I couldn't shake the thought that whatever Eleanor was up to would lead to more trouble than good.

Chapter 2
Cat

"Faeries are in tune with the natural world in a way that humans no longer are. When the moon is at its fullest, magic is thick in the air because change is taking place. If you pay attention to nature, you are bound to encounter the fae."

- The Modern Manual of Faeries by Eleanor Bishop

GRANDMA ARRIVED AT THE CAFÉ OUT OF BREATH, LIKE THE time we ran a mother-daughter 5K together and both ended up having an asthma attack. I sat up straighter in the booth where I was waiting and waved to get her attention.

Her eyes lit up when she saw me, and she waved back. She was dressed in the kind of apparel that only a grandmother can pull off: a T-shirt with crocheted straps and lace around the hem, a purple skirt that descended to her calves, and a felted handbag that was practically big enough to contain everything she owned. I smiled a little as she made her way across the crowded café, weaving her way in between tables, chairs, and customers snacking on pastries.

"Hi, sweetie," she said.

"Hey, Grandma."

She slid into the booth across from me, setting her purse down on the table with a loud clank.

She took a sip of water, ice cubes clinking against the side of the glass as she set it down. I observed. She looked pale—paler than the usual porcelain doll complexion that she and I shared—and had circles under her eyes that made me wonder how much sleep she'd been getting. Knowing Grandma, though, she would just brush off any concerns about her health.

"Did you find the restaurant okay?" I asked her.

"Oh, just fine," she said. "Very quaint. I like it."

I had been to this restaurant with a girl I liked a few months back, and although we broke up a few weeks later, the restaurant stuck in my mind. I had been here for many a cup of coffee since, enjoying perching at one of the tables by the window to people-watch. What set it apart was how the walls were plastered in maps—maps of America, maps of the world, maps that looked like they had been torn from an atlas and schlepped halfway around the globe. It made me want to leave this tiny village and have an adventure.

"Is this an okay birthday lunch?" I asked.

Grandma, busy arranging the silverware on her napkin, looked at me. "It's wonderful, Cat."

I smiled. The waitress appeared to take our orders. Grandma made sure to order extra butter on my waffle, just the way I liked it. She had been ordering for me ever since

I came to live with her at the ripe old age of eight, and nine years later I saw no reason to change our tradition, especially since ordering at restaurants made me nervous.

I relaxed when she left, leaving me and Grandma to wait for our food. Then I froze as Grandma asked, "How did you find this place?"

It was about twenty minutes' drive from home, not the kind of place I'd be likely to stumble across by accident. Grandma had no idea I had asked Angeline Maple out on a date, and I had no intention of letting her know. "A friend brought me here." Not exactly a lie. Angeline *had* been a friend—a friend I ended up kissing.

"Meg?" Grandma moved her fork a smidgen to the left to make it equal with the others. I was glad she was fidgeting because it meant she couldn't watch *me* fidgeting.

"Uh, I don't remember," I said, and hoped she would leave it at that.

Inspiration hit me, and I drained the rest of my lemonade and slid out from the booth under the guise of getting a refill. I hated lying to my grandma, but I didn't know how she would react. I'd always known I liked girls and only girls, and when I moved in with Grandma, I promised myself I would tell her when I turned sixteen. But over a year after I had reached that landmark, I still wasn't ready to tell her. She would probably be accepting, but as usual, the doubt lingered in my mind. My brain was always making me doubt things, even the love of my grandmother.

There would be time to tell her. I didn't have to do it right now. Certainly not today, because I wanted to make her birthday about *her*, not me.

Our lunch was waiting when I returned to the table, and I dug into my waffle with relief. Grandma had ordered French toast. "How does it rank?" I asked. She was on a mission to find the best French toast in all of Washington state, and I was helping her make an Excel spreadsheet to document her findings.

"I'd say a solid six," she said with her mouth full. I cringed.

"We can add it to the list," I said, spreading more butter atop my waffle.

"I got an email from a publisher this morning," said Grandma. My mouth was full of waffle so all I could do was raise my eyebrows to say, *go on.* "They want to turn my blog into a book and publish it."

"Holy shit," I said around the waffle. "That's amazing!"

"Don't swear with your mouth full," she chided. "My goodness, Cat."

"That's so great!" I said once I had finished chewing. "This is your first book, right? You've just had academic articles before?"

"Aside from my thesis, yes, this is my first book. You're sweet."

She meant her thesis from grad school, where she had studied faeries, or the Fae. I knew it sounded weird to most people but she researched it just like you would research anything else, and throughout her life, she'd gone on various expeditions to sites where the Fae had been spotted. She dealt in the mythical and was lonely sometimes because she didn't have anybody to talk to about it.

We ate in mostly silence. Neither Grandma nor I were the best conversationalist, which was just fine with me, since awkward silences were my specialty. But it was never awkward sitting in silence with Grandma. Just being near her was enough. She got me in a way nobody else ever had and didn't feel the need to fill a silence with empty chatter. I did have a question for her, though. "Where did you go this morning, anyway?"

Grandma took another bite of her French toast, in no hurry to answer.

"Just running errands."

"What sort of errands?" I asked. It was odd for Grandma to leave the house more than necessary because it made her nervous. Her anxiety had been passed down to me, which she often felt guilty about, but it wasn't like she had tried to give me a debilitating mental illness. Genetics are a bitch sometimes.

Grandma dipped a bite of French toast in the maple syrup. "Just errands."

Surprised, I asked, "Really? What errands?" She volunteered sometimes at the local community center, but that was on the weekend. The only other place she liked to go was Yarn Emporium, and we usually went together, since we were taking a crochet class.

I'll admit that I didn't have much interest in crochet

because I was never really into crafting, but I liked spending time with Grandma…and maybe the ridiculously-adorable teacher, a girl around my age, had something to do with my interest in the lessons. Not that Grandma knew *that*.

"Nothing in particular," she said. "Just some business." She fidgeted with the edge of her plate, not meeting my eyes.

"Are you okay?" I asked. I didn't want to probe; it was wonderful that she was running errands on her own, but I couldn't help but wonder what was up.

She looped her arm through her handbag. "I wouldn't say no to a little nap," she said. Her complexion had, if anything, gotten paler.

"Okay," I said, uncertain of how to proceed. I had taken the bus to the restaurant and was driving home with Grandma. Would she be okay to drive home? It wasn't like she was drunk or anything, but she was clearly out of sorts. Sometimes people got into crashes when they were too emotional to be driving, and my brain seized on this thought and began spinning it around like a hamster on a wheel. What if we got into a crash and it was my fault because I hadn't stopped her? *Take it easy, Cat.* But I couldn't take it easy. I'd never been able to. My brain, once it got started on something, could keep worrying at it for eternity.

I paid the bill and left a tip and guided Grandma out the door, my anxiety kicking up a few levels. What had I done, or what had happened, to make her like this?

As we walked to the car, which was parked just down the block, I picked at the hem of my white linen blouse.

Usually Grandma could tell when I was getting stuck in an obsessive spiral. She was always there to put an arm around me and squeeze me back into reality. She didn't have to say anything because her mere presence was comforting. But right now, it was like she was the one in the obsessive spiral. I'd never seen her like this; it was like she wasn't even there. Her spirit was somewhere else while her body walked through town with me. I pulled at a loose thread on my blouse, which snagged the whole thing, and now there was a random white thread hanging out. Great, I'd gone and wrecked it.

I reached for the amulet around my neck—a glass bottle filled with dried rowan berries, rosemary, marigold, and a few daisy petals—worrying the chain between my fingers. Grandma had given it to me when I had first moved in with her in an attempt to make me feel safer, and I had never taken it off. Usually me fidgeting with it was a cue for her to put an arm around me, but she didn't even notice.

"Grandma," I said quietly, my voice coming out weird.

She didn't even respond.

I said her name again, louder, and then tugged at her arm. She whirled to face me, and it took a moment for her eyes to focus on my face. "What's going on with you?" I asked.

"I'm just fine, sweetie," she said.

"You've been kind of spacey. Are you feeling okay?"

"I'm just having an off day. We all have them."

True, but something about this just seemed…strange. "Is something going on?"

"I want to get home and take a nap. I've got a headache coming on."

"I'll make you some tea." Grandma swore by herbal remedies, and they always made me feel better, or maybe it was just the love she put into them. "You want to watch a movie or something?"

"I just want to be left alone."

She didn't usually snap at me like this. It stung. "Okay. I'm sorry." I was just trying to help, but if space was what she needed, I could give it to her.

We had reached the car, and Grandma unlocked it and climbed into the driver's seat without another word. I slid into the seat beside her, fastened my seat belt, and tried not to worry about her the whole way home. Which, of course, never worked. The more you try not to worry about something, the more it sticks in your head. My life was a cycle of trying to chase worries away, but they always came back.

Chapter 3
Auri

"Several herbs that are particularly effective in protecting against magic are St. John's Wort, rue, rosemary, sage, rowan, and clover. If you can find a four-leaf clover, you will be extra secure."

- The Modern Manual of Faeries by Eleanor Bishop

Aidyn called while I was still at work.

"Oh dear," said the customer I was helping, a Black woman in her thirties with a small child strapped to her front. "Do you need to take that?"

"No worries," I said. "Sorry about that. Whoever it is can wait." I smiled at the kid she was holding, who was the spitting image of his mom. I was in the process of winding a hank of yarn into a ball, because if you tried to work directly from the hank you would end up in yarn tangle hell, a place I had been all too many times. I undid the yarn tying the hank together and draped it over the umbrella swift, which was a contraption that—true to its name—expanded into an umbrella-like shape to gently cradle the yarn in a large ring. Then I fed the end into the ball winder and started turning the crank.

The child watched me with complete fascination. "Do you like this?" I asked him with a smile.

"He's enthralled," said his mom with a laugh.

"Just like I was the first time I saw this thing." I exchanged a conspiratorial smile with the kid. "It makes my job so much easier."

"Honestly, I need to get one of those. I spend so much time rolling yarn into balls."

The swift spun around and around with the occasional squeak as I wound the yarn into a ball. "We sell these here, actually. They're $50, but I use mine so much. If you ever decide to invest." Before I got one, I had improvised by draping the yarn over the back of a chair or forcing my brother Aidyn to hold it around his forearms. Although he was very obliging, he was definitely glad to be released from his yarn-winding duties.

"Well, Caleb seems to be fascinated by it, so I better give it a whirl." She adjusted Caleb on her hip and he turned his head around to keep looking at the ball winder. "I've spent enough money on yarn today, I may as well keep it going."

It was true that Yarn Emporium was not a cheap store. If I didn't get an employee discount, there was no way in hell I'd be able to shop here. "Let me get that set up for you!" There were still three more skeins to wind. "If you want, you can go get a coffee or something and I'll have these wound when you get back."

She hesitated. "Really?"

"Yeah. It's no problem. Go relax." I waved at Caleb, who stared at me with mouth agape. His mom headed out gratefully to go get some caffeine from the coffee shop down the street, which left me a good twenty minutes to wind the skeins and listen to Aidyn's call.

He had left a voicemail, and true to form, it was short and sweet. "I need your advice. Call me." Click.

I dialed his number. He picked up on the third ring. "Aidyn."

"Auri. You didn't pick up."

"I was working. What are you up to that requires you to call me in the middle of my shift?" I was only fake-annoyed.

"I told you, I need your advice."

The first ball of yarn was almost all the way rolled, so I turned the crank the last few times and pulled the ball off the winder. "What do you need?"

"How do you ask someone out on a date?"

I dropped the ball of yarn. "Are you dating?'

"I'm asking the questions here."

The ball of yarn had rolled under the shelves across the store, leaving a long tail of yarn for me to tidy. "Um, I think this is my business. My little baby brother, asking someone out on a date?"

"I am fourteen years old."

"You're a baby. You don't need to be dating."

"You went on a date when you were fourteen."

"I was fifteen. Aidyn! Who are you asking out?"

I could pretty much hear him rolling his eyes. "Would it

surprise you that much to hear that somebody asked *me* out and not the other way around?"

"Well they must be delusional," I teased.

"Clearly. But I have received an invitation to go to the movies, and I'm not sure if that counts as a date or not."

"No, I'm not surprised," I said. "You're decent enough, I guess. Who asked you?"

"A kid in my class." School had just let out last month. Maybe the kid had waited to gather up courage. But someone asking my brother out? Disturbing, from an older-sister perspective. "Texted me this morning."

"Oh, she has your number?"

"He."

"Sorry. When did he get your number?"

"I gave it to him."

Right. "Is he your friend? What's his name?"

"Is this the Inquisition?"

"You asked me for advice. I have to know some backstory." I squeezed the phone between my ear and shoulder and got to work on the second hank of yarn, this one a beautiful shade of magenta. "Do you like him? Is he your friend?"

"Yes, he's my friend. Otherwise I wouldn't have given him my number. Auri, pay attention."

Now it was my turn to roll my eyes. "Well, what's his name?"

"Alejandro."

"So you're friends. But going to see a movie? I dunno, that could be a date. It depends." When Loren from Yarn

Emporium had asked me out for coffee, I had a hard time figuring out if it was a date or not. "There isn't really a rulebook. Not even for straight people."

"Alejandro is gay. I know that much."

"Okay. Does he know you're not gay, though?"

"I thought you knew I was gay."

Wait, what? "You're gay?"

"Did you not work that out on your own?"

My brother had never been on a date or showed any interest in boys before. But…he had never showed any interest in girls, either. I guess I had just assumed that he was straight…which, now that I thought about it, was a dumb assumption to make. "I had no idea. Was it supposed to be obvious?"

"Mom knew without me telling her. I thought you did, too."

"I thought that 'gaydar' was a myth."

"I mean, it's not like you can *always* tell whether or not someone is gay, but sometimes you can get a pretty good idea. God, Auri, I knew you were spacey, but I didn't think you were *this* oblivious."

"Ouch."

"I'm kidding. Sort of. I really thought you knew."

"I mean, it doesn't matter to me. You know that. I'll love you no matter what."

He made a gagging noise on the other end of the phone. "Spare me the sentiments, please. I know you love me. Now show me you love me by giving me advice."

Aidyn had just come out to me, kind of by accident, and now he was asking me for advice on how to go on a date with a boy. "Uh, I've only done straight dating. I don't know how the social cues change when you're the same gender."

"Yeah, that's fair. But I haven't told anybody at school, so you're the only person I can ask."

"I'm sorry, Aidyn. Of course I want to help." I thought for a minute, yarn winder paused. "Uh, do you like him back? I don't want to pry, but you have to know going into the date so you don't hurt his feelings."

"I don't know, though. I know I like him as a friend. But…"

"That's okay. Just be prepared if he tries to hold your hand or something, that's all."

"Oh God." He sounded equal parts terrified and elated.

"My baby brother, about to go on his first date. I'm so proud."

"Stop it. Do I buy the tickets or does he?"

"Why don't you offer to buy the snacks if he buys the tickets?"

"That's reasonable. Okay. I'm going to text him back."

"Good luck, Aidyn. Uh, congrats, I guess. On getting asked out."

"Say hi to Loren for me." The line clicked off.

Of course he would tease me about Loren, who came to dinner once at our house for a painfully awkward meal. He had been cute and nice and everything, but there just weren't sparks between us, and both of us had ended up deciding to call it off. It had ended amicably enough that we could still work at Yarn Emporium together, though. I hoped Aidyn would have the same kind of luck.

What kind of sister didn't notice that her brother was gay? Was I really that dense when it came to relationships? I rolled the last two skeins while I was mulling this over and had them ready when the customer came back in. But my mind was far, far away, thinking about Aidyn and then darting back to that crochet shawl. I was going to tell him about it but his question was much more pressing. I could tell him about it later. First, I would try crocheting it.

These past two days had been quite the strange ones. I couldn't shake the feeling that it was going to keep getting weirder.

Chapter 4
Cat

"Never make a deal with a faerie that you aren't prepared to keep. They will always, always find a way to collect."
- *The Modern Manual of Faeries by Eleanor Bishop*

GRANDMA WAS SITTING AT HER COMPUTER BUSILY TYPING when I got home that evening from my four-hour shift at Freeze. I put the carton of strawberry-mango frozen yogurt that I'd taken home from work into the freezer (Grandma and I loved those employee perks). Then I went to check on her.

I didn't want to interrupt her while she was working on her book, but I was also worried about her, so I kind of just hovered in the doorway. When she really got writing, it took a lot to disturb her, so I wasn't surprised when she didn't notice me for a couple of minutes.

I gazed around her office while I waited. Our house was small, but Grandma and I had transformed it over the years we'd lived here into our own little haven. Spells hung everywhere—rowan berries woven into rugs, vials of salt hanging from the windows, horseshoes upside-down above every door.

Such was life when your grandmother was a faerie expert.

You can call me naïve for believing in it, but you can't grow up hearing what I did and not believe, not really. Not when you've read all the studies that your grandmother has written and been to so many of her talks that you could pretty much recite them yourself. I was probably the most knowledgeable seventeen-year-old girl in the area when it came to faeries and magic lore. After a while, it just becomes second nature to you. I guess it's like being raised in a religion, in a way. You believe what you're used to.

And it helps that I'd had my own encounter with a faerie a few years after I moved in with her. Seeing is believing, they say. If you saw what I saw, you would believe, too.

I shifted my weight, and a floorboard creaked. My shoulder hit the door, which jostled the string of bells hanging from the molding. The jingle of bells alerted Grandma to my presence, and she spun around on her rickety wooden stool.

"What's up, Cat?" she asked. It always took her a minute to pull away from her writing when she was particularly entrenched. Sure enough, her eyes were unfocused and she was clearly still buried in her work.

"Sorry to interrupt you," I said. "I just wondered if you were ready to do our ritual or if you wanted to do it later."

"What time is it?" We both looked to the clock on the wall, framed with holly branches. "How did it get so late? Yes, honey. I'm coming in just a moment."

I didn't move. Grandma did lose track of time sometimes when she got really into something, but she also didn't forget rituals. It was the full moon tonight and we always did something. It was important, she said, to honor the passing of time and the fluctuations of the planets and their moons. Faeries did this because they were in tune with nature in a way that most humans weren't, and it was one of the ways in which we were most different from them.

"How is your writing going?" I asked.

"Well enough." She turned back to her computer. "I'm doing some research that I need to finish up. So I'll meet you in the backyard in a few minutes."

It was clearly a dismissal.

"Okay," I said, hovering for a minute in case she changed her mind, but she started typing again almost immediately. Trying not to be offended, I padded down the hallway in my fuzzy socks. Grandma often let me hang out in her office while she was writing because she knew I was interested in this stuff, and we both liked the company. What was she researching that was so riveting? Did it have anything to do with why she was so distracted at lunch?

I could at least get the materials ready for the ritual. With a creak of the door hinges I opened the closet at the end of the hall. Nestled inside were our magic supplies as well as less interesting things like a broom and vacuum cleaner. I pulled out a mortar and pestle made of oak and gave them a quick wipe with a cloth to make sure there was no dust, then I stuffed a small container of salt into the pocket of my gray-and-white cardigan, which Grandma had knitted for me specially so that it would have big pockets to hold my stuff.

Heading outside, I realized it was darker than I had thought even though it was only 8:00 PM. We would have to move quickly to complete this before the moon rose, and again, I wondered what was up with Grandma for this to escape her notice. We picked all of our herbs fresh for our spells so I went into the garden to pick the necessary supplies. A pinch of rosemary (and a bit for me to suck on while I worked), a dash of salt from the container in my pocket, some sage, and a bit of mint to make it smell fresh.

I returned to the edge of the yard to mix all of this together, sitting on the wooden swing we'd hung from a tree branch. The leaves around me rustled while I mashed everything together with the pestle, enjoying the gentle sound of wood scraping against wood. The smell of mint relaxed me and I lost myself in the rhythm of the work and the feel of the swing beneath me.

Grandma didn't come out while I mixed the ingredients together. I took longer than usual on purpose because I wanted to give her ample opportunity, but she still didn't show up even when I made a ring of crystal quartz and sprinkled the herb mixture inside. The moon was high in the sky and it was time to start the ritual. I jogged inside to find her still typing away on her computer, looking more frazzled than ever. "Grandma?"

She whirled around. "I told you I would be out in a minute."

"It's been…fifteen minutes."

"Cat, this is important! Leave me be."

She never snapped at me like this. I blinked back the tears that sprang to my eyes. "What are you working on that can't be interrupted for our ritual?"

"I'm researching. It's important. Just leave me alone, go do the ritual yourself, I've shown you how enough times."

My lip trembled. What was up with her? I turned and left without another word. Of course I could perform the ritual by myself, but I wanted to do it with her. And if she wasn't here, she couldn't get the healing properties of the spell.

I stepped into the center of the ring and grounded myself, focusing on the moonlight that shone down upon me. Some people had the Sight, which meant they could see beyond. But faeries were visible to everyone if you kept your eyes open. The Sight just meant you had a little bit of magic yourself. Neither Grandma nor I possessed it, but we could still communicate with the Fae if we chose to. I lifted my hands to the sky to invite the moonlight to enter my spirit.

At first I had felt ridiculous doing stuff like this, but it all changed on my thirteenth birthday, when I saw a faerie in our very own backyard. I was taking our daily offering of a bowl of milk and piece of bread into the yard when I saw it, not ten yards from where I was standing now: a tiny being that looked like a cross between a troll and a garden gnome. It had furry feet, but it didn't look like a Hobbit; it was too short and squat. When it saw me looking at it, it froze in place, but I crouched gently and extended a hand to it. I set down the milk and scuttled backward, sitting and watching.

The creature remained frozen for several minutes until it

saw that I didn't mean any harm. From my knowledge of the Fae, which was pretty small at that point, I figured it had to be a brownie. They were creatures that lived in the human world and faerie world alike, and they helped humans with household chores sometimes if you left out food for them. Grandma didn't leave out food for that reason, she just did it to show her respect. "They just want to be noticed" was how she had explained it to me. "Everyone, deep down, wants someone to see them." Leaving out food for the brownies was our way of doing that.

Eventually, the one in front of me darted forward to pick up the piece of bread and then it vanished into the undergrowth. I didn't follow it; I ran inside and told Grandma what had just happened. And then I spent the rest of the day poring over her blog that detailed her encounters with the Fae.

So I knew that this yard had some magic in it, and it was that magic that I summoned that night. Throughout the ritual, I kept hoping that Grandma would come out to join me, but she never did.

And I didn't ask her anything more that night.

After I finished, I gathered the supplies, returned them to the closet, and then went to my room to read a book. Grandma was still in her office, typing, typing away.

Chapter 5
Auri

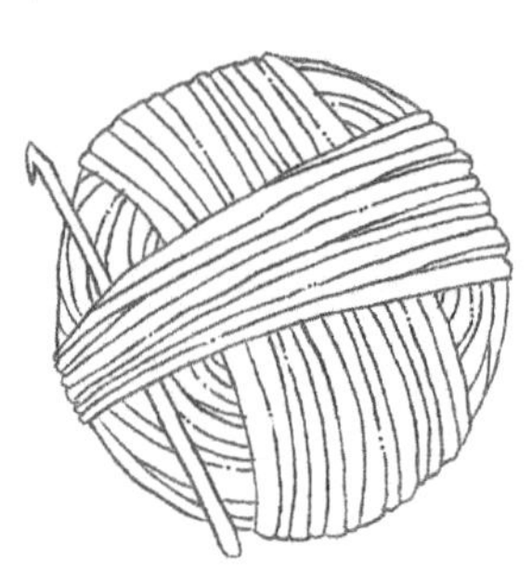

"Never give your name to a faerie unless you are prepared to give away your identity. Faeries have different ways of naming than we do, and if they know your full name, they have power over you. Nicknames are your friend."
- *The Modern Manual of Faeries by Eleanor Bishop*

I WOKE TO THE SOUND OF FROGS CROAKING AND CRICKETS chirping and lay there for a minute in confusion. I definitely hadn't been transported to the rainforest during the night. Then I realized it was my phone, ringing loudly enough to wake someone from a hundred-year sleep.

I reached for it, but my hand connected with nothing except the book I'd left on my bedside table. Nor was my phone charging in its outlet. I scrambled out of bed and embarked on a frantic search to find the sound of the rainforest, which eventually led me to the laundry basket. Evidently I had forgotten to remove my phone from the pocket of my jeans.

The caller ID displayed a picture of Genevieve Hafrey, modeling a crocheted sunhat she had made last summer with a huge smile on her face. *Wonderful.* I liked her a lot, but nobody wanted to talk to their boss first thing in the morning.

I touched the button and put the phone to my ear. "Hello?" I said, hoping I didn't sound too groggy.

"Auri!" exclaimed Genevieve. "Look, I'm sorry to wake you so early, but I need you to open today." I glanced at the clock. It was half-past seven, which left me barely any time to make myself look presentable and walk to Yarn Emporium, which opened at eight.

"It's my day off," I said.

Genevieve was quiet for a minute. "Loren ran into some bad traffic," she said. "Something's going on in his neighborhood. Lots of emergency vehicles, he said, blocking his driveway. He's not going to be able to make it on time…I don't want us to open late."

I sighed. It was true that it wouldn't be good for Yarn Emporium to open late on a Saturday, since it was our busiest day. We had a lot of classes today, including an introduction to weaving class that started at ten, and people tended to show up early to chat beforehand. I myself taught the crochet class at seven o'clock tonight. I understood; that didn't mean I wanted to get out of bed. The problem with working for an indie store was that sometimes you did have to fill in on short notice.

"Right. No, that's fine," I said, mourning my lack of sleep. I wouldn't have stayed up until one in the morning reading that fantasy novel if I knew I'd be waking up five hours later. "I'll be there in half an hour."

"Thanks, Auri," said Genevieve, her relief palpable. "I appreciate it."

"No problem."

I hung up and flopped back onto my bed, wanting to curl up and go back to sleep. Instead I got up, dressed, and took the thirty-minute walk to the village that housed Yarn Emporium. It was a slightly foggy day, and I shivered a little in my handmade sweater, cursing myself for not wearing a coat. Although I was tired, I liked the feeling of being awake before everyone else, like the rest of the world was frozen in time. Mornings felt full of possibility—that is, once I managed to drag myself out of bed.

I unlocked the door and stepped inside, half expecting Eleanor to pop out at me. The shop was deserted, and my footsteps echoed through the empty room as I went to turn on the lights. I flipped the sign to "Open" and set about organizing some yarn that had fallen off the shelves. Ani and I sometimes joked about yarn goblins emerging in the night just to make a mess for us to clean up in the morning.

Wandering into the back room, a flash of pink caught my eye. It was the project left by Eleanor. I picked it up, feeling the lightweight, shiny thread. It shimmered like it was from another realm, like there were little flecks of fairy dust woven into the fiber.

I picked up the bag and carried it to the front desk, where I sat down to await customers. In the meantime, I opened the bag and pulled out a huge skein of coral pink thread, a folded piece of paper, a small notebook, and a crochet hook so small that it looked more like a needle. Thinking this might be a nice way to occupy myself, I unfolded the piece of paper.

It was a crochet pattern, as I'd guessed, for the "Briars and Roses Shawl." I read it through. It was rated Advanced, and I could see that it would take a while to complete with the small hook and thread. I had never seen anything quite like the material before, not even the silk thread Genevieve had special-ordered from Japan last year that cost an arm, a leg, and your firstborn child. The otherworldly quality of the thread captivated me, and I immediately wanted to try crocheting with it.

Why not? I needed a new crochet project, having just finished a sweater I had made for the shop. It was good for business when customers saw the employees knitting or crocheting and often acted as an excellent conversation starter. Me choosing something from the Projects setup was probably the best thing I could do with myself. It was also the only way I could afford the yarn.

I studied the shawl. A quick row count revealed that Eleanor had stopped at Row 17; she hadn't gotten very far before giving up. I wondered why. I picked up the shawl and started crocheting—chain two, turn, double crochet—and then my hands went completely numb.

The shawl slid out of my grip and plummeted to the floor. I shook my hands, trying to wake them up. When that failed, I put them under my legs for a few minutes, and when I pulled them out they had regained feeling. They had probably just fallen asleep, but an uneasy feeling crept up on me. I suddenly felt rather ill, like the granola bar I'd scarfed down for breakfast on the walk here wasn't sitting quite right.

I put the shawl down, fingers still tingling.

Then I did what everybody does when they have weird medical symptoms: I opened up Google and started typing keywords.

weird tingling in fingertips
why are my fingers tingling
why do limbs fall asleep
how to wake up asleep limbs
numbness in fingers
signs of a stroke
signs of a heart attack

That wouldn't cause any concern if Genevieve checked the computer history. Definitely not. All of my searching revealed that a tingling left arm was a sign of a stroke. But I wasn't at risk for something like that; I was only sixteen and pretty healthy. I didn't even have seasonal allergies like most people I knew; flower pollen didn't bother me at all, even when it made other people's noses clog up and made them sound like a frog. Plus, both of my hands were tingling, not just the left one. So I closed the tab for "5 Warning Signs of a Stroke" and read a little bit about heart attacks before deciding I wasn't having one of those either.

The sensation was bizarre. My feet fell asleep all the time when I sat in a chair in a weird position. I knew what that felt like; it was like pins and needles in your foot and it hurt to walk for a few minutes until the sensation came back. But this feeling…it was more like my hands were disconnected from my body. Like when you wake up and you're in the dreamy land between sleep and waking, that split second when you're half-asleep and half-awake and you don't have control over your limbs quite yet. Or like when you get a cavity filled at the dentist and they pump you full of laughing gas and it feels like your body doesn't quite belong to you. My fingers were tingling, but in an uncanny, far-off way, like they weren't totally under my command anymore.

It had felt like something was taking control of my body… like someone was *making* me crochet.

And it wasn't like I had to be forced to crochet, either. I practically had to be forced to *stop*. A few years back, I crocheted twenty granny squares in one day and couldn't move my elbow for the next few days, and Aidyn threatened to tie my wrists together so I wouldn't be able to keep crocheting even though I was injured. Nobody ever had to force me to crochet. So why did I feel this way?

I hesitated, then picked up the shawl once more. If it happened again, then I would know there was a problem. Probably I was just overtired because I was up too late last night and had to get up early this morning. It was normal to feel kind of out of it when you were tired.

It was dumb to get worked up over a crochet project like this. What would Aidyn say?

With the thought of my brother's mockery in mind, I wrapped the yarn around the hook and pushed it through the next stitch. Pulled the yarn through. Wrapped the yarn around the hook again, pulled it through two loops…and the tingling shot through my hands again, stronger than before.

"Shit," I exclaimed.

I tried to keep crocheting, but it was hard when you couldn't properly move your fingers. It was like I was looking at them underwater, my vision distorted, and what would usually be easy stitches were twice as hard. And this shawl wasn't made of easy stitches, either; it was made primarily of bullion stitches, which were enough to make any crocheter shudder, mixed with complex clusters that formed a larger rose pattern over the finished shawl. As far as I could tell, anyway. Barely any of it was completed.

And at this speed, I would never finish it.

I kept going for a few more stitches, but anyone who has ever attempted a bullion stitch knows it isn't exactly smooth sailing. It's this godforsaken stitch where you wrap the yarn around the hook a million times (or thirteen, in this pattern), then you try to pull the yarn through every single one of those loops in one go. To put this in perspective, usually you only have to pull through two or three loops at once. Thirteen is nearly impossible. I had to work the hook through the loops with my fingernails and squint to even make out the stitches. No wonder Eleanor had abandoned this project, it was no fun at all. I crocheted to relax and exercise my creativity, not to torture myself with an impossible pattern.

I slid the yarn back into my project bag as the bells rang and a customer walked in. For the rest of the morning, I wound skeins of yarn into balls, organized the inventory, and helped customers pick out the right yarn for their projects, but try as I might, I couldn't get my mind off the shawl. And it was disconcerting.

It was 12:00 PM. Loren would be here soon, and then I could take off. I slipped on my cabled, cream-colored crochet sweater and put my phone in my pocket, then I packed up the yarn so I could show it to Aidyn. As I stuffed the yarn into the plastic bag in which it came, my hand brushed against a piece of paper in the bottom.

I opened it and was faced with a page of spidery, thin cursive. Pattern notes, perhaps? The pattern was certainly complicated enough to justify it, and I wouldn't mind some guidance. The note had yesterday's date on it.

Sweetheart, if you're reading this, I'm sorry.

I paused. From the sound of it, this was a personal letter of sorts, and certainly not something I should be reading. But curiosity had always been one of my biggest shortcomings, and my eyes flitted to the next line despite myself.

I love you more than anything. You have been my greatest blessing, and I am thankful for each and every day we had together. The day you came to live with me was the happiest day of my life, and you are more than I deserved.

I am so sorry to do this to you. I have struggled for years with depression, and I never told you because you have enough on your plate without me adding to it. Now, it's too much for me to handle. I know that I sound crazy, but I can't get it out of my head. I haven't eaten or slept in days. I need it to come to an end, and this is the only way.

I do not want you to be the person to find me. I have asked Mrs. Adkins to come over for a visit today so it will be her. I know this is not fair to her, but I want to protect you as much as I can. This is not fair to you, either, and I'm sorry.

I love you.

My heart dropped through my sandals. I had just discovered someone's suicide note. What in the world should I do now? Was it Eleanor's?

No, it couldn't be. I read it again.

The person was talking about something: *I can't get it out of my head,* they had written. Why was this note in with a bag of yarn? Was it from Eleanor when she'd dropped it off? I couldn't imagine how else the note had found its way in here. As awful as the thought was, perhaps she had dropped off the yarn in an effort to clean up before she ended her life. Eleanor wouldn't have wanted her granddaughter to suffer more than necessary.

But I didn't know for sure that Eleanor had written this letter. And I certainly didn't want to believe that I was holding her suicide note. *Don't jump to conclusions,* I told myself. *You don't even know that anything has happened to Eleanor.* In all likelihood she would show up tonight for class like she always did.

There was a sticky note on the back of the paper. The bright turquoise seemed at odds with the devastating content of the letter. On the note, the letter-writer had scribbled something. It was messy, as if she was frenzied, and I struggled to decode the loopy handwriting.

I can't get it out of my head, she had written again. *The tingling in my hands, the needle-sharp hook, the way it's taken over my every thought...It's cursed.*

Chills shot down my spine. I folded the note quickly, burying the turquoise inside, and stuffed it back into the bag. The letter-writer was obviously in mental distress when she wrote those words, and while it clearly had felt real to her, that didn't mean it was true. Curses weren't real. I didn't have to take it seriously.

But tell that to the goosebumps on my arms.

I slid off the high stool and tucked my hair behind my ears as Loren approached me. He was good-looking with light brown skin and striking brown eyes; today he was wearing a forest-green shirt with his dreadlocks pulled back into a ponytail. I was suddenly conscious of my own wrinkled linen shirt and jean shorts. I usually liked to dress nicely, with a crochet accessory or two, but getting dragged out of bed early did not encourage thoughtful fashion choices.

"Hey," I said. "Bad traffic?"

"The worst," he said. "Sorry you got called in, Auri."

I laughed. It sounded strained even to me. "Oh, no problem. You know me. Always willing to help." What was I even saying?

He wasn't listening, in any case. "It's quite sad, really. Did you see what happened?"

I tilted my head, unsure of what he was talking about. He pulled his cell phone out of his pocket and showed me a webpage. It was a news article titled "Woman Dies By Suicide with Granddaughter's Medication."

He scrolled through the article. A woman's body had been found yesterday by her own granddaughter. "It's awful, honestly. This is why there was so much traffic."

My heart stopped. I grabbed his wrist. "Wait," I said, and zoomed in on the picture. It couldn't be true, but I would know her face anywhere: it was Eleanor Bishop.

Chapter 6
Cat

"Children see faeries everywhere. Have you ever seen a child stop and stare something—an empty place in a parking lot, a meadow, a tree—where you can see nothing? The faster a child grows up, the faster they stop seeing faeries. But the Fae don't disappear from the world. They just vanish from your sight."

- The Modern Manual of Faeries by Eleanor Bishop

The house was quiet when I got home from my therapy appointment. I dropped my keys as I tried to unlock the door. Grumbling under my breath, I picked them up and fitted the hey into the lock. They jingled as I turned the knob.

"Grandma," I called, pushing open the door, "you home?"

No response. The house was quiet, my own voice swallowed up by the thick beige carpet and narrow walls. I checked for a fourth time that the car was locked. One of the many reasons I hated driving was that there were so many things to *check*. But as Stephen always reminded me, no matter how many times I checked, my OCD would never let me feel totally sure. He was right, but resisting the compulsion to check "just one more time" was easier said than done. That's why I saw him every week for therapy.

I kicked the door shut behind me and slung my keyring on the hook on the wall. "I'm home," I called. Still no response.

I extricated my phone from the back pocket of my jeans to check for the hundredth time: Grandma still hadn't responded to my texts. She hadn't been herself since our lunch, so I'd called into work sick in order to come home and check on her rather than working my typical post-therapy shift. Grandma would be annoyed. I didn't care. Although you would never be able to tell from her personality that she was seventy-three, I worried that she had fallen and injured herself, unable to reach the phone.

Something felt off, like the times when my OCD was at its worst—the times when I started out the door with my left foot first, or couldn't wash my hands before I ate, or didn't do a task *just right*. My meds took the edge off, but I still spent a sizable portion of each day feeling not quite right inside, no matter what I did. OCD is sometimes called the doubter's disease because it makes you doubt everything, especially your own mind. That's what I had been feeling from the moment I had walked in the door.

She wasn't in the kitchen or the living room. "Grandma," I called again, and knocked on her bedroom door. Three times, because odd numbers were good.

I opened the door a crack and peered inside. When I didn't

see her, I opened it all the way and stepped inside, making sure my green Converse didn't leave muddy footprints on the grayish-beige carpet. Such an ugly color. The bed was made, with five gigantic throw pillows fluffed on top. An empty laundry basket sat on the floor. No Grandma to be found.

I returned to the hallway and approached the bathroom we shared, counting my steps, my stomach in knots and anxiety at an 11 on a scale of 1 to 10.

I knocked, then turned the cheap, tarnished doorknob.

The contents of my stomach threatened to come up. There was Grandma, slumped against the wall, her head lolling against the cold ceramic of the toilet at an unnatural angle. I crashed down next to her, barely registering the pain in my knees, and shook my grandmother by her frail shoulders. She slumped into my arms, completely limp. My mind ran through the possibilities: stroke? Heart attack? Seizure? I pressed my fingers to the side of her neck to check for a pulse and found nothing.

Then I noticed the empty container of Lexapro on the floor. I stopped breathing for a moment. I had refilled my prescription for my OCD medication just the day before. It was now lying empty on the floor next to Grandma's limp hand, and I stared, unable to accept what I was seeing.

The empty bottle of meds. The strange behavior. Grandma had been delighted that I was working today, saying it was good for me to get out and do things, to work through the mental struggle. Was she really just waiting for an opportunity to…I couldn't finish the sentence, even though the evidence was right in front of me?

My hands were dialing 911 automatically as I tried to process, but I was shaking so badly, I could hardly manage. I hugged my grandmother tightly to me, feeling a terrible void where I should have felt grief. All I could think was that she couldn't have killed herself—it was impossible.

Her skin was clammy and the hue was all wrong. "Please wake up," I pleaded, knowing full well there was nothing I could do. I was six years old again, pleading with my dad to wake up as the wail of sirens drew closer, pinned under the wreckage of the station wagon. I knew what it looked like when someone was gone.

What were the odds that I would experience any of this *twice*? I was practiced enough to be calm when the paramedics arrived, although I couldn't stop tapping my fingers rhythmically on my legs: three on each side, repeated three times to avoid the number six. I opened the door and let them in, telling them where to find Grandma. As they filed in, the one at the end gave me a sympathetic look. My eyes dropped to the floor.

I didn't watch as they scooped her onto a stretcher, unable to stomach the way her limbs flopped. How long had it been since she died? Minutes? Hours?

They carried her out the door, stretcher bumping into

the narrow walls of our house, leaving marks as it went. I followed. We proceeded down the hall, and I prayed no neighbors had chosen this time to run their errands. They would find out eventually—from the news, if nothing else—but I wanted to avoid any shocked expressions at this particular moment.

The front door was open. I fumbled for my keys. I had to lock the door behind me. My world was crumbling, but I had to lock the door. The stretcher bumped against the door frame, leaving a mark. I would have to touch up the paint later. Grandma would know what shade of white it was. *I'll never ask her about paint colors again.* I closed my eyes against the nauseating wave of realization.

"Can I ride with her?" I asked as the paramedics loaded her into the back of the ambulance.

"No," someone said, at the same time another said "Yes."

They looked at each other. "Are you related to Ms. Bishop?" asked the first.

"I'm her granddaughter."

"Let her go," said the second. "There's enough room."

The first nodded. I relaxed a fraction. There was no way I would leave Grandma, not unless someone dragged me away. Had I locked the door? I went back and wiggled the doorknob. Yes, it was locked.

I climbed into the ambulance with the paramedics and the still, cold body of my grandmother. Her hand dangled off the side of the stretcher, fingernails still polished the same dark red as mine from our DIY manicure session. The thumbnail was chipped. I itched to retouch it, bothered by the unevenness.

The ambulance doors slammed shut. We began to move. I clutched my keys between my fingers, worrying at the onyx heart keychain that Grandma had given me one Winter Solstice years ago, the stone cool beneath my clammy fingers. Had I locked the front door? What if we came back from the hospital to a home invasion? What if Grandma didn't come back from the hospital at all?

One thought stuck with me during everything: *This is my fault.* And the pressing weight of guilt in my stomach, dragging me down.

Chapter 7
Auri

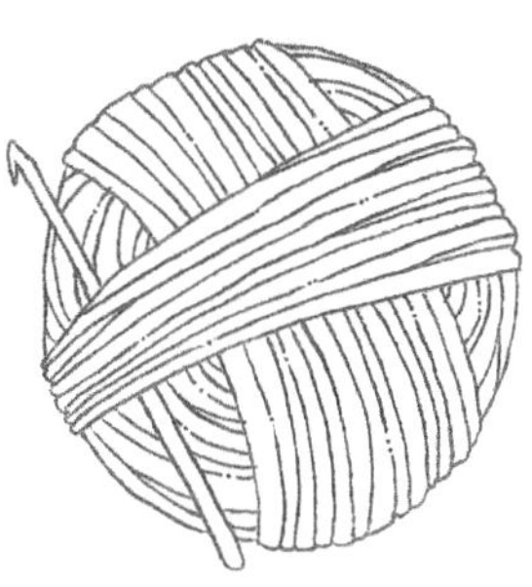

"There are many different names for them: fairies, fae, faeries, the Little Folk, elves, the Forest Folk. And that's before you start on the spelling variations. Whatever you call them, they are the same thing: beings from another world that touches ours in places at certain times. They are not of this world and they do not play by our rules. Don't expect them to."

- *The Modern Manual of Faeries by Eleanor Bishop*

I COULDN'T SEEM TO CONCENTRATE. MY FINGERS WOULDN'T stop tingling, no matter what I tried: lotion, running them under freezing-cold and then scalding-hot water, sitting on them, clapping loudly. This was the kind of thing better suited for a trip to the doctor, but that was too expensive. And what would I say, anyway? I tried to imagine how that conversation would go. "Um, Smart Medical Professional, I was crocheting and suddenly my hands fell asleep." What would a doctor say to that?

Then it came to me. My younger brother, Aidyn, was absolutely obsessed with all things related to medicine, and he would likely have some idea of what was happening. He had wanted to be a doctor practically from the day he was born, and it seemed like his nose was always stuck in a medical book, the likes of which would put me to sleep. He was fourteen but was already doing schoolwork several grades ahead. It was a little disconcerting to have your younger sibling coaching you on algebra, but I welcomed the help. Besides, he owed me one from the time I crocheted him an enormous plush dinosaur that had taken me a solid three weeks to complete.

It wasn't good protocol to call someone during a shift. I hated when employees did that, and I knew Genevieve would blow a fuse if she found out, but I felt I deserved a pass in this case. Loren was here now and taking care of customers. I dialed our home phone number.

It rang three times before he picked up. "You've reached the Davis Dwelling," Aidyn announced. "How may I direct your call?"

"Davis Dwelling?" Despite my worries, I smiled.

"You liked 'Davis House of Horrors' better, then?"

"No. You're going to get the cops called on us, Aidyn," I told him.

"I think Dad took care of that for us," he said. I winced. "So what can I do for you, my elderly sister? Did you call just to hear my lovely voice?"

"I called in spite of that," I said. "I need medical advice."

"Ah." I heard drawers opening and closing. "So you just wanted to use the free doctor at your disposal."

"I can't exactly call the real one," I said.

"A quality substitute." The kitchen drawer shut with a clang. "What's wrong with you, anyway?"

I wasn't really sure how to explain this one. "Something weird happened to me this morning. I..."

"Did you look in the mirror?" Aidyn's voice was filled with glee.

"Shut up," I said. A customer wandered around the corner, and my eyes widened in embarrassment, hoping they didn't think I was talking to them. I smiled at them and lowered my voice. "This is serious. I think I've happened upon one of those weird events you always ramble on about."

Aidyn was obsessed with National Geographic's *Weird But True* books when he was younger, and he was an expert on medical anomalies, the kind that blur the line between sci-fi and reality. "Go on," he said.

I explained my encounter with Eleanor, the suicide note, and the strange tingling in my hands.

"Tingling, huh? What does it feel like?" he asked. Leave it to my brother to take all of this without question. "Like your hand had fallen asleep, or that you dipped it in a bucket of cold water, or something else?"

"Like I lost all feeling in it," I said. "I guess like when you sit on your foot for too long and it falls asleep."

"Hmm." He was quiet for a minute.

I listened as he flipped through pages in a book, probably one of his thick medical tomes. "Aidyn, I'll see you soon, okay?"

"Adios, sister," he said, and the line clicked off.

Chapter 8
Cat

"Faeries can lie, but they are not so quick to lie as humans are. Their culture favors the truth, whereas ours encourages pretending to be someone else. Faeries are also very good at telling when you are lying. If you must tell a falsehood to a faerie, look them in the eyes while you do so and speak smoothly. They will be taken in by your confidence, so summon all the confidence you can."

- The Modern Manual of Faeries by Eleanor Bishop

You would think that finding Grandma's body was the worst part. But plenty of other things kept piling up after that, wanting *their* turn at being the worst part.

First was the fact that I spent four hours at the police station while they grilled me on how Grandma had behaved during the last few weeks of her life. In office No. 13, to make things worse. I knocked on the wooden door frame as I went inside to offset the damage done by thirteen. But then I had to keep knocking on wood to hold off the bad luck, and the officer interviewing me looked at me funny every time I rapped on the table with my knuckles.

The officer interviewing me was a balding man, what little was left of his hair turning gray. His nametag read *Officer Reynolds*. He pulled up a chair for me, wooden with gray cushions, and started the interrogation.

"Can you tell me your full name, please?" he asked.

"Catherine Bishop," I told him.

"Your license says you're seventeen. Is that right?"

I nodded. He slid my driver's license across the table to me. I picked it up and fiddled with the plastic edges. It was a truly unflattering picture; my red hair was sticking up on one side, my freckles made it look like I had chicken pox, and my lopsided smile did not look attractive in a photograph.

Then the real fun started. "Did you notice any changes in your grandmother's behavior?"

"No." I hadn't. I felt that he was judging me for failing to notice my grandmother's depression—what kind of granddaughter did that make me? Guilt rose up in my stomach. I tilted my head to the right, tapped the arms of my chair, tried to arrange my feet just right on the thin gray carpet. My sock just wasn't *right* inside my shoe, and no matter how much I wiggled my toes, it wouldn't lay flat.

"Did she go anywhere unexpected?"

"Not that I'm aware of." I tried to think, but my thoughts were like wading through molasses, and that damn sock was wedged between my toes. "She went on an errand by herself, but she does that sometimes."

"Where did she go?"

"I don't know." I wished I had pressed further when I

asked her what errand she had run before our lunch date.

Officer Reynolds turned a page in his notepad. He wrote with a slant, like he was in a hurry. "Do you have a family history of mental illness?"

I pressed my lips together. Where could I start? "I don't know about my mom," I said, hoping he wouldn't ask for more details. "My dad died when I was six. Car accident." I twisted my fingers together. "I have OCD, so one of my parents probably had it too. I'm not sure, though."

His pencil didn't stop moving throughout this whole explanation. "Do you live with your grandmother, Catherine?"

"Cat." Nobody but my mom had ever called me Catherine. "Sure. Cat."

"Yeah. I've lived with her since I was eight. After my dad died." I lowered my gaze to the floor, where the floor was scuffed from chairs being moved in and out. If my sock situation didn't improve soon, I was going to throw something across the room.

"But your mother was still living at that point?"

I nodded. Before he asked, I told him: "She was unable to cope with my dad's death. So my grandma took me in." It was the truth, albeit a nicer version of it.

"I see." *Scribble, scribble.*

I couldn't take it any longer. I yanked my foot onto my opposite knee, untied my Converse, and threw it onto the floor. My sock was twisted and stuck between my little toe and the toe next to it, and I whisked it off my foot, experiencing instant relief as my foot met the air. The officer looked at me like I was crazy, but I was *going* to go crazy if my sock didn't get fixed. He could think whatever he wanted. I carefully pulled the sock back onto my foot and arranged it so that the seam laid perfectly flat against the top of my foot. Then I slid my foot back into my shoe and did up the laces, double-knotting them as always.

"You okay?" he asked.

"Dandy."

He lowered his gaze back to the paper. I crossed and re-crossed my ankles. I just wanted to go home.

And my sock was already bothering me again.

***

But I couldn't go home. Another thing to add to the "worst things" list. As a minor, I couldn't stay here by myself. A social worker named Lindsey took me home just long enough to grab some clothes from my room.

I shoved underwear, jeans, socks, and a stack of blouses into a tote bag. On the front of the bag was a cartoon crab holding a beach umbrella. Grandma had bought it for me when we visited the ocean last year. Something about the smiling crab brought tears to my eyes, and I turned the tote bag inside out so I wouldn't have to look at it. Then I felt bad for the crab, and guiltier than before. Inanimate objects didn't have feelings, and I *knew* that, but somehow I ended up feeling bad for them anyway. It was infuriating, knowing something was irrational but feeling the anxiety anyway, and I just wished my body would catch up with my rational thoughts.

I sat on the edge of my bed and tried to overcome the rising wave of panic. I dumped everything out of my tote bag and turned the bag right side out again, so the crab would be happier. I didn't realize I was crying until a tear dripped onto my bedspread, leaving a splotch on the light blue fabric. In situations like this, the only thing that helped my anxiety was getting Grandma to tell me everything would be okay. Now I didn't have her, and it made me feel like nothing would ever be okay again.

I curled up on my bed, pulled my stuffed sloth out from underneath my pillow, and cried. Partly for Grandma, and partly because I couldn't see an end to this guilt and panic. When I was in the middle of an OCD spell, there was nothing that could shake me out of it. But in this case, no compulsion could ease the pain and guilt of Grandma's death being my fault.

It was all my fault.

I had as good as killed Grandma.

Simon the sloth soaked up my tears, and I buried my face in his fur.

I heard footsteps in the hallway, and I quickly straightened up, wiping my face. Lindsey stepped into the doorway. "Are you almost done, Catherine?"

"Almost. Sorry," I said.

Her face changed into one of pity when she saw I'd been

crying. "You take as much time as you need, honey," she said. "You need any help?"

"I'm fine," I said. I put Simon in the top of the tote bag and stood up. "I'm good to go."

"You sure?"

I nodded, taking one last look at my room. I wondered who would buy this house after it went on the market. Maybe nobody, because it was haunted. If so, I would be back to clean out my room (and the rest of the house, because the work would probably fall to me), but it wouldn't be the same. Without Grandma, it wasn't home anymore.

I followed Lindsey down the hall, giving my door one last pat to say goodbye.

The third thing on my ever-growing list of unfortunate events was seeing my family again.

Grandma moved to Washington to get some "well-deserved peace and quiet" in her retirement, and after I joined her, I got to partake in that peace and quiet. It was beautiful out here, all tree-covered hills and houseboat-filled lakes and mountains that still wore a coat of snow even in the summer, and I didn't miss the East Coast for even a minute. I hadn't seen my extended family in years, not since Mom had left and nobody stepped up to take care of eight-year-old me. After that, I didn't particularly care to see them.

If I were just a year older, I wouldn't have to lay eyes on them, but as a minor, I wasn't allowed to continue living on my own. I would be living with Aunt Stephanie for the time being, until other arrangements could be made.

I didn't dare ask what the other arrangements would be.

Stephanie was my dad's sister. All I remembered about her was that she always wore absurdly large earrings that I tried to tug on when I was younger. True to memory, when I met her in the lobby of the Paramount Hotel, she was wearing silver hoop earrings that looked more like bracelets, and I wondered briefly if she had any pets or children that would try to play with them. You couldn't get away with earrings like that if you had a cat. I'd always wanted one, but Grandma was allergic. I could get one now, I realized, and was immediately flooded with guilt for even thinking about it.

Stephanie rose to her feet when she saw me and gave me a tight-lipped smile. "Catherine!"

I didn't smile back. I didn't feel like it.

"Stephanie Bishop?" asked Lindsey, who had accompanied me. "I'm Lindsey Jacobs. It's my job to ensure Catherine gets to the right place."

She held out her hand for Stephanie to shake. She did, showing off her smooth peach-colored fingernails. "It's a pleasure to meet you," she said. Then she turned to me. "Catherine, I'm so sorry, my dear."

I hated being called Catherine. I held my tote bag awkwardly in front of me, not wanting her pity. What did you say to someone who pretended you didn't exist as a child and you hadn't seen in years? Nothing polite. I was suddenly fearful I would yell out something offensive right here, right now. I tapped the tile floor with my toe to help ease the irrational fear, but it clung tight like a child who doesn't want to be set down, as intrusive thoughts always do. Although my therapist, Stephen, always said there's no such thing as a bad thought, some thoughts just felt nasty to me and I didn't want them in my head. "It's your actions that determine your worth, not your thoughts," he had told me, but it was hard to remember that when you were held in the grip of a scary, intrusive thought. And now I didn't have Grandma to talk me through them anymore. Somehow I doubted that Aunt Stephanie would be particularly comforting, or even understand at all.

Lindsey cleared her throat. "I'll just need you to sign a few things," she said to my aunt. "We can look at the papers right here."

"Of course." Stephanie didn't take her eyes off me. She looked like my dad's side of the family, with dark hair, brown eyes, and pale skin. She was wearing a pantsuit that would make a politician proud. "Catherine, you can head up to our suite, okay? Here's your key."

I took the key from her without saying anything, wanting to scream at her, *My name is Cat!* I took the elevator to the sixth floor, grateful that I didn't run into anyone else along the way.

The key was to Room 613. Six and thirteen were my

least favorite numbers. The universe was trying to tell me something, but it was nothing I didn't know already. Things couldn't get any worse.

Chapter 9
Auri

"Contrary to popular belief, holy water, crucifixes, or any other religious relics have no effect on the Fae. Because they do not subscribe to any particular human religion, and their realm exists apart from ours, they cannot be affected by human beliefs. If religious symbolism gives you more presence of mind and feeling of security, by all means wear it. But the Fae will not stop because of it."

- The Modern Manual of Faeries by Eleanor Bishop

IT WAS BROAD DAYLIGHT, BUT I STILL KEPT MY HAND ON the pepper spray in my pocket as I walked home. Yarn Emporium was about a half-hour walk from my house, which meant an hour of being slightly on edge every day. The village in which the store was situated was lovely, but my commute involved a lot of walking on the side of the road and through less-than-stellar neighborhoods. A second car, though, was not in the budget. A first car barely was.

The driveway was empty, which meant Mom was at work— no surprise there. I slid the key into the lock and pushed open the door. Aidyn was sitting on the floor of our tiny kitchen with a medical book propped open on his knees, his blond hair falling over his face and brushing the side of the long nose he had inherited from Mom. I had called him before I started home to update him about my findings on Eleanor Bishop.

"I discovered some stuff," he said by way of greeting. "Follow me and I can show you."

"Hello to you too," I said. "You're not gonna tell me about your date?" I locked the door behind me, tossed the key into the bowl by the door, and followed him down the hall to his bedroom. It was right across from mine.

"There's nothing to tell. Except, apparently, that I'm gay. I still can't believe you didn't know." Aidyn flopped onto his bed with the family laptop. It had the slowest Internet in the world and all sorts of food crumbs wedged under the keys, but it was infinitely better than no computer. I sat on a beanbag chair, watching as he clicked around for a bit. "I looked up that article," he said, "the one you were telling me about this morning. Is this it?"

I looked at the screen. "Yeah, that's it." The suicide had been all over the news. "I know her. She's one of our regular customers."

"Damn, really?"

"Yeah. She's really sweet. Has a granddaughter my age."

"Do you know her granddaughter's number? Or contact information?"

"Her name is Cat. That's all I remember." Aidyn knew I was horrible with names. "And I don't want to bother her, either. Since she's going through hell right now."

I didn't tell him about the suicide note, because it was too raw. I would give it to Cat when the time was right. Would seeing the note help her, or just make her hurt more? There was no guidebook for this sort of thing.

"Maybe she'll want to hear from you. Have a little support."

"I would, if I knew her number."

He shrugged. "So that's a no-go for now. Well, I looked up Eleanor Bishop, and I found some stuff on her. Not as good as getting in contact with her family, but it's a start. But first, the question you asked me about." His voice was matter-of-fact. "What's up with your hands doing the thing? Are they still tingling now?"

"Not right now. But they felt so weird earlier."

He took my hand and examined it, turning it over and poking at my palm. "God, Auri, your hands are cold."

"I just walked home from work."

"Are you sure the tingling wasn't just your ice-cold hands that match your ice-cold heart?"

"Ouch." He knew my heart wasn't cold; he'd seen me cry too many times.

"Right. See, I've been confused as to your whole medical debacle. I can't find any evidence that suggests your hand-tingling experience is related to a disease. An allergy, of course, makes the most sense, but let me see the yarn."

I pulled it out of the plastic bag and handed it to him. He pulled a strand loose and studied it closely. "There was no label," I told him.

"Is that normal?" he asked.

I shrugged. "Yarn comes with labels, yeah, to tell you fiber content and all that. So if you're allergic to wool, you can avoid it. But this was used yarn, so…"

"No label," he finished. "Shame. Still, you've been crocheting so long, you've probably worked with something similar to this, right?"

I nodded.

"And you're not allergic to wool or anything?"

"No." Luckily. All the best yarn at Yarm Emporium was animal fiber, and you just couldn't beat a cozy woolen sweater in the chilly Washington winters. Alpaca yarn was my favorite.

"I don't think it's an allergy. All the same, let me know if your hands act up again when you're crocheting it, okay?" He went back to the computer.

"I'm not going to *keep* working on it," I said, shocked. After everything this morning, especially that note, I wanted as little to do with that shawl as possible.

"Mm-hmm," said Aidyn, like he thought otherwise. Before I could protest, he went on: "If Eleanor Bishop is the woman who left the note, I figured I'd find some information on her. She seems to be a pretty private person, but I found a community center that she goes to." Aidyn opened a new tab and typed in a link, and the Tacoma Community Center website popped up. "See, she's on the Donor list, and she leads a yoga class on Wednesday."

"Cool," I said. The community center was one of those things that looked fun but was just out of our price range.

"Well, I clicked around the website, and she seems to be pretty popular. Like, read this." Aidyn clicked the "TCC Rummage Sale" button.

From what I could tell, it was a big annual rummage sale that happened at the beginning of summer. It had made newspapers and was a big hit, the article informed me. There was another section for "This Year's Sale," which had taken place about two months ago. A banner at the top of the page read, "Thank You to Our Volunteers." I was about to push the computer back to Aidyn when a name caught my eye: Eleanor Bishop!

"Awesome," I said. "So we know she volunteers at this rummage thing."

"Yes. What I was thinking is we could go and ask around at the center to see if anyone knew her." I was already shaking my head. "Come on, do you have any better ideas?" said Aidyn, looking exasperated. He slammed the computer shut and leaned against the wall.

"I don't know. I don't think we're going to find anything." This whole procedure sounded so tiring, and I wanted nothing more than to curl up in bed and crochet...*oh no!* I sat bolt upright, the beanbag shifting beneath me, as I realized the only thing I wanted to do was work on the shawl.

"What?" Aidyn was looking at me oddly.

"Just kidding. I think you're right. We should go to TCC," I said. "Tomorrow's my day off, should we go then?"

Aidyn eyed me suspiciously. "Okay," he said, "tomorrow works for me."

"Awesome. Now, I'm going to bed," I said, standing up and tripping over a textbook that had been left on the floor. I stepped on a *National Geographic* magazine and slid into a globe, which I tripped over, and crashed into the wall. "Your room is a disaster, you know that?"

"Not as bad as yours," he said, looking smug. I rolled my eyes.

I walked next door into my room and instantly felt calmer. True, it was a glorified closet, but it was mine. I had painted the walls a light turquoise, and the wall across from the door had an ocean mural on it. Aidyn and I had painted it last summer when we were looking for something to do. My bed was unmade, and there *was* a mess on the floor—mostly yarn—but it still calmed me. I tossed my bag onto my bed and curled up next to my giant throw pillow.

It took approximately twenty seconds for me to realize that there was no way I could stop thinking about that shawl.

So I got up, put my pajamas on, and did my normal evening routine. I did thirty jumping jacks in an attempt to tire myself out. Then I did fifteen push-ups, although admittedly the kind with your knees bent due to my lack of upper body strength. I meditated for ten minutes and tried to stop thinking about that cursed shawl.

Aidyn's muffled voice made its way through my wall. "Auri, what are you doing in there? I'm trying to write a paper."

"Sorry," I yelled back. My limbs itched to move and it pained me to sit still, kind of like after a long day of sitting in the same spot and trying not to fidget. I squeezed my pillow a few times, but when that failed to relieve my anxiety, I did the only thing that would.

I opened the bag and pulled out the Briars and Roses Shawl. I knew Aidyn would say "I told you so," but I put the hook back in the loop and crocheted the rest of the row. It couldn't be so harmful, could it? If the problem was being obsessed with the shawl and not being able to think of anything else, like Eleanor Bishop said, the obvious solution had to be *finishing* the shawl. I was so pleased with my answer that it took me a minute to realize the obvious flaw in my plan: this pattern was nearly *impossible.*

I had crocheted many difficult things in my life, the hardest being a multicolored mandala blanket that had taken me about six months of working on it every day to complete. But this beat them all. The pattern was well-written, but the thread was thin and it used a tiny hook. I had never been good at thread crochet.

I wondered where Eleanor had gotten this shawl. I doubted she had designed it herself, because of the problems she was having with it. Then that left the question of when she had gotten it. In that time, she had only crocheted seventeen rows, and it seemed like she had been working on it a lot, from that Post-It note.

"Great," I whispered to the room. It was obvious I couldn't just power through and rapidly crochet this thing. Well, I would just take it one row at a time.

Maybe I was only dwelling on the shawl because I thought it was cursed. A sort of reverse psychology thing, perhaps. It would be easy enough to finish the blasted thing and be done with it all. The real issue here was the tragedy of Eleanor's death and what to do about her suicide note, not a supposedly "cursed" shawl. How stupid was that?

Chapter 10
Cat

"A horseshoe, when placed open side-up above a doorway, acts as an effective deterrent for the supernatural. Never turn it open side-down or the luck will fall out."
- *The Modern Manual of Faeries by Eleanor Bishop*

THE LACE COLLAR OF MY DRESS ITCHED LIKE THE DEVIL, AND I clasped my hands tightly together to keep from scratching my neck. I tried to look like I was praying. The chain of my necklace had gotten twisted around and I fidgeted, moving the clasp to the back of my neck like it was supposed to be, and then toying with the tiny glass bottle itself, shifting the berries and leaves inside.

The crowd rose to their feet, and the minister began reading something from the Bible. I probably looked bored out of my mind, which was not the appropriate reaction at your grandmother's funeral. But Grandma would have hated this. She wouldn't have chosen a Christian funeral, which was exactly what she was getting right now. She would have wanted something outdoors, where she could be connected to the earth…something with plants, but not cut flowers.

Something natural and nature-filled. *Spiritual, not religious* was how she'd always described herself and how I felt about myself too. She would never have wanted this.

I tapped my fingers on the back of the pew in front of me, soothed by the feeling of the rough wood on my fingertips. I couldn't get rid of the rock of guilt in my stomach. I had done so many things wrong: I snapped at Grandma too much, I didn't pull my own weight, I wasn't grateful enough for all she had done for me. Now I could never go back and redo it. What was tugging at me the most, though, was that I had misled her about my sexuality. I was finally comfortable with myself being a lesbian; what I regretted was waiting too long to tell Grandma, thinking she would always be around. Now I would never get the chance.

I fidgeted with the ends of my hair, tugging a strand loose out of habit. The dark red stood out against my black skirt. I forced my gaze to the white marble urn on a lace tablecloth, which was barely visible through the flowers placed around it.

Grandma would have hated it. She had faithfully tended her plot in the community garden, yielding a bountiful harvest of cherry tomatoes, zucchini, and carrots every summer, and scoffed at gardening for aesthetic reasons. Sometimes her garden was the only thing that could get her out of the house. My lips twitched as I pictured her reaction to this flowery monstrosity, as she would've described it.

The small crowd of mourners plunked back down into their seats, like a somber stadium wave. I adjusted my skirt to cover my knees, crossing my feet at the ankles. My ballet flats rubbed painfully at my heels. If it were up to me, I would have worn my favorite green Converse, but Stephanie was appalled at the idea.

She was seated next to me, wearing a black pantsuit for the occasion, the perfect somber mourning expression on her face. She had tried to take me shopping for a funeral dress, but when I wouldn't leave the bathroom, she went out and bought one on her own. It was a size too small and was giving my neck a rash. "You need to be respectable for your grandma's funeral," she had told me, but I knew Grandma. She would've found it hilarious had I shown up to her funeral in everyday clothes and Converse.

"You okay?" Stephanie whispered, as if she could sense what I was thinking.

"Yeah." One of my uncles was speaking to the group about how close he had been to Grandma. That was a lie; neither Grandma nor I had seen Uncle Byron in years.

"Eleanor Bishop was a wonderful mother, grandmother, and friend," said Uncle Byron. "She will be missed, but she will be remembered forever in our hearts." He paused for a minute, probably to make himself seem moved.

I scowled. If it were up to me, I would've planned a small funeral for Grandma, without all these insincere relatives. But my mother had been put in charge—which struck me as ridiculous. I was the closest to Grandma and knew her better than anyone.

But if I knew her that well, why hadn't I seen the signs of depression? Why hadn't she been able to tell me how deeply unhappy she was? I chewed my lip, tasting blood.

Uncle Byron finished his speech and pulled out a handkerchief to wipe away nonexistent tears. I stood. My palms clammy with sweat, I made my way to the front of the room.

I opened my notebook, a Moleskine one from Grandma that I carried everywhere, and placed my hands on the podium to steady myself.

"I'm Cat Bishop, Eleanor's granddaughter," I started, and the mic let out a deafening shriek, causing half the congregation to clap their hands over their ears. I knocked my notebook off the podium in surprise, Grandma's eulogy falling to the ground. The minister leaped up to help me readjust the microphone. "I'm so sorry," I said, feeling my face flood with color.

"You have nothing to apologize for," he said, and handed me the Moleskine.

I stood there, clutching my notebook, as his words registered. I had everything to apologize for. Grandma's death was my fault—if I had seen the warning signs, I could have prevented it, could have gotten her help. Grandma had done everything for me, taking me in after Mom up and left and making sure I had as normal a childhood as possible. She even showed up to the mother-daughter events at school, despite how uncomfortable she must have felt surrounded by the young moms. Sure, she was a little strict, but she had loved me like a daughter…and I had failed to see how miserable she was. She had been the world to me—why hadn't I been enough for her?

The stares of the congregation now felt hostile and accusatory. I was sure every person was thinking the same thing. First my mother had left, now my grandma had killed herself—there must be something wrong with me.

I bolted from the podium, unable to remain in the room a second longer.

I hid in the bathroom for as long as I could. The bathroom of a funeral parlor, as it turns out, isn't any nicer than your typical public restroom. You'd think they might have separate bathrooms so people could run off and cry in peace. At the very least they should have quilted toilet paper. I stayed in there, counting the ceiling tiles in groups of three, until Stephanie came looking for me.

"Catherine, honey, are you in there?"

Her high-heeled shoes were visible under the stall door. I knew my shoes were, too, and she would recognize them. Sighing, I emerged.

"Oh, sweetie." She pulled me into a hug, enveloping me in a overpowering cloud of flowery perfume. Startled, I pulled away as quickly as I could. She nodded understandingly. "Are you okay?"

"I'm fine," I said, which couldn't be further from the truth. But she nodded and didn't say anything more. I didn't blame her. "

"Aren't you coming to the reception?" she asked, only her

tone of voice made it clear that I didn't have a choice.

I wasn't in danger of crying anymore. But the last thing in the world I wanted was to see my mother. If it were up to me, she wouldn't have even been invited to the funeral. Yes, Grandma was her mother, but family isn't just blood relations—it's about the effort you put in. I didn't know the last time Mom had gone to visit Grandma. And after she had abandoned me, I didn't think she deserved to be here. I certainly didn't want to be in the same room as her.

But I followed Stephanie to the reception room. At the very least, there would be food.

It was a sea of black and gray. It seemed like every relative I had was here. They probably just wanted in on the inheritance. Well, they would be disappointed there— Grandma and I definitely weren't wealthy. I dodged condolences as I made my way through the room, parting the crowd of fake mourners.

The food was at the back. So were all the little cousins. They looked up at me nervously as I walked over. Their parents had probably warned them that their cousin Cat would be sad. I smiled at them and went straight for the cheesecake.

A little girl with her hair in two braids sidled up to me. "Try the chocolate," she said.

"Okay." I smiled at her. "Is chocolate your favorite?"

"Yeah. Mommy said not to eat too much, though," she said, looking dejected. My smile grew.

"Just don't make yourself sick," I said, and slid a chocolate-chip cookie onto her plate. "Your grandma would love this."

She scampered off with her cookie. Little kids I could handle; they were so well-meaning and innocent. Grown-ups, on the other hand, I could do without, particularly the variety of grown-ups that were here now.

As I was piling three slices onto my plate, I heard an all-too-familiar voice from behind me, and my stomach dropped through the floor. "Catherine?" The voice was tentative, like it wasn't sure how I would react. Truth be told, I wasn't too sure either. I slowly turned around, balancing the cheesecake and fork on my plate, and came face-to-face with Natasha Bishop.

My mom.

Chapter 11
Auri

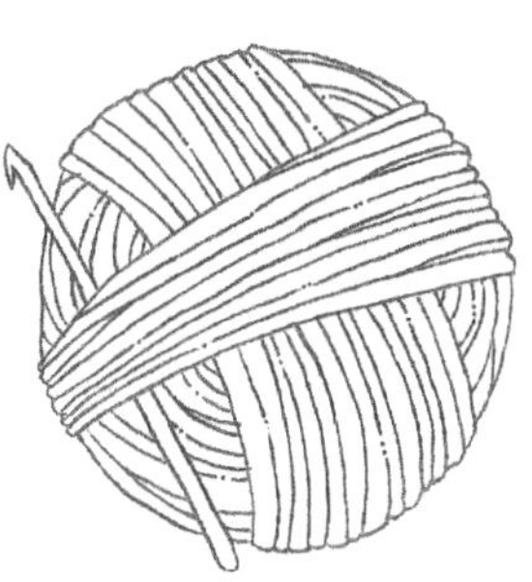

"People call me childish or crazy for my belief in the Fae. I call them foolish for not accepting what would be right in front of them if they opened their eyes and mind. Just because you deny something doesn't mean it goes away. It just means you're unaware of it. And being oblivious to the Fae does not protect you from them. It makes you vulnerable."

- *The Modern Manual of Faeries by Eleanor Bishop*

WHEN THE ALARM SOUNDED, I ROLLED OVER AND FROZE. There were bloodstains on the pillow. *Did I have a nosebleed in the night?* I wondered. Then a stinging pain in my left hand alerted me to the real source of blood. The hook was so small that it was actually sharp, and my long stint crocheting had caused the skin to rip off my pointer finger and leave a bloody welt. I cringed.

I sneaked to the bathroom and washed out the wound. It stung like a dozen hornet stings, which unfortunately I had experienced several years ago during a particularly memorable game of hide-and-seek at a family reunion. I put a Band-Aid on it and hoped it wouldn't get infected. How would I explain that one to the doctor? He would tell me to stop crocheting, and that wasn't an option.

For all my insistence that this wrap couldn't possibly be cursed, all the evidence was pointing in the other direction. But if that was really the case, then who had done it? And how? Could there really, actually be some magic at work here? I couldn't believe in magic anymore, I was sixteen years old. But the feeling this shawl gave me was just too odd to be explained. Fairies, though? There had to be a rational explanation.

Magic didn't happen to a girl like me.

That afternoon, Aidyn and I took the bus to Tacoma Community Center. It was an hour-and-a-half ordeal that involved two transfers and a whole lot of frantic navigation on our part, as neither of us possessed a sense of direction. We had to contend with one particularly chatty stranger who insisted on making conversation for the entire bus ride. Eventually, though, we got off at the correct stop and walked the ten minutes to the community center in the boiling-hot sun.

"This way," said Aidyn. I followed him through the front doors into a bright, large entryway with a reception desk, cushy-looking chairs and couches, and an enormous skylight. I shivered in the air conditioning. "So, do you want to look around or what?"

"I thought I'd just ask that person," I said, gesturing to the green-haired girl at the reception desk. Aidyn snickered. I looked at him, eyebrows raised.

"What?" she asked. "You're just going to walk up to her and go, *hey, do you know about this addictive crochet wrap that killed a person who went to this rec center?*"

"No," I said, rolling my eyes, "I'm going to ask her about the rummage sale. And try to be discreet."

"It's not like I bellowed it from the rooftops," said Aidyn, but he did lower his voice. "You sound more suspicious when you're whispering, you know."

"I guess, but still, I think we should keep this quiet."

"Sure." Aidyn gave me a push and I tripped over my own foot, stumbling up to the desk.

"Hello," said the girl, whose name tag read *Hi, my name's Eloise.* "How can I help you?"

"Hi," I said. "I just wanted to ask if you could tell me about the rummage sale?" I pulled a piece of paper out of my back pocket. It was a bit crumpled from the bus ride, but when I unfolded it, the writing was still perfectly legible: it was a brochure about the annual sale.

"Sure!" said Eloise, adjusting her textbook hipster glasses. She wore bright green lipstick that went with her hair, and I was transfixed by the shape of her lips, outlined perfectly by the lipstick. It was hard to bring my attention back to what she was saying. "Well, it took place two months ago, so you've got a bit of a wait for the next one. Did you want to donate something?"

"No," I said. "Um, I have an…*aunt* who goes here, and she was telling me about it." *So lame.* But Eloise didn't bat an eye. Of course, there was nothing wrong with asking about the sale, but I didn't know how to work in the Briars and Roses Shawl without sounding weird.

"Yes, it is pretty popular," said Eloise. "It started when TCC first opened about, oh, thirty years ago, and it's just taken off from there. Have you been?"

"What?"

"Have you been to the rummage sale?" Eloise twirled a strand of hair around her finger, and I followed the motion with my eyes, distracted.

"No, I haven't." How to bring up the shawl? "Um."

"Well, do you want to sign up for any classes while you're here?" She kept the smile plastered on her face, but I could guess what she was thinking: *What does this girl want?*

An opening! "Yeah, actually, I was wondering if you had any yarn classes here?"

"Yarn classes." Eloise turned her gaze down to her computer and began to type. "Like fiber arts?" I nodded. "Yes, actually, we have a beginning knitting class, beginning crochet, spinning, weaving, and—"

"Great!" I said, bringing my hand up for a thumbs-up and accidentally slamming it on the underside of the counter, right on my bandaged finger. I tried not to wince. "Actually, I'm more interested in thread crochet. Do you happen to have any classes about that?"

"Thread crochet? Hmm. Let me see." The typing sounds resumed.

While she was occupied, I dug in my bag and pulled out the Briars and Roses Shawl, which I set carefully on the counter.

Eloise looked up at the clanking sound from the crochet hook, and she laughed. That was not what I'd expected. "Are you sure you haven't been to our rummage sale?" she asked. I nodded, puzzled. "Because I know for a fact that your lacy thing was for sale there."

My heart leaped—now we were getting somewhere! Not only did Eleanor Bishop attend TCC, but it appeared that she'd purchased this shawl from their sale. I couldn't wait to tell Aidyn, who would probably say "I told you so," as he so loved to do. "Really?"

"Yes! We have a big yarn selection, but this was on top. I remember because of the color—that's my favorite shade of pink." She ran the fabric of the shawl through her fingers.

"That's nice," I managed. "Do you know who donated this?" In an effort to not appear too nosy, I added, "I'm having some trouble with the pattern, and I'd love to ask for help."

"I don't know," she said. "I'm sorry." What could I say now? I was saved from concocting a reply when Eloise said, "I have an idea, though. You could post something on our bulletin board over there." She pointed. A gigantic corkboard was tacked on the wall, and it was filled with notices, advertisements, flyers, and various papers.

"Thank you!" I smiled at her. "You've been so helpful. I'll do that." I paused. "Actually, can I ask you one more thing?"

"Sure," she said.

"This might sound weird, but did that shawl just make your fingers go numb?" I shifted to the other foot, nervous.

She looked puzzled. "No, not that I noticed. Why?"

"Ah. Must just be my allergy, then," I said, doing my best to appear nonchalant. She nodded and handed me the shawl.

I scooped the shawl back into my bag, walked back to Aidyn, and sat next to him on the couch, which was actually quite comfortable. There were too many throw pillows. What was it with elderly people being obsessed with throw pillows? Both of my sets of grandparents had enough to fill a hot tub. "Any information?" he asked.

I told him what I'd learned. He leaned his head back against the couch and thought for a minute. "So what are you going to put on the board? 'Young Crocheter Seeks Previous Owner of Magic Obsessive Crochet Wrap'?"

"No." My hand found its way into the bag, where I fiddled with the shawl, feeling the threads slide against each other.

"'To the Owner of That Weird Pink Crochet Shawl Thing: Attention, I Need Your Help! I Am Obsessed with This Thing!'"

"You're not helping." I pulled the shawl out and arranged it on my lap. I might as well crochet a little while I was waiting, I mused, until I figured out what to write. As I made the stitch, the hook brushed my injured finger and I bit my lip.

"What'd you do to your finger?" asked Aidyn, glancing over at it. "Papercut?"

"Yeah," I said, although I didn't like lying to my brother. He made an indistinct grunt, and I could tell he was thinking. That was fine with me. It gave me more time to crochet. My right fingers were getting blistered from holding the tiny hook, and as I finished the row, one of the blisters burst.

I quickly tucked the finger under my other hand, hiding it from Aidyn. Blood seeped out, and I fumbled in my bag for a Band-Aid, thankful I'd had the foresight to bring them. I had a feeling I'd go through quite a few more Band-Aids before, and if, I finished the wrap.

After I bandaged up my finger, I went back to crocheting, and Aidyn walked off. Fifteen minutes and several very sore fingers later, he appeared with a handwritten sign, which he held up in front of me:

Attention, All Rummage Sale Participants!

I bought a pink crochet shawl from this sale, and I'm having trouble with the pattern!

Would the donor please email me so we can discuss where I went wrong?

REWARD of $20 if you help me make sense of this thing!

Contact Auri Davis.

He put my phone number at the bottom, and we hung it on the bulletin board next to some "Lost Dog" and "Piano Lessons" posters.

Then we took the bus home. Although I would've loved my own car, I was grateful to take the bus today, because it meant I could crochet while someone else drove. Aidyn looked at me but thankfully didn't say anything, and our commute home was a quiet one.

Chapter 12

Cat

"Stones that naturally have holes eroded in them, commonly known as "hagstones," have magical properties. Thread them on a string and wear them around your neck to use the power of nature to protect yourself. Looking through the hole in the stone will give you the ability to see through enchantments and can offer you a glimpse into another realm."

- The Modern Manual of Faeries by Eleanor Bishop

Mom looked just like I remembered her, except more youthful. Happier, probably, without me around anymore. I couldn't help but stare at her.

"Catherine. You've grown so much," she said, just like Aunt Stephanie had said.

I found my voice. "That's what nine years does to a person."

Her face fell. "I can't believe it's been so long," she said. "You've gotten so beautiful."

Of all the things to say…and it stung, too. If I'd been prettier when I was younger, would she have stayed? "It's plastic surgery," I said. It looked like Mom didn't quite know if I was joking or not. "Botox does wonders," I said, and wiggled my eyebrows to accentuate the lines in my forehead.

"Oh, Cath," she said.

"Don't call me that." She didn't even have the right nickname. I had never been a Cath; it was Cat or nothing. But she didn't have the right to know that.

"You were always such a silly thing." She looked like she wanted to pat my shoulder or something. I stiffened up and took a half step away, and she took that as an answer.

"Too silly for you, apparently."

Mom pressed her lips together, the same expression I'd worn on my own face countless times, and that Grandma had also. I didn't realize Mom did it too. "Catherine, I know it's been a while since I saw you, but I wanted to be here for you."

Too damn late, I wanted to say. *Where were you nine years ago?* But instead I just looked at her, waiting for her to realize the stupidity of her comment.

Stephanie walked by and gave me a reassuring smile. I would much rather have been talking to *her*, and that was saying something. Mom was still staring at me.

"You're grown up," said Mom, and I was alarmed to realize there were actual tears in her eyes.

A thought floated into my head, unbidden, of me stabbing the fork into Mom's eyeball. I was horrified at myself for thinking it, and even more horrified that it actually sounded appealing. I twitched my right hand three times, then tapped my hip. The feeling was still there, though, so I set my fork down in the used dishes tray so that I wouldn't have access to it. The violent intrusive thoughts were the worst because they made me feel so guilty and afraid of myself.

That left an uneaten piece of cheesecake on my plate. A piece of cheesecake that I *really* wanted to eat.

"You're not still twitching, are you?" asked Mom, who had been watching this whole time. "I thought you'd outgrow that."

"You don't outgrow OCD," I said.

She pursed her lips. "It's just such a silly thing. I thought for sure it was just a little-kid thing, that it would be gone by now."

"Little-kid thing?" I said, incredulous. "*Mom*, it's a mental illness. I can't just make it go away."

She didn't seem to accept this answer. "You were always so stubborn as a kid. Always reorganizing your stuffed animals and carrying hand sanitizer everywhere you went. You have no idea how difficult it was."

I stared at her. "You're kidding, right?" We held eye contact. "I think I had a pretty good idea!"

"I kept telling you to just snap out of it!" she said. Her voice was getting louder, exceeding the polite funeral volume, and people were starting to look. Well, good. Let her make a fool of herself; I sure didn't care what these people thought of me. "I thought that shrink would tell you to pull yourself together, but that was just a waste of money."

I had seen that therapist, Ella, right after Dad died.

She diagnosed me with OCD in five minutes flat (as well as Generalized Anxiety Disorder). I had all the symptoms of OCD: intrusive obsessive thoughts with compulsions to try to get rid of the obsessions. But Mom said it was "utter bullshit" and wouldn't take me back. It wasn't until a few years after I moved in with Grandma that I actually started treatment. You can't outgrow OCD. All you can do is learn to cope with it. Mom wasn't exactly the epitome of patience, though, when it came to a mentally ill daughter.

"They told you exactly what was wrong with me. It wasn't a waste of money." Wasn't my mental stability worth anything to her? When she had *seen* the meltdowns I had when it was time to go to school but my socks just weren't fitting right, or when I couldn't go through a doorway because I had stepped with the wrong foot first. It wasn't like I was trying to be difficult. I would've much preferred not to have a mental illness at all, because it was pretty much just hell. But Mom had always treated it like a personal offense.

"It's all in your head!" she exclaimed.

"It's a *mental illness.* That's kind of the *point.*"

"I knew you living with Eleanor was a terrible idea. She's just been encouraging you."

"No," I said, and my voice was loud this time too. "She, unlike you, actually *cared.* She gave me a childhood and actually *loved* me, which is something you never did." Everyone in the room was looking at us now, the little cousins gathered in a group looking fascinated. Mom looked dumbfounded.

I delivered the final blow: "And I never want to speak to you again."

———

The first time I saw Dr. Stephen Trevor, at the age of eleven, was the scariest day of my life. And that's saying a lot for somebody who's been worrying probably before she was even born. I just knew that something was wrong with me but I didn't know what, nor did I know if it could be fixed. I looked back pleadingly at Grandma in the waiting room, but she shooed me into Stephen's office with an encouraging smile. Stephen's practice specialized in anxiety disorders. He diagnosed me with Generalized Anxiety Disorder and Obsessive-Compulsive Disorder in under five minutes, just like Ella had all those years ago.

I thought he must be wrong because I wasn't a very organized or tidy person, nor did I wash my hands more than a normal person. He nodded like he heard this all the time. "That's what most people think OCD is," he told me. "And it's true that for some people it manifests like that. But what OCD is really about is intrusive thoughts. And from what you and your grandma have told me, it sounds like you experience those, right?"

"Yeah," I said uncertainly. "I don't like talking about them." They were the weird thoughts that popped up when I least expected them. Things like, *Put your hand on the iron.* Or *Grab the wheel while Grandma is driving and steer the car off the road.* Or *Punch that random person in the face.* Thoughts I didn't want to be having and didn't agree with but that popped into my head nonetheless.

"Why is that?"

"Well, they sound crazy." Stephen leaned back in his chair, waiting for me to say more. "I mean, they make me sound like I'm a bad person." Guilt pooled like lead in my stomach. "Maybe I am a bad person."

"Ah, so the thought creates a feeling. A bad feeling." I nodded. "And you want the bad feeling to go away, right?"

"Yeah."

"How about we use hand-washing as an example? For a person with contamination OCD, they might have the thought that they've been exposed to germs. Maybe they were on the bus or they touched a shopping cart. Or maybe there was no trigger at all—maybe they were just on the couch at home watching a movie. Whatever the case, they think, *There are germs on my hands and I might get sick.* That's an upsetting thought, right? How does that make them feel?"

"Anxious, I guess."

"Exactly. They want to make the anxiety go away. So what might they do?"

"Wash their hands?"

"Bingo. The thought of getting sick—that's the obsession."

"And the hand-washing is the compulsion?"

Stephen made finger guns at me. "You got it."

"But hand-washing really does get rid of germs. So they're not wrong."

"That's the interesting part," said Stephen. "OCD is often based in reality. But it's taken to the extreme. Washing your hands is a good thing. Obviously. Please wash your hands." I snorted. "But when you wash your hands over and over and over, that's not helpful, right?"

"But I don't wash my hands that much," I said. "I don't really worry about germs that much, to be honest."

"So let's talk about something that does affect you. Your grandma said that sometimes you're late for school because you can't get your socks to feel right."

"Yeah."

"Can you tell me about that?"

I didn't want to. "It sounds like I'm crazy."

"You're not crazy, Cat. I can promise you that I will never judge you for anything that you tell me in here. And I bet it won't be the first time I've heard it, either."

It turned out Stephen was right. Six years later, I'd still never managed to surprise him with anything that I said, no matter how crazy I thought it sounded.

"The good news is that whatever the theme of OCD, we use the same treatment," Stephen continued. "It's called ERP. Exposure Response Prevention. Basically, we want to resist the compulsion. Because every time you give into the compulsion, you're feeding the cycle of OCD." I bit my lip. I didn't like the sound of that. "Have you ever heard of exposure therapy?"

"Yeah."

"Can you tell me what you know about it?"

"I think it's like when somebody's scared of spiders and they spend time with spiders until they aren't scared of them anymore."

"That's the idea. We're doing exposure therapy by exposing you to your obsessions and then preventing the compulsion."

I *definitely* didn't like the sound of that. "But won't that just make the OCD worse?"

"Actually, giving into the compulsions is what feeds the cycle. Every time you have an obsession and do the compulsion, it tells the OCD that it was right. So every time you have an obsession and *don't* do the compulsion, it actually breaks the cycle."

I nodded slowly. "It sounds kind of scary, though."

"We'll start small and go one step at a time. You call the shots on this. You're in charge."

"And it works?"

"It absolutely works. It's all about learning to tolerate discomfort. Every time you do, you're pushing back against OCD. And over time that muscle will get stronger and stronger. Does that sound like something you'd like to try?"

It was. Even though it didn't sound like much fun. But along with the medication that a psychiatrist at the same practice prescribed, at least now I had a fighting chance. And it never would've happened if Grandma hadn't gotten me the mental health care that I needed.

Grandma had given me my life back in so many ways. How could I ever repay her?

———————

Grandma was a packrat. I learned this after I was charged with the task of going through her things. I would have liked to believe it was because I was closest to her and therefore the best person for the job, but it was probably because nobody else wanted to do it.

My extended family had flown home, with the exception of Aunt Stephanie, who was staying around until Grandma's belongings had been sorted to keep track of me. After that, it would be time to find "alternate arrangements," as Lindsey had said. I tried not to think that far ahead, but it became my new obsession: imagining a future with a strange family, or being schlepped from home to home. I would be eighteen in less than a year and would be free then, but the thought of making it by myself in the world filled me with anguish.

In the meantime I was sorting out Grandma's things, making piles of stuff to donate. But I couldn't bring myself to get rid of anything. I was a bit of a hoarder myself, yet another symptom of OCD, and it was doubly hard because these things had belonged to Grandma. If I threw them away and regretted it later, there was no going back.

I found her purse in the hallway, hanging up next to the door. I dumped the contents onto the living room floor and giggled despite myself—I didn't know it was possible to fit *that* many things into your purse. The side pockets were like a miniature pharmacy, holding a tiny bottle of hand sanitizer, a pouch of Kleenex, cough drops, nail clippers, antiseptic wipes, Band-Aids, antibiotic cream, and Grandma's inhaler. The rest of the purse was filled with an assortment of things: menus, business cards, crochet hooks, even a rolled-up pair of socks. Apparently Grandma shared my paranoia about not having something when we needed it.

I started sorting the pile of papers. As I shuffled the stack, a thin, white piece of paper fluttered to the ground. I set down the pile and picked it up. It was a receipt from Yarn Emporium. Unremarkable, by all accounts, as she often bought yarn there. We even took a Saturday evening crochet class there. I wasn't too interested in crochet, but I *was* interested in the ridiculously adorable teenage girl who taught the class. Auri. She had the cutest upturned nose, eyes the color of the sky, and unruly blonde hair that often stuck up on one side, which I had to resist the urge to smooth down behind her perfect ears. And she always smelled like flowers, but not harsh and cloying like my aunt's perfume—more like the light scent of daisies in a meadow. Yeah, I had it bad.

Cute teacher aside, if something was important to Grandma, it was important to me. Even if seeing Auri was also a powerful motivator.

The remarkable part about the receipt was that it was dated the day before Grandma had died. The receipt said something about thanking her for her donation. What did she donate? It wasn't like Grandma to get rid of yarn.

I stood up, leaving the contents of her purse strewn on the floor. Nothing could bring Grandma back, but at least I could find out where she went on her last day. I knew I was clutching at straws, but I hoped it could tell me *something*. A little closure was better than nothing.

Yarn Emporium was a short drive away. I grabbed Grandma's keys from her purse.

Chapter 13
Auri

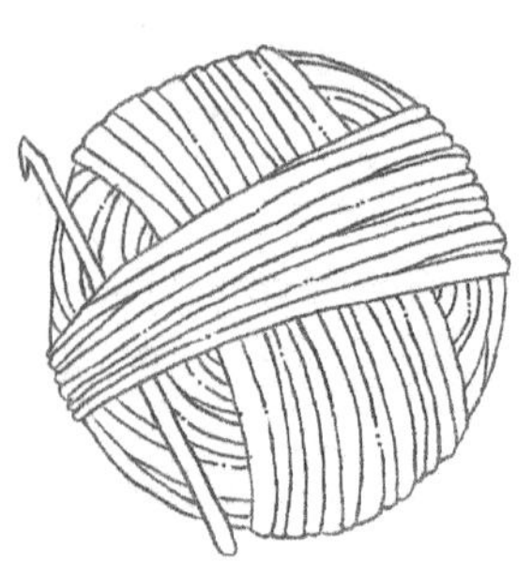

"The Fae don't think of language the way we do. They have the ability to speak the language of anyone they're communicating with. If humans were better at listening—truly listening—deep down in their spirit, they too would possess this skill. But when was the last time you stopped to truly hear the world as it is?"
- *The Modern Manual of Faeries by Eleanor Bishop*

My head propped on my hands, I was fighting to stay awake when the bells rang to signal a new customer. I bolted upright and plastered a smile onto my face, just as my phone made a buzzing noise. "Hello," I called to the customer, a tall red-haired girl. "Can I help you find anything?"

The girl let the door close behind her and walked up to the counter. I pinched my leg to try and wake myself up. "I'm not sure," she said. When she met my eyes, my eyebrows shot up in recognition. It was Cat.

I didn't know what to say. Did she know that her grandma had come here? Did she know that I knew that her grandma was dead? I waited too long to say anything, and she drummed her fingers on the countertop, one at a time. "I don't know where else to go," she said, voice barely audible.

And my heart broke for her.

"I heard about your grandmother, Cat. I'm so sorry for your loss," I said, wishing I had something better to say.

She closed her eyes for a few seconds, like she was trying to keep the pain inside. "Thank you, Auri. I didn't know if you had heard."

"I saw it on the news," I said. Then, without really thinking about it, I covered her hand with my own. Her fingers stilled. "I'm so sorry. Is there anything I can do for you?"

She turned a deep red color that almost matched her hair. Realizing that I had just grabbed her hand without invitation, I removed it quickly. But the flush remained on her cheeks. "Maybe you can help me," she said quietly.

"I'll do anything I can," I said.

"I don't know. I don't know what I expected, coming here." She curled her hands into fists and rested them on the oak countertop. "It's not like you know why she did it."

The note. I need to tell her.

"But Yarn Emporium is one of the last places she visited, and I guess…I don't know. I just had to see it for myself."

My thoughts were churning: did Cat know about the Briars and Roses Shawl? "I'm really sorry about your grandma," I said again. I couldn't imagine that kind of pain, didn't know how Cat was standing here and functioning. "Actually, I think I may know why she was here."

Her eyes lit up a little, but it looked like she was trying to rein in her excitement. Not get her hopes up, probably. "Really? I knew it was a long shot, coming here, but…"

"You thought maybe there would be some clue?" I finished.

Cat nodded.

"Actually," I said, "I think I can help you." An idea was formulating. Cat needed to figure out what was behind her grandma's death; I needed to save myself from the same fate. Even if I wasn't in the same situation, there was something about her that made me want to help. I couldn't help wondering why I had waited so long to talk to her outside of crochet class. There was something about her that intrigued me in a way I didn't have words for. "My break is in twenty minutes. Can you hang out until then?"

Cat hesitated. I saw her hand go to her pocket where her car keys were sticking out a little. "Yes. I can do that," she told me, and I wondered just what she was thinking.

Cat and I walked to the Starbucks down the street. She ordered a white chocolate mocha and I got an iced caramel macchiato. We found a cozy booth by the window, and Cat started telling me about the last days she had spent with her grandmother.

"It's strange how clearly you remember things," she mused, wrapping her hands around her coffee to warm them. "It was her birthday. Seventy-three years old. I teased her mercilessly," she said with a small laugh. "I brought her out to lunch, but she was acting a little…off."

"How so?" I asked, taking a sip of my drink, ice cubes clinking against my teeth.

"She went out on some errand," said Cat, "but I didn't know where she went. That's the weird part. What was she doing at your store?"

She fumbled for something in her pocket, then slid a receipt onto the wooden table top. A date was written at the top, and I immediately recognized my own handwriting.

"Eleanor brought in a project donation a few days ago," I said, and I told her what had happened, weird behavior and all. She was quiet, listening. I took a breath and asked, "Can I tell you something crazy?"

"Crazier than what's already happened?" One side of her mouth quirked upward. "Go for it."

I showed her my bandaged fingers, one of them bloodstained. She winced and curled her own fingers to her palm like she knew the feeling. "You pick your fingernails, huh?" she asked.

"Not really," I said. "This is from crocheting."

"Yikes. How did you manage that?"

"It's your grandma's shawl," I said. "Honestly, I think… this sounds crazy, but I think it's cursed." I summarized the shawl situation, including what Aidyn and I had done at the community center, but I left out the suicide note. I didn't want to hide it from her, but I also didn't feel comfortable breaking that news to her. I would give it to her soon.

My phone let out a croaking noise from in my bag. Cat's eyes followed the sound. "Do you want to check that?" she asked.

"If you don't mind," I said, typing in my code. "It might be something about the shawl." Sure enough, I had a new email with the subject line "Rummage Sale Shawl." *Finally!* "Oh, excellent. We got a reply."

I quickly scanned the contents. It was from a woman named Nerissa—no last name. She informed me that she had been given the shawl as a gift—"It's a long story," she wrote—and had then donated it to the rummage sale. "If you want to meet me at the rec center, we can have a chat about it, but I don't know how much help I'll be."

I handed the phone to Cat so she could read it. "Do you want to come with me?" I asked. "It might be helpful."

"Yes please," she said. "Can you see if she's free tomorrow?"

I quickly fired back a reply, and Cat and I finished our drinks in relative silence. She kept tapping her fingers on the table; they were slender and delicate, a few freckles sprinkled atop them, and I found myself wondering what they would feel like laced through my own. The thought startled me. She was good company. I knew from our crochet lessons that she was sweet and a quick learner, but I didn't expect her to be this easy to hang out with. I glanced over at her to find her deep in thought, studying the clouds. Probably thinking about her grandmother. Then she looked at me and caught me staring, so I smiled.

"Thank you for your help, Auri," she said, taking one

last drink of her coffee. "It was really nice to get out of the house."

"My pleasure," I said, and I meant it. "I'm glad you came along. And I'm sorry about your grandma."

"Thanks. Me too." Cat sighed. "I just can't believe she would have killed herself. I thought she was happy…" She grew quiet, like she hadn't meant to say it out loud. "She didn't even leave a note."

My heart sank. I had known this moment would come, but I wasn't ready. I just couldn't give it to her right now. Not here, at Starbucks, surrounded by strangers. I would wait for a better time. Until then I would keep the note safe for her. "It's not your fault," I said. I knew that for sure. "You can't blame yourself."

"I wish that were true."

I hated seeing her in pain. "My aunt died by suicide about ten years ago. I saw how much it hurt my mom. She said a lot of the same things that you're saying. But it wasn't her fault either."

"Thank you for saying that."

I wished there was more I could say. I wished I could take away her pain. "I wish I could do something."

"I'm just glad I'm not alone right now."

"I'm here," I said, feeling woefully inadequate.

Cat closed her eyes and took a long, quivering breath.

"Are, uh, you okay? Can I…" What could I do? "Get you a glass of water?" *Brilliant, Auri.*

"A glass of water would actually be nice," she said.

So I sprung up to fetch it for her, grateful for something to do. By the time I had returned with a cup of ice water, she was wiping her eyes. "Thanks, Auri," she said.

"Of course," I said. "I'm really sorry."

Cat took a sip of water, the ice cubes clattering around her teeth. "I just can't believe she's gone."

"She loved you so much," I said. "Anybody could see that."

Tears shone in her eyes. "I loved her so much too. I just… Ugh." She wiped her eyes on the sleeve of her ivory sweater.

"She knitted you that, didn't she?" I asked to try and distract her.

She nodded. "A few years ago."

She shrugged. "It's nice yarn."

"Knitting someone a sweater. Now that's true love."

She gave a watery smile. "I wish I had known how she was feeling. That she was hurting this much. Even before the shawl got added to the mix."

"There's no way of knowing what's going on in somebody's head," I said. "And, I think, mental illness is one of the hardest things to understand."

Cat laughed under her breath. "You have no idea."

"We'll figure it out," I said. "Believe me, I never thought I'd be suggesting that there's actual magic at work here. But a curse doesn't seem so far-fetched anymore." Even as I said it, an image of the shawl floated into my head, and my fingers twitched as if reaching for a crochet hook. I slid my hand into my bag to play with the fabric of the shawl, longing to keep working on it.

"My grandma always believed in magic," said Cat. "Magical thinking, that's what she called it." She smiled ruefully. "It would be just like her to stumble upon a curse."

We exchanged numbers so I could call her if Nerissa got back to me. Then we parted ways. But I kept thinking about her.

Chapter 14
Cat

"It may seem strange that some people can see the Fae while other people in the same family cannot. But people can be vastly different, even when they're related. Is it so strange to think that extends to the realm of the magical, too?"

- *The Modern Manual of Faeries by Eleanor Bishop*

WHEN I GOT BACK TO THE HOTEL WHERE STEPHANIE AND I were staying, there was a police car parked out front. I froze, thinking back to the days where I didn't have to worry if they were there for me. I wasn't a prisoner, though. I shouldn't be in trouble for anything.

Still, I nervously tapped my fingers on my legs three times as I walked into the lobby. Lindsey was there. I recognized her by her long, black hair, which was pulled back into a ponytail. Stephanie was standing next to her, taller than Lindsey by a good six inches, although her high heels did play a role in that. My mom's side of the family ran tall, that was for sure—I'd been five foot ten since I was fifteen. I used to feel self-conscious about my height, but Grandma had always told me I was statuesque, and seeing myself through her eyes helped me embrace it.

What am I going to do without her?

"Catherine! Where have you been?" my aunt exclaimed, *click-clack*ing over to intercept me. "I was so worried about you!"

I doubted that. She was probably just worried that she would get in trouble if I went missing.

"I just went to the yarn store," I told her. "I didn't mean to worry you." I really didn't care.

Lindsey walked briskly over to us. "Catherine, I'm glad to see you're all right," she said. "Next time, please don't run off without telling someone where you're going."

I didn't realize I was under house arrest, I wanted to say. Instead, I nodded and apologized.

I was left with Stephanie, who was looking at me like she didn't know what to do with me. "You went to the yarn store, honey?"

"I wanted to return some yarn that Grandma had," I said, to prevent further questions.

She gave a brisk nod. "That's good. I'm glad to see you're organizing her things." She paused, sighed, and said: "I think it would be best if you stayed here, in the hotel, until we can make other arrangements." There they were again, those "other arrangements."

"You mean I can't leave?" I said, sure that I had misunderstood.

She dithered. "It sounds bad like that, I know. It's just that you're not in the best frame of mind, and I worry about you when you run off on your own. You're only seventeen, honey. Teenagers don't always have their best interests at heart, and I would hate for you to do something you'd regret. It runs in the family, you know, and the influence Eleanor must've had on you…I just worry."

It took me a minute to sort through this speech. Then I realized what she was saying. "You're worried I'm going to off myself, too."

"Oh, sweetie."

"She didn't 'influence' me." I crossed my arms. "Suicide isn't catching, you know."

"Of course not. But with your own mental illness…"

What was it with my family and their fundamental misunderstanding of OCD? "I have obsessions. They don't make me kill myself!" I was devastated, yes, but not depressed.

"Whatever you may have, Cat, I'm going to insist you stay here," said Stephanie. Her tone made it clear that this was the end of the discussion. "It won't be for very long."

I let out a huff of frustration. In her mind, I was probably acting exactly as she expected: the rebellious teenager who couldn't be trusted. "Fine."

As I walked to the elevator to go to the sixth floor, which would always set me on edge, I made sure Grandma's car keys were still in my pocket.

Auri texted me later that night. I was laying on my bed, the door between suites cracked open just a little at Stephanie's insistence, reading a book I had gotten at the hotel gift shop. When my phone went off, I dropped the book on my face in surprise.

For months, I had tried to work up the courage to ask Auri for her number, but it had taken a death and a curse for it to finally happen. I quickly read the message, my stomach filled with nervous flutters.

Auri: Nerissa just replied. She's meeting us at Tacoma Community Center tomorrow morning at 10. Work for you?

I tried to ignore the butterflies and typed back.

Cat: Sounds good, I'll see you there. Thanks!

I closed my phone. Then I had the terrible feeling that I had accidentally sent that text to the wrong person. What if I texted Stephanie by mistake and she confiscated my phone? *Relax,* I told myself. *You don't even have Stephanie's phone number.* But I double-checked anyway to assuage my nerves. I hadn't been this nervous texting someone in, well, as long as I could remember. Auri had no idea.

I set my alarm for eight the next morning. When it woke me up, I quickly turned it off so as to not wake Stephanie. Then I shoved all the clothes I owned into a backpack and stuck Simon the sloth on top for good measure. Whatever happened, I didn't plan on coming back here.

I turned on the shower in the bathroom between our adjoining suites. Then I locked the door. With any luck,

Stephanie would hear the running water and assume I was taking a shower. That would buy me a good twenty minutes. I darted back into my room, grabbed the keys, and made a beeline for the elevator.

My plan was to pick up Grandma's car and drive to the community center. With any luck, we would get some helpful information from Nerissa, and then maybe we could solve this whole mess. After that…well, I would figure it out from there.

I didn't know if I had what it took for a life on the run, but what other choice did I have? All I had to do was make it until I was eighteen.

I got into Grandma's car, which smelled of sage from the sachet tucked into the glove compartment. It smelled like Grandma. Tears sprang to my eyes. But if I started crying, I would never stop. I pushed the tears down and focused on putting the keys into the ignition and starting the engine.

The community center was about twenty minutes from our house. I hated driving, even when I took the back roads. I always had a lingering fear that I would hit a pedestrian, or that I would get into a car accident…maybe even on purpose. I knew it was just my OCD talking, but it didn't make driving any more enjoyable.

The intrusive thoughts were the worst part of OCD for me—the fear that I would lose control and hurt somebody, drive my car off a bridge or straight into the concrete barrier on the highway, mow down a pedestrian…the possibilities were as endless as my brain was creative.

The suicidal intrusive thoughts were extra scary because I didn't want to kill myself—at least I didn't think I did. So why were these thoughts popping into my head? It took me a few months of seeing Stephen before I was brave enough to tell him about it. He told me that a thought was just a thought. Everybody had weird thoughts. Like when you're standing on a high place and you think *What if I jump?* even though you have no intention of doing so. But a brain with OCD holds onto those thoughts and obsesses over them. "Your brain's job is to make thoughts. They don't have to mean anything," he told me. So now when I got those random, disturbing thoughts, I tried not to hold onto them, to let them pass like a leaf floating down the river. Well, this river was all white-water rapids, and the leaves were full-grown trees.

One of the worst things about OCD was feeling so alone. If I tried to tell anyone about the intrusive thoughts, they would think I was crazy. They would think that I wanted to kill myself or hurt somebody else even though I didn't want that at all. I didn't want anyone to be afraid of me. Even if sometimes—*all the time*—I was afraid of my own thoughts.

I was relieved when the brick building came into view. I parked the car, locked it, double- and triple-checked that I had locked it, and started for the building.

Chapter 15
Auri

"Faeries can enter the dreams of humans if they choose to. If you have a reccurring dream, pay attention to the symbols and the people within. There may be a message for you."

- The Modern Manual of Faeries by Eleanor Bishop

THE NEXT DAY DAWNED BRIGHT AND EARLY. MOM DIDN'T need the car today, so she let me take it out and I drove, yawning, to the rec center. The Briars and Roses Shawl was nestled next to me, and every so often I reached down to touch it, just to make sure it was still there. I pulled into a parking spot next to a smart car, bouncing off the parking curb.

"We're here," I announced, fully aware that rather than talking to myself (which I did on a regular basis), I was talking to the shawl. "Ready to meet your previous owner?"

The shawl did not reply.

I scooped it up and made for the air-conditioned hall, which was filled but not packed with people. Cat's long dark red hair was visible from across the hall, and she looked up and waved when I entered. I waved back and threaded my way through the throng of people, plunking down next to her on the couch.

"Hey," I said, weirdly self-conscious.

"Hi," she said. "How you doing?"

"I feel like I should be asking you that. How are you holding up?"

She shrugged, and a flicker of emotion passed over her, but she didn't elaborate. "Hanging in there. Thanks for coming."

"You're welcome," I said. "We're going to figure this out."

I got up to buy two cups of iced tea from the little café in the lobby so that we would have an excuse to lounge around. I set mine on the floor and continued the next row of the shawl, Cat watching me closely. Her brown eyes were enormous in her freckled face, and I found myself captivated by the way her eyelashes—the same dark red as her hair—fluttered when she blinked.

"That looks hard," she said with a laugh. I smiled but kept crocheting. "You're good at it, though. How long have you been crocheting?"

"About eight years," I said, which did sound quite impressive. The hook pricked my finger—why was it so sharp?—and I winced.

"So did you teach yourself or what?"

"My aunt taught me when I was eight," I said, watching a bead of blood well up on my fingertip. "I was at a family reunion and got really bored, so I went to hang out with the grown-ups, and Aunt Lily took pity on me. I barely put down the hook for the next week."

"I'd like to get better at it," said Cat. "It was never really my thing, but Grandma loved it so much…maybe I'll keep taking lessons." She blushed, looking at me quickly. "I mean, if you still want to teach me."

"You're good at it," I said. "You caught onto the basics really fast."

She gave me a tight smile. "It's easy, the way you explain it. I looked forward to that class every week."

I nudged Cat and pointed to a lady who was walking around, craning her neck like she was looking for someone. "Do you think that's her?"

We studied the woman. She looked to be in her sixties with pale skin and hair so white it seemed to glow. She wore enormous silver wire-rimmed glasses. Her blue floor-length dress swished as she walked, and she carried a tote bag that said "I'd Rather Be Kayaking." All in all, she was nothing like I had expected, and judging from Cat's incredulous expression, she felt the same way.

The lady turned and saw the shawl sitting next to me. Her face brightened and she made a beeline for our couch. I found myself sitting up straighter. "Might you be Auri Davis?" she asked.

"Yeah," I said, standing up. "Thanks so much for meeting me here." We shook hands; her grip was so strong it felt like she had broken my already-battered fingers. "This is my friend Cat." I glanced over at her.

"I hope you don't mind that I tagged along," said Cat.

Nerissa shook her head. "Oh, of course not! I was thrilled to get your email, Auri. Truth is, I've been wanting to talk to someone about this wrap."

"Do you want some tea, ma'am?" I said, gesturing to my untouched cup. She laughed.

She made a face. "Please call me Nerissa. Ma'am makes me sound old." She plucked the cup from my hand and took a sip, then shuddered. "So sweet. I never could get used to that."

Nerissa pulled over a chair and sat down, facing us. "Do you mind if I take a look at this?" she asked, and I handed her the wrap. She gently tugged it between her fingers, admiring the lace like she was greeting an old friend. "I hoped I would never see this again."

"Why not?" I asked, trying to sound casual but mentally screaming at her to give us some answers.

"Well," said Nerissa, "I got this yarn at my fiftieth birthday. For a gift. You asked for information about this shawl, and I can give it to you, but it's a bit of a strange story."

Cat looked at me like she was trying to tell me something, but I wasn't sure what. "Please do enlighten us," I said.

"Oh, well, if you're sure..." While she talked, she folded up the Briars and Roses Shawl with expert hands. "I wasn't too concerned about a party, to tell you the truth. If I had had my way, I wouldn't have invited anyone—just too much hassle, and too much money! But my sister insisted. She's always been into celebrations, but I haven't. So we quickly slapped together a guest list. I picked a couple of friends, and she invited *everyone*—you know, the obligatory extended family members.

"At my birthday dinner, a strange woman showed up at the door and demanded to be let in. I didn't know who she was, but figured maybe she was one of my extended family members…you know, some second cousin once removed that I'd forgotten. I didn't want to offend her. She was insulted she hadn't been invited, and, well, what could I do?" Nerissa squeezed the shawl between her hands. "So, yes, I invited her in."

"Who was she?" asked Cat, who was listening intently. I half-expected her to start taking notes.

"That's the thing," said Nerissa, "we don't know. I asked my friends later, and they had never seen her before. We thought maybe she was just some random person who had decided to crash a party. Or maybe she was mad. I don't know."

"So where does the shawl come into this?" I asked, genuinely curious now.

"It was a gift. It wasn't until later that we realized the stranger must have left it."

"Huh," said Cat. She took a sip of her iced tea. "Do you know why?"

I had a sinking feeling that I *did* know why, but it was a preposterous thought: she had wanted to curse Nerissa. That was ridiculous; curses didn't exist, they were the stuff of fairytales. But I couldn't shake the idea.

"You know, I *don't*," said Nerissa. "But here's the thing: this wrap has been really bothering me."

I perked up. "Me too," I said, and she smiled.

"Of course it is, dear. You posted a notice begging for help!" Nerissa held up the shawl to illustrate her point.

"No, not because of that." I hesitated, looking to Cat for support. She nodded encouragingly. "It's because, um, this shawl is, like…taking over my life."

Her eyes lit up. "I know just what you mean."

I had been hoping she would say that. "Did you experience it too, then?"

"Well, I was never much of a crocheter," she said, "but I watched some YouTube videos and managed to get about a row done, and—"

I interrupted. "Did your hands go numb?"

"Pardon?" She looked confused. "My hands did tingle a bit, when I first started…is that what you mean?"

"Yes!" A piece of the puzzle seemed to *clunk* together in my head. "That's it, then. This shawl is cursed!" I wished I hadn't said that so loudly; the room quieted and heads turned toward me. I slouched and looked at my knees.

Nerissa laughed, and my heart sank—did she not believe me after all? "That's an interesting theory, Auri." Why had I made the mistake of telling her? "I have to say, it doesn't seem out of the question."

Cat slid her hand into mine and held it up for Nerissa to see. A tingle shot through my arm, even though her hand was quite warm. I tried to pull away, but she held on. My heart beat faster, like someone was pumping me full of adrenaline. "Check out the Band-Aids," she said, with an apologetic glance at me. "That's what happened to her from crocheting. She's been crocheting for eight years, and how many rows did you get done? Five?"

I nodded, curling my fingers under my palm to hide them.

"That was in s few days," added Cat. "I don't think this is going anywhere good. Nerissa, I think this is why my grandmother died. It's because she was so distracted with this shawl thing." She bit her lip. "She killed herself," she said quietly. "And I don't know why. So the question is, can you help us?" Cat let go of my hand, and I let it hover in midair for a second before clasping my hands together on the gray sofa.

Nerissa paused for a long moment; I held my breath. "I don't know what I can do," she said, "but I'll do my best. After all, the shawl did a number on me too. Do you wonder why I donated it? I've been going to yoga every day to try and forget about it. I've hung on for a year, but then again, I only crocheted one row."

I sighed in relief. "Thank you so much," I said, slumping back against the couch. "Now what do you think we should do?"

Chapter 16
Cat

"Faeries trade in secrets and riddles. Be careful what you tell them. The more they know about you, the more they have to use against you. In the age of the Internet, faeries can take advantage of humans more than ever because they know so much about you. The more familiar with you they act, the more danger you'll be in."

- The Modern Manual of Faeries by Eleanor Bishop

Nerissa's story made everything line up. I knew it was irrational, but I couldn't help but hope that the shawl really *was* the reason Grandma had died. It would be so much easier to blame it on something else rather than think it was my fault. The thought had been pulsing at the back of my mind for days now, and it made me feel sick. But the lack of a suicide note and Nerissa's story about the shawl were making it seem like there was an outside influence here.

Auri's fingers were twitching, a motion I was all too familiar with. "You look like you're crocheting," I said.

She paused. "I guess you're right. Hey, Nerissa, would you mind handing that to me?"

Nerissa handed the shawl to Auri, who relaxed like she'd just regained a missing part of herself. It reminded me of my own sense of relief when I could indulge in a compulsion to make the obsession of the hour go away. In this case, it was a much more visible example while mine was all inside my head. But engaging in my compulsions only made the OCD cycle worse. What if it was the same for Auri?

"How's it feeling?" asked Nerissa. Auri didn't look up from her crocheting.

"Painful, honestly. But not bad." Her fingers were moving so quickly, it hardly looked like she was crocheting at all. During all our lessons, I had been in awe of how fast she was. Even more so than Grandma, who was immensely talented but burdened with arthritis in her fingers.

I wasn't sure where we would go from here. All I knew was that I couldn't go back home. "Nerissa," I asked, "where did you have that party again?"

Nerissa fixed her gaze on me. She had the uncanniest eyes I'd ever seen, a silvery-blue color that made me feel as if she could read my thoughts. "Oh, it was a wilderness retreat center up in North Cascades National Park," she said. "Beautiful place, really."

"Anything unusual about it?" I asked.

"Apart from being rather secluded, no, nothing comes to mind."

"Do you think we could find something there?"

Nerissa tilted her head, considering. Auri spoke up. "Kind

of a reach, isn't it? I get where you're coming from, but the party was a few years ago, right?"

She was right, but I couldn't think of anything else to do. Tracing the previous owners of the shawl seemed to be the most logical thing to do. I said as much. Nerissa was nodding. "I share your opinion, Cat. I don't know what we'd be able to discover there, but I'd be happy to show you girls the center."

That caught Auri's attention. She looked up from the shawl, fingers poised mid-stitch. We exchanged glances. "Take us to North Cascades?" she asked, her apprehension evident.

It did sound like a stupid idea: two teenage girls getting into a car with a complete stranger and heading for another city. Any number of things could happen. I didn't care so much about myself—I would do anything to find out what had really happened to Grandma—but I didn't want to drag Auri into things. "Can I talk to you for a minute?" I asked Auri.

We excused ourselves from the conversation and I led Auri to a spot at the side of the hall, behind a large potted plant with a red-and-white ceramic mushroom in the dirt. My heart leaped to be so close to her. "I know this idea sounds crazy," I said, "but part of me thinks we might find something."

"Yeah," she said, "the inside of a human trafficking ring."

I bit my lip. There were plenty of horrifying images in my head, too.

Auri sighed. "I know, Cat. Believe me, I want to find out what's going on just as much as you do." She paused at the look on my face. "I'm sorry. This must be so much harder for you…I know what happened with your grandma…"

"Don't feel guilty about that," I told her. "If we're going to do this, I don't want you going along out of a sense of duty."

She tucked a strand of blonde hair behind her ear. I longed to be able to do that for her. God, she was beautiful, the way she bit her lip when she was thinking, the way her eyes were the color of the sky. I wanted to touch her so badly it hurt. "My instincts are just screaming at me that this is a bad idea."

I nodded. "Mine too." But my instincts were really just screaming at me to kiss her. I stamped them down with difficulty.

"You know," she said, "we could always go on our own." I considered the idea, leaning back against the wall. "You have a car, right?"

I wanted more than anything to say yes, that we could do that, but fear stopped me short. "It's my grandma's."

Auri watched me closely. "Would you be comfortable using it?"

"Grandma wouldn't mind, if that's what you're asking." She encouraged me to drive anywhere. The problem was my damned anxiety. But I had never told anyone about it, besides Grandma. "I don't know if I can drive so far."

"Nervous?"

I nodded once, worried she was judging me.

"I get that. I was scared when I first learned how to drive," she said. "Since Mom's always using the car to get to work, I barely ever get to practice." Relief flooded through me, along with a tinge of shame for having so quickly misjudged her. "You don't have to. But if we did go, I'd be with you the whole time. I'm a good navigator."

I took a deep breath and slowly let it out. Now that I didn't feel pressured, by her *or* myself, I could actually imagine doing it.

Auri put a hand on my arm. Her touch sent a wave of butterflies through my stomach, and all my focus went to where she was touching my skin. This cemented my resolve. "I'm not making any promises," I said, "but maybe we can give it a go."

Her face broke into a wide smile, one that lit up her whole face. I wanted nothing more than to kiss her, and it took all my resolve to keep a platonic distance and not grab her hand when she removed it from my arm. "You can do it," she said. "Let's go."

We explained to Nerissa that her offer was very kind, but we didn't want to inconvenience her, so we would just go by ourselves. Auri, who had appointed herself navigator, asked for directions. North Cascades was about three hours from Tacoma, probably more when you factored in traffic.

"I have a map in the car," she said. "Why don't you follow me down to the parking lot so you can hit the road after I find it?"

"You go ahead," said Auri. "I'm gonna stop in the bathroom before we go." She gave me a gentle nudge toward the door.

I followed Nerissa down the path to the parking lot. The outside of Tacoma Community Center was beautifully landscaped, filled with Japanese maples and flowers of all colors. Grandma and I had spent hours in the garden together, growing vegetables that we would cook into casseroles and pasta dishes. Her zucchini bread was legendary. Even though she didn't like purely decorative plants, she had helped me build fairy gardens when I was younger. The fairies left notes for me in the snapdragons, which I kept for years. Grandma swore she didn't write them, but that was just the kind of thing she would say.

"Here we are," said Nerissa, jolting me from my daydream. For a moment I was surprised that it wasn't Grandma next to me, and I had a brief moment of pain.

Nerissa's car was a PT Cruiser that looked like it had seen one too many road trips. The bumper was held on with duct tape, and a deep gouge on the side revealed peeling orange paint. She fumbled around in her purse. "I just have to find the keys," she said.

It took her a long time. Finally the car doors unlocked, and she opened the one to the backseat. "Come help me find it, Cat," she ordered. I obliged, leaning into the backseat and expecting to find a mountain of stuff to dig through. But the backseat was pristine, like the car had just come from a dealership. A *very used car* dealership.

An alarm sounded in my nervous system. "Nerissa?" I started to get out of the car as fast as I could, but something sharp jabbed me in the side of the neck. I yelped, slapping at the spot.

Nerissa was holding a hypodermic needle with a few drops of liquid dripping from the tip. It didn't look like any drug I had ever seen, though: it was glittering like molten silver. "What did you do to me?" I tried to exclaim, but my lips felt numb, like they had been pumped full of Novocain.

My legs weren't responding anymore, and my knees buckled. Nerissa caught me mid-fall and shoved me into the backseat. I felt the panic rising inside me, but all I could do was move my eyes back and forth.

The last thing I heard before that stuff claimed my consciousness was Auri's voice as she approached the car... and Nerissa giving her the same treatment.

Chapter 17
Auri

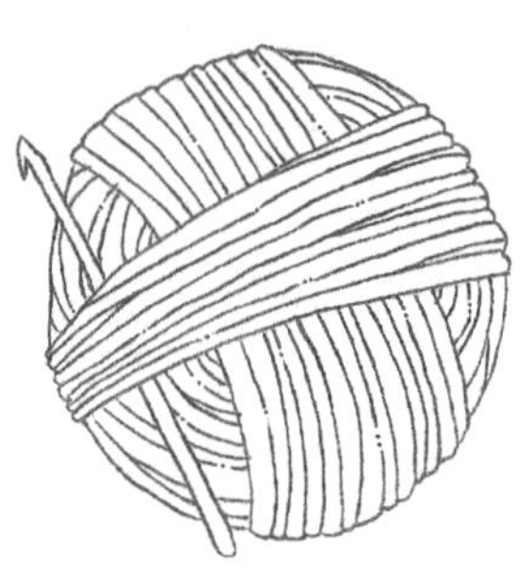

"Faeries favor the isolated places where humans don't go: the ocean, the forest, the caves. In these places, if you are quiet and listen very carefully, you can catch a glimpse of magic."

- The Modern Manual of Faeries by Eleanor Bishop

I WOKE UP TO THE WORST HEADACHE OF MY LIFE, WHICH felt as if two people were pounding rocks on either side of my head. My eyeballs felt like they were about to pop out from the pressure. I groaned, not moving.

The ground was swaying under me, like I'd fallen asleep in a hammock.

I started to feel uneasy.

I cracked open my eyelids to find myself looking at the inside of a car. My wrists were tied together, and I was squashed into the footwell of the backseat. Next to me, Cat was in the same position, but she was fully conked out.

My unease kicked into full-fledged panic. I shot upright, but I was so dizzy that I flopped right back down again. My memory slammed back into me: coming down to the parking lot to find Cat sprawled in the backseat of Nerissa's car, and then something sharp poking into my neck. She had kidnapped us!

I slowly eased myself to a sitting position. I was wedged behind the passenger seat, so I could see Nerissa in the driver's seat. "Where are you taking us?" I asked, my voice hoarse.

Her silvery eyes met mine in the rearview mirror. "Awake, I see."

It might have been smarter to pretend I was still asleep, so I could try and catch her off guard, but it was too late for that. Besides, I was tied up and barely able to see straight. "What did you give me?"

"Oh, nothing that won't wear off in a few hours," she said cheerfully. The car swerved as she made a lane change. Looking out the window, I saw we were on the expressway. My heart sank. Judging by the light, it was early afternoon; we had to be miles away from home by now.

"You might find the dust quite enjoyable," she added. "Most of us do."

I'd never taken them myself, but I was fairly familiar with all kinds of drugs thanks to the less-than-stellar neighborhood Mom, Aidyn, and I lived in. I knew there were nicknames for them, but this was a new one to me. "What is it?" I asked, then cleared my throat.

"Faeriedust. You wouldn't have heard of it."

I fidgeted with the cord around my hands. It was thin nylon rope, but it was wrapped around my hands so many times that I doubted I could wriggle free, even if my muscles were responding properly. How many hours would it take to wear off? And just where was she taking us? I was half glad Cat wasn't awake to experience this. But the other half of me didn't want to go through it alone.

I was spared my mental struggle when she groaned and started stirring.

"Cat," I said. "Can you hear me?"

"Mmm." She twitched and opened her eyes. I saw the moment she recognized our situation, the moment her brown eyes widened and took in the scene. "Oh my God. Auri..."

"It's okay," I said. Which had to be extremely convincing coming from the girl tied up in the backseat of a car.

"Nerissa! Open the door!" exclaimed Cat, wriggling to sit up.

Nerissa glanced at us in the mirror. "Struggle all you like. We have a good three hours more to go."

Cat pressed her lips together tightly, and I suddenly knew what she was after. "Nerissa, she's going to be sick."

Nerissa looked unfazed. She rolled down the window. Cat's body heaved, and she turned away from me to throw up out the window. She collapsed back against the wall. Sweat was beading on her forehead and she looked even paler than usual, making her dusting of freckles stand out.

"Are you okay?" I asked. I felt pretty crappy from the drug, yes, but she was taking it worse than me.

"I feel awful," she whispered, and was sick again.

"She's having some sort of reaction," I said, springing

into action. I used all my willpower to push myself off the floor and slide onto the backseat. I would have hit Nerissa if it weren't for the divider between front and backseat, like police cars have. *Not* standard issue for a PT Cruiser. "I don't know what's in that drug, but she's reacting to it."

"That's impossible," said Nerissa.

"Look at her!"

Cat was curled up and looked like she might be starting to have a seizure. Anguished, I tried to pry off the rope with my shoe, but all I succeeded in doing was hurting my wrists. "Do something!" I exclaimed.

Nerissa mumbled a curse under her breath and made a sweeping right turn onto the next freeway exit. There was nothing I could do to help Cat. I nearly dislocated my arm trying to get my phone out of my pocket, but I couldn't reach it. If something happened to her, it would be all my fault; I had pulled her into this situation. The car screeched to a halt in the parking lot of a Chevron gas station, and Nerissa rushed around to Cat's side of the car.

I wanted to make a run for it, but if I did that, Cat might not get the help she needed. I didn't trust Nerissa, but she was Cat's best chance right now. Nerissa opened the door and scooped Cat up effortlessly, even though Cat was as tall as the older woman. She pressed a hand to Cat's forehead and began chanting something under her breath.

"You're kidding me," I said. "That's the best you can do?"

"Shhh," said Nerissa sharply. Her chant was rhythmic and soothing, a cross between a lullaby and a hymn. She kept her hand pressed to Cat's forehead, and as I watched closely, I saw a faint glow spring up from the palm of her hand. It absorbed into Cat's skin like a luxury lotion. Cat stopped seizing, and her head lolled onto Nerissa's shoulder.

My stomach filled with fear. Was she still breathing?

Then she coughed and sat up. She didn't seem to have the energy to push away from Nerissa, but she turned her head and blinked at me. "Auri," she said.

"I'm here." I scooted over and slid my bound hand into hers. Her fingers curled around mine, and her eyes closed again.

"What happened?" I demanded for the fifteenth time. Cat was asleep with her head on my shoulder, hand still in mine, and Nerissa was cruising down the highway again. So far, she had been ignoring my questions, but I would not be dissuaded. "You said it was impossible for someone to be allergic to the drug. But Cat was."

She shifted, snuggling closer to me in her sleep. I squeezed her hand.

"Stop pestering me," said Nerissa. "I'll answer your questions later. Your situation doesn't change even if I do entertain your questions."

"No, you'll answer them *now*," I said. "You know I won't leave it alone."

I rested my head on Cat's. Her hair smelled like vanilla, and it sent tingles through me. If she woke up, she would likely move away, and I found myself not wanting that—probably because it was comforting, given the stressful situation. That was all.

"Fine." Nerissa raised her chin. "Where I come from, this is a very popular…medication of sorts. I'm sure you have them here, too. The difference is that we don't have medication like yours where I come from. We're more natural, I suppose you would say. Whatever Cat had in her system reacted poorly with the drug. I merely dissolved the existing medication in her body."

I briefly wondered what medication Cat was on, but it wasn't my business and it didn't matter right now anyway. "What do you mean? Where are you from?" I asked. What place didn't use medication at all?

"Feylinn," she replied. "We'll be there in just over an hour. Now I want you to be quiet."

"What's Feylinn?"

"Do you want me to give you another dose of faeriedust?"

"Not really."

"Then shut up and make sure your friend doesn't have any more problems."

She wouldn't be having problems at all if you weren't drugging her, I wanted to shout. But even though I wasn't always the sharpest tool in the shed, I knew you shouldn't torment somebody who had kidnapped you.

I knew that we had to get out, though. When you get kidnapped, your odds of survival went *way* down if the kidnapper managed to take you to another place. If we could get out of the car and make a run for it, we could get help before she took us to…wherever Feylinn was. Images swam through my head of being locked in a cellar for months, tortured and abused, all because I had been dumb enough to meet up with a complete stranger. You don't think of a middle-aged woman as being the perpetrator of these crimes. But I guess it was a painful lesson in not judging a book by its cover. Literally everybody can be a danger, yippee!

Chapter 18
Cat

"If you ever happen upon an unnaturally straight road in the forest, do not follow unless you're prepared for what you may find. These energy paths, called ley lines, are places where our world touches the faerie world. When the ley lines intersect, a person or faerie may cross from one world to the other. But visiting another realm comes at a price, and you should never go unprepared: once you go through, you may never come back."

- The Modern Manual of Faeries by Eleanor Bishop

I PRETENDED TO BE ASLEEP FOR FAR LONGER THAN I SHOULD have just so I didn't have to move away from Auri. To feel her hair tickling the side of my head and smell her flowery perfume was intoxicating, and I didn't want it to end. But I wanted to see where we were going, so I finally lifted my head off her shoulder and peered out the window with blurry eyes.

"Oh, good," said Auri, stretching her shoulders as best she could with tied hands. "I was starting to think you were pulling a Sleeping Beauty."

I blushed, both at the word "beauty" and the thought of Auri waking me up with a kiss. "Sorry to use you as a pillow that long," I mumbled, sure that my face was flaming red.

I might have imagined it, but Auri was blushing a little herself. "Don't sweat it. Nerissa says we're almost there."

Nerissa was telling the truth for a change. It took us twenty-one minutes to get there, wherever "there" was. During that time, Auri told me everything that had happened, from when I passed out to when Nerissa revived me. She asked if I had any memory of it. I could only remember flashes of it, like bits of a barely-remembered dream: a warm hand on my forehead and what could only be described as magic flowing through my whole body. For a brief moment, it had felt like my blood had been replaced by tingling warmth.

"Cut the whispering," snapped Nerissa.

We did. But I didn't stop mulling it over. Grandma had always been a believer in superstition, avoiding ladders, black cats, and throwing pinches of salt over her shoulder to ward off evil. She helped me leave offerings to the "fairies" in our backyard, and in return, they left me notes.

She called it "magical thinking." It was the idea that the world was filled with magic, but most people chalked it up to coincidence or natural phenomenon. Grandma, however, recognized it as little bits of magic, the most that we humans would ever experience. And after I got over my skeptical phase as a youngster, I began to believe in it myself.

I had just experienced more magic in the last hour than most people would experience in their entire lifetime.

We were driving on a narrow road bordered by trees with hardly anyone else in sight. It was the kind of road that appears in horror movies. It was approaching evening, and the sky was beginning to darken.

Nerissa slowed down. There was no destination in sight. Instead she pulled off the road and sent us crashing through the plants at the edge.

I grabbed Auri's arm without thinking. Nerissa took us careening through the grass, and then drove straight into the forest. Auri put her hand on mine; her pulse was fast, although not as fast as mine had just gotten.

Although my stomach was in knots, I wasn't as afraid as I should've been, knowing this was how I would die. A secluded forest in another state was the perfect place to dispose of a body: two bodies, in this case. I wondered if it would be painful. Maybe she would use magic. Wouldn't that be a story to tell Grandma when I saw her again. My heart leaped a little as I imagined our reunion in the afterlife—it wouldn't be long now.

Nerissa parked the car near a copse of trees. Auri squeezed my hand tighter as our captor got out and came around to open our doors.

"We can do this the easy way or the hard way," said Nerissa. "I need you to walk with me a ways. I would prefer not to carry you, but if necessary, I'll drug you and do that." She gave an impatient sigh. "Which will it be?"

I knew which it would be for me. I couldn't tolerate the drug.

Auri, apparently, was thinking the same thing. She slid out of the car onto the forest floor and I followed her.

Nerissa grabbed my arm roughly and used more cord to tie Auri and me together. My skin tingled at the contact, and I felt like the worst person in the world for thinking that. Who thinks about their crush when they and their crush are about to die?

The cord pulled at my wrist, and I winced. Auri gave me a sympathetic look.

"After you," said Nerissa, and pushed us in front of her.

The forest came to life the deeper we walked. The sound of birds chirping echoed down through the trees, and when I looked up, a butterfly flew past, wings open in an explosion of orange and red. I could hear the wind whistling through the trees, which most people thought of as a lonesome noise but I found peaceful. I had spent many a day sitting by myself and listening to the wind. Sometimes Grandma and I sat together in the garden and just listened, and it was incredibly comforting.

After a few minutes, Auri piped up. "Where are we going?"

"You'll find out soon enough."

"We're going with you anyway. You may as well tell us," she said.

I tapped her hand with the back of mine. Did she really think it was wise to annoy the captor?

Nerissa was right on our heels, forcing me to walk faster than I liked. The forest was thick with brambles and branches, all trying to trip us. If we were following a trail, I didn't see it, and I had no idea how Nerissa knew where to walk. Obviously she'd been here before. The question was, what lay at the end of our journey?

There was a feeling here, though, the same thing I felt when Grandma and I were casting a spell in our backyard for the faeries, or leaving cookies out for the mythical creatures in our neighborhood. The feeling of something simmering beneath the surface of the world you can see, just waiting to be noticed. And then I realized what we were doing. This had to be an energy path, like Grandma had told me about.

My thoughts were interrupted when Auri's foot caught on a root and she pitched forward, yelping. Out of instinct, I grabbed her around the waist as best I could to keep her from hitting the ground.

My face immediately warmed. "Careful," I said, helping her back to her feet. "Are you okay?"

"Yeah." She was still clutching my shoulder. When she saw that I had noticed, she quickly let go. I knew I wasn't imagining it this time: her face was distinctly red. From embarrassment, I was sure.

"No problem," I said, attempting to look unruffled. "These woods are hard to walk in. I used to go on hikes with my grandma and one of us was always tripping over something." I didn't want to embarrass her.

"Humans are so clumsy," said Nerissa. She prodded us forward.

If she was speaking so dismissively of humans, what did that make her?

We emerged into a clearing, and despite the danger, all thoughts of unease or evil vanished from my mind. All I could do was stare at the incredible sight in front of me. I heard Auri gasp and felt her grip my arm tighter.

There was a large stone well in the middle of a grassy clearing: a perfect wishing well, like you would see in a fantasy movie. It was covered in moss like it had been there for a very long time, like most things in the Pacific Northwest were, but somehow even more vibrant and alive. The clearing was bordered by trees of all shades of green; pine trees, willow trees, trees I didn't know the names of. I could see the sky through a gap in the branches overhead, and though it was still overcast, there were no clouds in this particular patch. It was like someone had taken a fairytale scene and brought it to life in front of me, and so much beauty made me feel kind of dizzy.

The odd thing was that the well was surrounded by a ring of daisies, all equidistant from each other. I couldn't imagine them growing that way naturally.

Grandma's voice rang in my head: *A faerie ring.* Unease ran through me. I remembered all the fairytales she had told me: once you entered a faerie ring, you would never leave. There were tales of young men seeing a circle of beautiful women dancing, going to join them, and being eternally bound to the faerie realm—tales of children on their way home through the woods getting caught in a faerie ring and returning home a hundred years older.

"What is this?" asked Auri. Her jaw was slightly agape and her eyes were wide as she glanced around the meadow. I knew I wore an identical expression.

"Our destination." Nerissa grabbed Auri's arm and marched forward, dragging us with her. My heart sped into overdrive.

Our eyes met and we had a minute of unspoken communication: *Let's go. Quick.*

But when we turned to run, an invisible wall slammed up in front of us. My shoulder burned from where I impacted with it. We spun around, and Nerissa was standing there, hand outstretched and palm glowing.

Magic.

I heard Cat take a sharp breath as Nerissa came toward us. Her hand wrapped around my arm and I was powerless against her, magic coursing through my body. She dragged us to the well, and I felt chills rush through my body as we crossed the daisy line.

My pulse pounded in my head, nearly drowning out all other sounds. We were trapped. The faerie ring acted as a circular wall, holding us captive.

"I need you to step into the well, Auri," said Nerissa, so calmly she could've been commenting on the weather.

"What?"

Nerissa severed the cord tying us together. My wrists

instantly stung. "There are some very powerful lines of energy that intersect here. And I need you to drop into it."

The ley lines. It was true. All this time, Grandma had been right.

Auri stumbled forward like she'd been hit by a gust of wind. She hit the well, knocking the air out of her, and frantically grabbed for the wooden pole supporting the roof. Her fingers stretched out, grazing the wood, and she held on for dear life. I rushed forward, grabbed her other wrist, and pulled as hard as I could. But the wind was so strong, like a vortex pulling us toward our death.

"Let go!" Auri screamed at me. "We'll both die!"

There was no chance Nerissa wouldn't kill me, too. I was not going to leave Auri. How deep was the well? Would we die just from falling, or would we end up drowning in the freezing cold water, looking up at the sky? I had read that you could see stars in the sky from the bottom of a well, even if it was the middle of the day. That wasn't a bad thing to see before you died. But I wanted to save Auri at the very least.

Auri screamed, losing her grip. I caught the wooden beam, using all of my strength to keep both of us from falling. She clutched my hand with a death grip. But bit by bit, my fingers loosened from the wooden beam. I focused every smidge of my energy on keeping my hand clenched, but then a stabbing pain shot through my fingers. Nerissa had hit my fingers with something sharp. I let go reflexively—

And then I was falling backwards, tumbling over the stone edge of the well, plummeting into the abyss. Darkness closed around me and I could see the sky above as I fell.

Chapter 19
Auri

"When it comes to how to spell their name, it's a question of personal choice. I personally choose to spell it "Fae" as that is the most established spelling and eliminates confusion. The capital letter lends respect, which is an intelligent thing to show a faerie. But truthfully, the Fae have bigger concerns than our human grammar conventions."

- The Modern Manual of Faeries by Eleanor Bishop

I ALWAYS HEARD ABOUT PEOPLE'S LIVES FLASHING BEFORE their eyes. I would have liked that; I would have preferred to relive my childhood memories right before my life ended. Picnics with Aidyn, long evenings marathoning TV shows while I crocheted, the day I got a job at Yarn Emporium and didn't stop smiling for the next week. It would have been comforting. Instead, while I was falling through the earth, a different image swam into my mind. It was the Briars and Roses Shawl, the bane of my existence. For a fleeting second, I saw it in its finished state, delicate roses twining their way up the side of the shawl, framed with lacy edging that let the sun shine through the holes. I saw it so clearly, it was like it was right in front of me.

Then I got the wind knocked out of me again, the bottom of the well slamming into my back. I bumped my head against the ground and just lay there for a moment, trying to remember how to breathe.

It took a moment for me to realize what was wrong.

I had fallen down a well; why was I resting on grass?

I opened my eyes and took in my surroundings, unable to believe what I was seeing. I didn't see stone surrounding me and water at my feet as I had expected. Instead—impossibly, ridiculously—I was lying *next* to a well identical to the one I had fallen down. But the rest of the world had changed.

I sat up gingerly, head pounding.

The sky was gray like a storm was about to come, teeming with clouds dark as my mood. The trees were thicker and taller, pinning me in. The ring of daisies was still there, but the flowers were wilting. When I looked closer at the trees, some of them had brown leaves and pine needles like they were dying. It didn't look like the same forest from earlier, but there was no possible way I could be somewhere else. Maybe Nerissa had knocked me out and dragged me here. But why would she go to all that effort?

The worst part was that Cat was here, too, sprawled in a heap next to me. I'd known there was no way *I* could escape, but I'd hoped Cat, at least, would be able to get away. But here she was, and I couldn't help being a little relieved to see her, which made me feel guilty. *Where is "here," anyway?*

Nerissa had untied both of us. Clearly she didn't think we could put up much of a fight in this state. Well, she was right.

I had a sudden, awful thought: was Cat…alive? The way she was sprawled, I couldn't see whether or not she was breathing. I put a hand on her still-warm wrist and felt for a pulse. Then I released a breath as I felt her heart beating faintly. Not dead yet.

Then I saw Nerissa standing next to the well—except she had changed. Her ears ended in two points, poking through her hair. They were perfectly tapered like in every picture you see of fairies. Her hair, which had been plain white before, now looked like moonlight itself, as if each strand had a slight glow.

She was looking around, faintly smiling at her surroundings. Like she had just come home.

I wondered if I could scramble away before she noticed me, but I didn't want to leave Cat. Besides, I had no idea what had happened. I stood up. Nerissa's head snapped around to face me. Her gaze was striking; her eyes looked like something from a different world.

This is a different world.

I tried not to stare at her, but it was beyond my capabilities. She noticed. "You're confused," she noted. "I'm sure you're wondering what's going on."

"Nerissa, what…"

"Welcome to Feylinn, Auri," she said, an expression of complete contentment settling on her face. "I promised you answers, and now you'll have them. Tell me the truth: if I'd told you this before, would you truly have believed me?"

Had I fallen into a fantasy world? "I'm sorry," I said automatically, more out of a sense of self-preservation rather than any guilt. It wouldn't do to anger my possibly-fantastical captor.

"I don't blame you, truthfully," she said. "But Auri, I hate your world. I hate it."

I watched. Nerissa paced the grass, kicking aside Cat's feet as she went. I flinched on my friend's behalf, but she made no move to hurt her so I forced myself to stay put, to take a deep breath and not panic. Villains always talked about their evil plans. She might very well reveal something.

"It's so stifling," Nerissa went on. "No imagination. Everything dull and somber and…*ordinary.*" She spat the last word like it was a curse. "No wonder you humans are discontent, if that's how you live."

"We get used to it," I said automatically. How was I holding a coherent conversation?

"I suppose you do," she said. "But I don't." She stalked off, muttering something about "telling Elide never again." Elide? I filed that name away.

Maybe it was impossible, and completely ridiculous, but it looked like I really *had* fallen into some sort of fantasy world. Like when Alice fell down the rabbit hole and appeared in Wonderland. Maybe a normal person wouldn't have jumped to that conclusion, but I had read too many fantasy books to discount that option.

Still, when I went to push my hair out of my face and felt the pointed tip of my ear, I very nearly had a heart attack.

I bit my lip and poked the tip of my ear again. The cartilage narrowed to a delicate point, protruding from my dark blonde hair. I hated having my hair in my face, but it just didn't want to grow much longer than chin-length no matter how hard I tried, and it never stayed tucked behind my ears. That is, before now. Apparently having pointed ears was an excellent way to make sure your hair stayed out of your face. The practical sides of being an elf or a faerie that nobody tells you about. I poked at them, then pinched the tip with my fingernails. A sharp pain shot through me, and any doubts I had vanished.

There was no reason my ears should suddenly be pointed. I didn't know of any medical condition that suddenly caused someone's ears to become pointed. Aidyn, the smartest person I knew, had not once told me about an incident of someone's ears becoming pointed; I'd asked him after finishing my latest fantasy novel. And if Aidyn declared it impossible...

That left me with two clear possibilities.

I could be dreaming. I wanted to rule out this option because my dreams were never this realistic. In my dreams, whenever I thought about the possibility that I could be dreaming, I usually woke myself up. That was the key to lucid dreaming—realizing you were asleep. In books, people were always pinching themselves to see if they were awake. That had never worked for me, but the truth was it seemed very unlikely that I was dreaming right now.

I had to admit it to myself.

I had fallen into Fairyland.

Although it scared me to admit it, the pointed ears weren't the only change that had happened to my body. Everything felt so much clearer, like the moment when your ears pop when you're on an airplane and you can hear clearly. Or like putting on glasses in the morning and having everything come into focus. *Oh God, is that why I don't have bad eyesight? Because I'm a faerie? Can faeries even have bad eyesight?* This was a strange, unfamiliar land, so I should have felt out of place…but instead it felt like coming home. It felt like I *was* home for the first time in my life.

The air smelled of flowers, a scent that had always comforted me, and it was just easier to breathe, like the air was purer and easier to process. I felt lighter inside, like a weight had been lifted from my shoulders. In a strange way, it felt like I belonged here. But rather than comforting me, this familiar feeling sent me into a tailspin of panic. Because *why* did I feel this way?

What was happening to me? What would happen to Cat? The questions spun through my head faster than I could put words to them. I put my hands over my eyes and pressed hard with my palms until my vision dissolved into swirls of colors, trying to ground myself in a situation that wanted to flip me head over heels. Panicking wouldn't solve anything. I had to keep my head so that I could find a way to save me and Cat.

My phone! My eyes flew open. Nerissa was about ten yards away and appeared to be talking to a tree. It didn't exactly fill me with confidence about the sanity of our captor, but at least she wasn't paying attention to us, which meant I could see if my phone worked here. I pulled it out of my pocket and powered it on, and it still worked. Hope soared in my chest. I swiped to open the keypad and dialed Aidyn's number as fast as I could type it. There was no way I was going to try to explain this situation to the emergency line, they would never believe me…but Aidyn would. He knew what was going on. I would tell him, and he could get the authorities involved if he had to, and then we would be rescued.

But the phone didn't even ring once. I held it away from my ear, thinking maybe I hadn't pressed "dial," but I had— it just wasn't working. The hopes I had tentatively built came crashing down like a house of cards when the cat walks by.

Could I text him? Quickly, I typed "help" and sent the message, but my phone immediately started pinwheeling and I knew it wouldn't go through. In fact, the only apps that worked were the ones that didn't require WiFi. I opened the camera app and snapped pictures of Nerissa before she noticed what I was doing. Then I took a picture of Cat passed out on the ground, to show what Nerissa had done, and a selfie for good measure, because nobody would believe me about my ears otherwise.

Now that I had proof to show, I slid the phone back into my pocket and started looking for anything I could use as a weapon. But all I had were the clothes I was wearing and my light gray backpack, containing a water bottle, granola bar, headband, used tissue, three tampons, and the crochet shawl.

The shawl!

It looked different here too; the yarn shone in a way that had only been suggested back home, the silver tendrils seeming to waver in the light. Maybe I could poke Nerissa in the eye with the crochet hook or strangle her with the yarn… but no, it was too thin and it would break. It wasn't like I could kill her with what I had on hand. And I was too small to hold my own in a fight.

Maybe Cat had something. I knelt beside her and brushed the red hair back from her face, making sure she was still breathing. Her ears were still rounded…no points. Her breath was warm on my hand and her lips parted slightly when I touched her cheek. Hopefully she was having pleasant dreams because she was in for one hell of a shock when she woke up.

She was a human in a faerie world. What would that do to a person? Was she in danger?

Chapter 20

Cat

"All faeries are repelled by iron. Even half-fae are sensitive to it. Faeries cannot touch iron without immense pain, and if they come in contact with it for long enough, they will suffer grave damage and even death. If a person is half-fae, they can experience allergic reactions to the iron and become ill if exposed to it for too long, but it will not outright kill them like it will full fae. For this reason, it is useful to carry an iron amulet when attempting to ward off the Fae."

- The Modern Manual of Faeries by Eleanor Bishop

My whole body hurt. I kept my eyes closed, not eager to return to the world of the living. I felt the sun shining on my face, although the sky had been overcast a few minutes ago, and I heard faint birdsong. I knew immediately that we were far from any familiar place.

Auri's hand was on my cheek; I could tell from the light smell of flowers. So she was okay. I decided to feign unconsciousness for a few more minutes in case there was information Nerissa didn't want me to know. It was pretty clear, from how she had spoken to Auri in those last few moments at the well, that her primary target was Auri and I was just along for the ride,. And with that, it all came flooding back: The faerie ring. Nerissa. The well had transported us somewhere. Where the hell were we?

Auri spoke. "Last I checked, we were in Washington. How did we get here?"

"I should think you'd have figured that out already, Auri. You must not take after your bloodline as much as I thought."

"Bloodline?"

I heard Nerissa walk closer. "Lineage."

"I know we came through that well-thing," Auri said. "But…"

"That well-thing! It's *the* Well. Capital *W*. Show some respect!" With how Nerissa had reacted, you'd think Auri had just insulted her entire family. Maybe she had. "*That well-thing*. You humans."

Auri pressed on. "So is it some sort of transport?"

"Yes. Yes it is." Nerissa sighed. "It connects the human world with the world of the Fae."

A pause. I tried to keep cool, to control my breathing. *World of the Fae?*

"You're unconvinced that I'm telling the truth."

I didn't have to be convinced, but I didn't know about Auri. Grandma's magical thinking had prepared me for this. But this was more than magical thinking—I was in an honest-to-God magical *land*.

"I don't have to prove myself to you, but we do need to

wake up your companion," Nerissa mused. I cracked open my eyes a smidge.

Auri instantly put her hand on mine, putting herself between me and Nerissa, who was walking closer. My chest tightened at the gesture. A situation like this was a sure-fire way to see how much someone cares about you, and Auri's instinct had been to protect me.

"Oh, don't worry," Nerissa continued. "If I was going to hurt her, I would have done it already, don't you think? I'm just going to wake her up. Simple bit of magic."

Auri hesitated. Her hair was disheveled, but other than that, she looked unharmed. She pulled back enough so that Nerissa could step closer and place her hand on my forehead again. She didn't say any incantation; there were no flashes of light or sparks. But it was the same feeling as before: a tingly warmth running through my veins. It gave me an extra burst of energy, like caffeine straight to my system. I couldn't have kept my eyes closed even if I had wanted to.

I opened my eyes and saw Auri, her light blue eyes fixed on me anxiously. "Cat!" she exclaimed. "Are you okay?"

"What's going on?" I asked, doing my best to sound bewildered.

"Well, we…" said Auri, looking like she had no idea how to begin.

"Where are we?" I sat up and took in the scenery. I didn't have to fake my amazement: it was like we'd landed in a faerie garden.

"We're in Feylinn. To me, it looks like we're in…fairyland."

Auri shook her head incredulously. "I never thought I'd say that."

"I never thought I'd hear you say that." I raised my eyebrows at her. "It kinda looks like that to me." Auri nodded. She seemed to be thinking of something else, but was hesitating. "What?"

"There's one more thing."

I hadn't heard Nerissa say anything else. I waited expectantly. Auri swallowed hard, then pushed her hair back from where it had fallen over her face, and I gasped. The tips of her ears were pointed. Any shreds of doubt disappeared from my head: we were undeniably in a fantasy world.

"I know. Impossible, right?"

"Very few things are impossible," said Nerissa. My eyes widened when I got a good look at her. She had changed, her white hair turning to a silvery moonlight shade and her skin becoming almost translucent—and her ears were pointed too. I had a sudden thought and touched my own ear, and was mildly disappointed to find it unchanged. *You thought you were special, did you?* I didn't think it was possible for Auri to be any more beautiful, but she was stunning as a faerie.

Auri looked like she was going to cry. She bit her lip, blinked quickly a couple of times, and helped me to my feet. "Why did you bring us here?"

"I wasn't lying about the shawl," said Nerissa. "I told you I would bring you to the place where I got it. That's the reason I sent Auri down the Well." She looked disdainfully at me.

"I didn't plan on bringing the human, but there isn't much we can do about it now."

"Don't call her that," Auri said.

"Human? Well, she is." Nerissa raised her eyebrows at Auri. "Coming to terms with your own Fae situation, are you?"

Auri touched her ear, going pink. She pulled the tendrils of hair over them, self-conscious.

"This is not how I thought this day would go," she said. I giggled despite myself. I peeked at her out of the corner of my eye; the corners of her lips were turned up slightly.

We were far away from home, in a completely impossible, definitely magic situation, but I vastly preferred it to going home. We were both freaked out and trying to process what was happening. Our lives were probably in danger. But at least we were together. I tapped my right leg three times and felt my anxiety settle a little. I wasn't alone in this. In fact, I was accompanied by the cutest, sweetest girl I'd ever met. I couldn't believe I was checking her out at a time like this.

Auri gave a quick, almost imperceptible raise of her eyebrows. I got her unspoken message: *Let's tough this out, go along with Nerissa, and find a way out when we can.*

"Now then," said Nerissa, "no time to waste. I'm going to take you to Elide's castle. She's been looking for you for a while, Auri. Three days' walk. You'll get a nice tour of

Feylinn in the process." She fixed a glance on me. "You're one of the first humans to ever set foot in Feylinn. Enjoy it while it lasts."

I tried not to read too much into that comment. After all, she hadn't outright said she would hurt me. But it was hard not to worry. *At least she isn't threatening Auri,* I figured. I had no idea how I could defend my friend against a bunch of Fae. Especially if they all had magic.

Nerissa took a few steps away from us, walking toward the forest. Dead branches cracked under her feet. I wondered where she was going; she was heading directly toward a copse of trees. Then something stirred in the tree—the branches moved as if in the wind, but the air was still.

Right before my eyes, a figure melted out of the tree. If I hadn't been paying close attention, I would have missed it altogether. They walked to Nerissa's side, and I got a good look at them. Their skin was light brown, the color of the tree bark, and their hair was a range of different shades of green. From a distance, I couldn't tell if the figure was male or female, if trees even had genders.

The tree-figure gestured emphatically around them, pointing to the tree and to me and Auri. Nerissa gestured back. I would hate to go up against either of them. I caught a few muffled words from Nerissa: "It's your duty, Hemlock."

Hemlock seemed to accept defeat, shoulders slumping a bit. The two of them marched over to us.

"Introductions," said Nerissa, clapping her hands together. "This is Auri Davis. As we discussed earlier." She nodded at me. "This is her human friend. She's staying with us until we cross the Aethelney."

"I'm Cat," I said, although they both ignored me.

"Auri, this is Hemlock. You won't be speaking to each other much, I'm sure, as the nymphs don't associate with humans." She sniffed. "Of course you're not human," she said to Auri, "but you came straight from Terrin, so you might as well be."

Not human? Well, that wasn't surprising, given her miraculously pointed ears.

"This is hard to accept for your world, but tree nymphs don't have genders," explained Nerissa. "You don't need to try and guess Hemlock's."

I nodded. It made perfect sense to me; I didn't see the sense in arbitrary labels if a person didn't care for them. I couldn't imagine Hemlock caring about labels at all; trees just existed, didn't they?

I catalogued the nymph's name: Hemlock. Of course. A poisonous name for an intimidating tree warrior. The nymph was wearing clothes that looked like they were made out of leaves. Their skin was ridged like bark, and they were taller than normal humans—at least seven feet tall. I was at least half a foot taller than Auri, but Hemlock still towered over me. They looked, well, like a tree in human form. A tree who was glowering down at us.

Auri spoke up. "It's nice to meet you, Hemlock." She nodded her head in respect. "Nerissa, you said Terrin—what's that?"

"Human world." She made a face. "You're in Briarwood Forest now. Nobody comes here if they can help it; the only thing south of the Aethelney is the Well, and we don't much like interacting with *your* kind." It was directed at Cat, and I had never heard such hatred in someone's voice.

"We haven't had humans here for centuries," said Hemlock. Their voice was lilting and made me think of sunlight breaking through tree branches, like the dappled light we had seen in the forest. In *Terrin*. "I'm sure many will be interested."

"Sure enough," said Nerissa. "I didn't mean to bring her along. But I couldn't get rid of her without someone noticing; she's like a parasite, just tagging along..."

"Shut up!" Auri exclaimed. All eyes snapped to her, and she followed her outburst with a much quieter comment: "Don't call her that."

"It doesn't matter," I said softly, although it meant a lot that she had spoken up.

"I'm sorry, I didn't realize you were so attached." Nerissa didn't take kindly to being told to shut up. "How long have you known this human, Auri?"

"Who cares how long I've known her? That doesn't mean I want you to call her names." Auri was fiercely loyal.

"Of course, Your Highness," said Hemlock.

Nerissa shot them a look. So did I, but an incredulous one. First Auri was a faerie, then she was a princess? Maybe they were just messing with us. I didn't know if they had a sense of humor. I was bad at detecting sarcasm even when

I was dealing with fellow humans; I didn't stand a chance with faeries and tree nymphs.

I tasted blood, then realized I had been chewing my lip without realizing. I put a hand to my face and it came away with blood on my skin, pale as your stereotypical vampire. I wiped it on my jeans surreptitiously.

"Let's start moving," said Hemlock. "It's a solid three days' walk to Windermere Castle; I'm sure Elide wants the girl as soon as possible."

Nerissa nodded assent. "And Northpass?"

"It's not far out of the way," said Hemlock. "Just after the Aethelney River."

"Perfect." Nerissa smiled.

I exchanged a look with Auri. There was no way in hell I was going to let them take us through the forest; they could just kill us and dump our bodies anywhere. *Think, Cat. What do you have that could be used as a weapon?* Auri must have seen the desperation in my eyes because she drew closer to me and asked, "What are you thinking?" I wasn't sure myself. But then my fingers closed around something in my pocket that made my heart skip a beat.

It was an iron nail. I had completely forgotten.

Grandma insisted on me carrying around protection amulets, and since my OCD thrived on rituals, I was happy enough to oblige. Except it turned out this particular ritual, unlike everything else OCD made me do, was helpful. The Fae were allergic to iron, for lack of a better word. And being stabbed by a nail would hurt anybody. I palmed the nail and covertly returned my hand to my side.

Nerissa was only a few feet away, absorbed in her conversation with Hemlock. I had to do it now before I completely lost my nerve. I swiftly closed the distance between us, gripped the nail between my fingers like I'd been taught in self-defense class, and swung for the soft part of her throat right above her collarbone.

Hemlock shouted a warning. Auri screamed. And the nail stopped a fraction of an inch from her skin. She caught my wrist in an invisible hand, and no matter how I struggled, I couldn't break away.

"What were you thinking?" exclaimed Nerissa, stumbling back from me.

The force around my hand tightened, and although I tried my best to hold onto the nail, eventually it pried my fingers open and the nail fell to the forest floor. Immediately a circle of shriveled-up grass sprung up around it, forming a perimeter that had been killed by the iron. *It really does work. Grandma was right.*

She was right about it all.

"I should kill you right now," hissed Nerissa.

"No!" yelled Auri, who was being restrained by Hemlock. She was no match for them, but she still made a desperate attempt to wriggle free, lifting her legs off the ground and kicking as hard as she could. The nymph barely reacted when her feet connected with their knees. "I won't go anywhere with you if you hurt her!"

"Bringing iron into Feylinn?"

"I can't believe you didn't notice," I said, although I was trembling on the inside. "If you're all-powerful, why didn't you notice I had iron on me?"

Nerissa pressed her lips together firmly. "I don't owe you an answer."

"Yeah, but you're going to tell me anyway, aren't you?"

Of course she was. She didn't want to appear weak. "Aurora was my concern," she said, jerking her head to Auri. "Let her go. Let her do her worst. I didn't think you, a puny human, would be any trouble."

Not so puny now, from the way she looked at me. Had I made things worse for myself? Certainly. As long as they weren't any worse for Auri, I didn't care. I hadn't been able to save Grandma, but I wasn't going to let another person I cared about get hurt.

"How do you have knowledge of the Fae?" asked Nerissa, grudgingly curious.

"I don't have to tell you anything."

"You're..." She blew a breath of air from between her teeth. "Let's just keep going."

Chapter 21
Auri

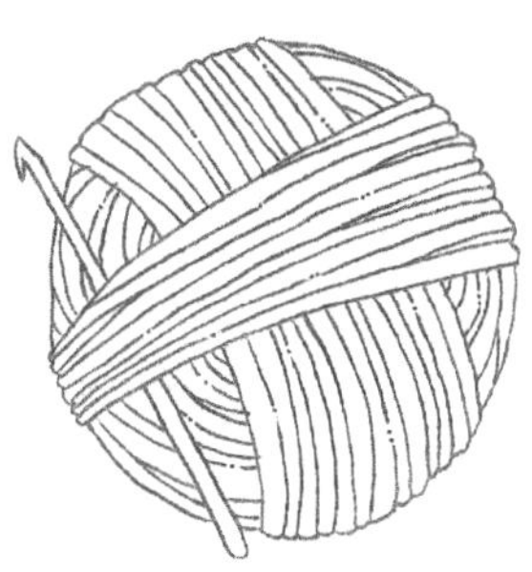

"There are stories of how the Fae mate for life, but they are only stories. In reality, the faeries are more like humans than we would like to believe. They fall in and out of love just as carelessly as we do. The faeries are not so attached to labels as we are, though, and would not think twice about having more than one lover of any gender. It is a freer world there, and if humans ever want to be as carefree as the Fae, they would do well to open their minds a little."

- The Modern Manual of Faeries by Eleanor Bishop

It was evening, nearing dusk, just like it had been in the human world. *In Terrin*, I reminded myself. If I was to survive here, the least I could do was try to learn their language.

I didn't know if time worked differently in Terrin than it did in Feylinn. Maybe the Well was a time warp and if I ever made it back home, I would be as old as Rip Van Winkle. I hoped with all my heart that wasn't the case. But I didn't know anything for certain.

Hemlock and Nerissa fell into formation, Hemlock leading the way and Nerissa following us and keeping us in line. Were we really just going to walk to Aethelney? It seemed like there should have been an easier, more magical way to get there. But Hemlock started walking, so the only thing to do was to follow suit. Three full days of walking. I worried that I couldn't manage it. I had never done more than running the mile in school. Now I wished I had run that Turkey Trot like Aidyn was nagging me to do, even though I couldn't think of a worse way to spend a holiday. I hadn't spent enough time with him, too focused on my own life, not even realizing that he was gay. I would die knowing I was a terrible sister.

We walked out of the clearing where the Well was located. As we went, we descended into the darker forest, with trees entwining overhead and blocking out the sun. How long until it would be too dark for me to see? I was sure the faeries wouldn't have that problem, being magical and all, but hopefully they would have some consideration for Cat and myself. The group tightened to form a line, and I fell in behind Hemlock.

"We're going to follow the ley line," called Nerissa from where she was leading the pack. "That'll take us to the Aethelney River, and after we cross it, it's a straight shot to the castle."

"Ley line?"

"I've heard of them," said Cat quietly. "Grandma taught me about this stuff. Ley lines are basically concentrated energy that forms a very straight path. Where they intersect, it's a place of great magic power. That's what they say, anyway.

I never thought it was real like this."

"Where they intersect…" I said slowly. "Do you think the Well was an intersection point?"

"Smart girls," said Hemlock. I didn't realize they were listening. "Three of them intersect there. That's why we could build a portal."

I filed this information away. We would have to get back to the Well to get back to our world. But maybe there were different portals at different intersection points. Was this an alternate version of North America? I asked as much.

"The continents are shaped differently here," Hemlock said. "Our world developed differently. But we've been here from the beginning, same as you."

"Why don't you tell her a little more, Hemlock?" said Nerissa sarcastically. "Tell them everything they need to stage an escape?"

Hemlock bowed their head and said no more. But this was enough information to get my mind buzzing.

I wondered what Crochet Fanatic's latest post had been. She posted free patterns every Friday, and I hadn't checked in my hurry to get out the door. Well, I would look when I got back. *If you get back,* persisted that annoying little pessimistic voice, the one that found the dire side to every situation. *Shut up,* I told it. Was it normal to be thinking about blogs when you were kidnapped, miles away from home, in a completely unfamiliar magical place? I didn't know anyone I could ask. Well, that wasn't actually true: I had Cat.

I nudged her. "How you doing?"

"Just peachy." She was focused on the path ahead as it wound through the trees. "You?"

"Same."

Her lips formed a tight line. "I guess we're in for a long hike, yeah?"

"The nature hike to end all nature hikes," I supplied. "Wait until my brother hears about this. He gives me such a hard time for never exercising."

"Really?"

"Yeah. He ran his first half marathon when he was thirteen. I never heard the end of it." I thought back to all my extended family sending him congratulatory cards. He completely deserved it, but it was a little disconcerting to be the non-athletic older child. "He wanted me to put a 13.1 bumper sticker on my car when I got one."

Cat giggled, the peal of laughter breaking through the shadows in the forest. I saw Hemlock stiffen at the noise. The conversation was good for me, though, and Cat was making just as much of an effort to keep it going. We both needed a distraction. "Did you do it?" she asked.

"My mom put one on her car. Figures. She does stuff like that to make up for never being home."

"I'm sorry," said Cat. "It's rough to not have your mom around."

"Yeah. But she's a great mom," I told her. "After she got divorced, she had to take two jobs to be able to feed me and Aidyn. My brother. Between that and Yarn Emporium, we get by just fine."

"Why'd your parents split up?" She glanced at me. "If you don't mind me asking."

I grimaced. "Our dad wasn't exactly an amazing person. He hit her sometimes, and they argued so loudly that one day someone finally called the cops." A horrified expression was spreading across her face with every word I spoke. "He went to jail for a couple years, and we haven't seen him since, but she has a restraining order just in case."

"That's awful," she said. "I'm so sorry. I can't imagine how hard that was for you and…your brother, right?"

"Yeah. His name is Aidyn." I bit my lip. "Mom worked so hard to support the three of us, since we weren't exactly getting child support from him."

Cat nodded. "She sounds amazing."

"She is." I missed her. It had been two days since I had seen her, between Yarn Emporium and her packed work schedule. I hadn't told Aidyn where I was going. Would Mom think I had run away? She had to know I would never abandon our family. But what if…

"Damn it." My foot caught on a root, but Cat grabbed my arm before I could fall.

"Is this going to be a regular occurrence?" she asked.

"Afraid so," I said, my cheeks burning. "It's…there's so many things to trip…"

"It's okay." I could hear her smile even as I looked to see where to take my next step. "I don't care, I can be your crutch."

I didn't know what to say to that, letting her words hang

in the silence. Why did the thought of holding her hand fill me with nervous energy? I'd never had a thought like that before. Not about a girl, anyway. I knew what it was like to get butterflies for boys, like Loren. But I didn't think I could feel that way about girls. At least, I never had before. So why did holding Cat's hand fill me with the same tingly feeling that Loren's crooked smile had?

It had to be the strangeness of our situation, that was all. Cat was comforting because she was familiar. Girls could check out other girls without it being a thing. Right?

The sun was beginning to slip beneath the horizon. I could just make it out in a gap between the trees. The shadows were lengthening, casting darkness onto us. I could still clearly distinguish the path, though, and I didn't take my eyes from it, not wanting to trip again.

"It's really dark anyway," Cat added. "I can't even see where I'm going."

"What?" Now I looked at her, the path forgotten. She didn't look like she was kidding. But it was just a little overcast and shadowed. I could see clearly.

"I mean, the sun set," she said. "My watch says it's nine thirty."

"Your watch works?"

"Yeah. It's battery-operated. But what do you mean? Isn't that why you're stumbling?" Her eyebrows were creased in confusion.

"Um," I said, "I can see just fine."

It took a minute for that to sink in, for her to realize I

wasn't messing with her. "You're serious," she said. "What are you, a cat?"

Hemlock spoke up. "There are some benefits to being Fae." They didn't turn around, but tilted their head. They appeared to be thinking about something, perhaps deciding how much to say.

"I see that," I said. "Anything else I should know? Can I stick to walls, or throw flames?"

"I hope so," said Cat.

Hemlock didn't laugh. "No."

"Shoot," said Cat. "I thought things were going to get interesting." She elbowed me in the side. "You don't even have wings. What kind of a faerie are you?"

That was exactly what I was wondering. "Yeah, how *can* I be Fae?"

"Hemlock," said Nerissa. Her voice was pleasant enough, but that one word was enough to strike some fear into the tree nymph, who tensed up, shoulders rising a couple inches.

"You have Fae ancestry," said Hemlock. "That's all you need to know for now."

As we continued on, I tried to watch out for Cat so that she wouldn't trip. It had to suck to be walking in the pitch dark.

"I'm probably some genetically flawed Fae or something. They shipped me off to the human world—excuse me, *Terrin*—because they were ashamed. Or something."

"But you'd think you would remember it," she mused. "I don't know."

"I don't know."

We had bigger problems than my heritage. Of course I would *like* to find out how I was part Fae, but it wasn't my priority right now. It would make a great question to ask Mom when I got back home…and Aidyn would be dying to do some research.

Just keep thinking that way—when *you get back home, not if. You will find a way home. Both you* and *Cat.*

It seemed that Hemlock was going to keep us marching through the night. My legs protested at the thought, and my stomach growled.

As the only one of us with night vision, and not being too steady on my feet anyway between clumsiness and fatigue, I figured there was only one thing to do. I slid my hand into Cat's. She intertwined her fingers with mine, squeezing back.

I wasn't going to lie and pretend I was unafraid of the forest at night. It was sinister, intimidating, and altogether not somewhere I wanted to be after dark—even with my newfound Fae capabilities. So it was nice to be able to feel Cat's hand in mine, to remind myself I wasn't alone. Her hand was warm and reassuring, and I couldn't deny it this time: it made my heart skip a beat.

I guided us around trees, holding back branches, following Hemlock. Neither of us spoke. What more was there to say?

In the dark, things come out that you wouldn't notice

during the daytime. In a way, it was a blessing to have things hidden from me. Things like this didn't exist in Terrin. Or if they did, I didn't know about it and I didn't want to. I tried to keep my eyes fixed on the path ahead, but out of the corner of my eye…I noticed things that I wished I couldn't see.

Long, colorless talons scraped against a tree trunk, making a *screeee* noise that set me on edge. Cat tightened her grip on my hand when she heard it. I squeezed my eyes shut when I saw unnaturally long and thin fingers hanging from a tree branch—but no, they were toes, and I could see something dangling from the tree like it was a bat.

Then I banged my hip on a tree and swore, pain shooting through my body. My eyes flew open. "Stupid tree!" I cursed at it.

"What—" began Cat.

"Shh!" hissed Nerissa, gripping my arm. She turned to the tree. "I'm sorry, honored nymph, she's from Terrin and had no idea what she was saying."

I had insulted a nymph. My heart, which was already down in my stomach, sunk even lower. *Nicely done, Auri.*

Nerissa's nails dug into my skin. I took that as my cue. Looking at the bark, I said, "I'm sorry. I didn't mean to offend you. That was entirely my fault." I held my breath. I didn't know protocol for a situation like this. Would the tree punish me? Kill me? Had I just committed a horrific offense? Death seemed a steep price for swearing at a tree, but it was a nymph, and rules were different here than back home…

"No apology is necessary from my princess." The voice was soft and soothing, like Hemlock's.

"What?" *Her princess? Was that directed at me? She had to be mistaken—*

Then Nerissa dragged me away down the path, and I dragged Cat by default.

"Wait!" I gasped. "What did it mean? Was it talking about *me?*"

Nerissa's silence was answer enough. So we just walked.

Chapter 22
Cat

"A simple spell to protect yourself against magic while you sleep: Boil 2 cups water and place in a large mug. Tie a piece of twine three times around the handle of the mug and place three pebbles in the water (be sure they are clean or you will be drinking muddy tea). Sprinkle in dash of salt and rosemary. Stir in one teaspoon honey with wooden stick. Let cool six minutes and then drink swiftly before going to bed."

- The Modern Manual of Faeries by Eleanor Bishop

WE SET UP CAMP IN A SMALL CLEARING JUST BIG ENOUGH for all of us. For a minute I expected Nerissa to produce a tent from thin air, or at least a sleeping bag. But either such luxuries didn't exist here or she didn't want to spare the effort.

I sank to the ground under a canopy of leaves. The grass was soft and tickled my palms. My feet throbbed and I was sure I had sweated about a hundred gallons.

"Don't get any ideas about running off," warned Nerissa. She looked at us, expressionless. "Besides, you won't know where to go. It would be an incredibly stupid idea to run off."

That was what I was worried about.

I stretched out on my stomach, sighing as the tension in my limbs subsided. I loved being out in nature, but I didn't care for camping. It made it hard to perform all the necessary OCD rituals: I couldn't set my alarm, lay out my clothes for tomorrow, and brush my teeth for exactly 53 seconds before going to bed. Plus, there was too much dirt, and I couldn't stand the feeling of it on my body.

And what was I going to do without my Lexapro? I hadn't gotten a chance to refill my prescription after Grandma had…I swallowed hard and tried to push the image out of my mind. I had a few doses with me at all times in my purse, but that wouldn't last me more than a couple of days. Withdrawal was going to be rough, which I knew from the time there was a supply chain shortage on SSRIs and had to go a week without my meds, causing dizziness, hand tremors, and something called "brain zaps" that felt exactly as unpleasant as it sounded. I did *not* want to be going cold turkey when I needed my meds now more than ever.

I worked up some saliva so I could swallow one of the small white pills without water. The Lexapro always tried to stick to my tongue. Then I lay there with my nose pressed into the ground, inhaling the smell of the earth. I figured that, at least, would be the same as back home, and I was looking for anything that would be the smallest bit comforting. Dank, mossy, and smelling of pine needles…plus something else, a spice or something I couldn't identify. Fine, so even the ground was foreign.

Auri sat down beside me, hugged her knees to her chest, and looked thoughtfully at the branches swaying overhead.

"You okay?" I asked.

She nodded. "You?"

"Just fine."

There was something comforting about this, about checking up on each other and pretending that everything *was* okay, that made it easier to handle. It was like when I was babysitting and had to take a huge spider outside—it was easier to be brave when you had to be for someone else. I was trying not to freak out for Auri's benefit, and I could tell from the set of her jaw that she was being brave on my behalf, too.

I was scared, but this felt right, somehow. Like a final homage to Grandma. I was closer than ever to answers. Nothing would bring her back, but maybe I could understand what had driven her to end her life.

The wind whipped through the trees, sending leaves rustling and branches creaking. Auri lay next to me. I wished I had the advantage of seeing in the dark so I could make out the expression on her face.

"What are you thinking about?" she asked, voice soft.

You.

"I don't know. I don't know what to think." *Why do you keep holding my hand?*

"Me neither."

Silence. I worked up the courage to move my hand a few inches to the right, but just then, she spoke again.

"I'm worried about my family," she admitted.

I nodded. "It must be awful to leave them at home."

"They probably think I abandoned them," she said.

Now I did put my hand over hers. "Auri, I don't know your family, but I do know you." I felt my face heating at the comment; I had known her for about a year, but not *that* well. "And you don't strike me as the kind of person to run out on someone. Your family must know that."

Her hand trembled. "Thank you."

I reminded myself that as far as I knew, Auri was straight, so her holding my hand didn't mean anything. She certainly wasn't flirting with me. But that didn't stop me from wanting to scoot closer.

Screw it, I thought, *what's the worst thing that could happen?* I moved over to her side.

She rested her head on my shoulder; her hair still smelled like flowers.

"How are you holding up?" she said. It took me a minute to comprehend.

"What do you mean?"

"With your grandma," she told me. "I don't know how you're plugging along so well. I didn't want to bring it up in case you didn't want to talk about it…but I wanted you to know that I'm here. In case you need anything."

"Thank you." Plenty of people had offered condolences to me at the funeral, but Auri's was the only one that felt sincere. I didn't want to talk about it. But for the first time I felt like if I wanted to, I could.

I woke with my heart racing. For a minute I lay there unsure of what was happening, and then I remembered where I was. I found myself shivering in the early morning cold.

I opened my eyes and realized Auri's arm was around me. She had rolled over in the night. I laughed and gently pulled myself away, sitting up and groaning at the ache in my muscles. I smoothed down a strand of her hair. She rolled over, yawned, and continued sleeping.

That was just as well. She would never have to know she had cuddled up to me in her sleep. I stood and whacked my head on a low-hanging tree branch. Biting back curses, I ducked under the offending tree limb this time and straightened up into the early morning fog.

The forest looked like a dream itself, with mist clinging to the leaves and the grass dewy and cold as it soaked through my shoes. I stretched, gazing upward at the clouds that promised rain later.

The silence was eerie. I never knew how much I relied on birdsong in the morning until all I heard was my own breathing and the snap of twigs. Shivers crawled along my spine. I looked toward Nerissa for encouragement, feeling relieved when I saw she was still there. She was my captor, but at least she would protect us from anything sinister in the forest.

At least until she brought us to this Elide person she kept mentioning.

I rubbed my hands absentmindedly on my pants. I had dirt under my fingernails, and the feeling set me on edge. My fingers were twitching involuntarily at the sensation; I absolutely hated the feeling of dirt, flour, sand, or anything of that nature. It made me shudder and want to climb out of my skin.

I unzipped my backpack and went through the contents. Maybe there was something inside that would help. Sure enough, I unearthed a travel-size container of hand sanitizer and frantically used it to scrub at my hands. I couldn't quite get all the dirt away. I smoothed lotion onto my palms, trying to relieve that awful dry feeling, and jumped when I felt someone touch my shoulder.

"Auri!" I exclaimed. "You scared me."

"Sorry," she said. "Bad dreams." Her hair was disheveled from sleep, and there were dark circles under her eyes. "Mind if I use some of that?"

I handed it to her.

"You came prepared, huh?" She raised her eyebrows, as if asking me why I was carrying all this stuff around.

I paused. *Because I have OCD and I can't leave the house without it.* Well, that wasn't exactly right. What would Stephen say? *I can technically leave the house without it, but I feel like I have to have it on me.* But telling people I had a mental illness was scary. Honestly, in a way it was scarier than coming out as a lesbian because people tended to react weirdly when they found out I had OCD. They never knew what to say. And I didn't want to lose the comfortable rapport

I had with Auri. So I decided to go for a version of the truth.

"I have some anxiety issues. It helps me feel more prepared to have this stuff."

"That makes sense. I guess it paid off, huh?"

She said it with no judgment, and I wondered if maybe it would be okay to tell her.

We continued walking soon after. It was chilly at first, but I soon grew warm thanks to the exercise and the rising sun. I wished I hadn't worn long pants. At least my legs weren't getting scratched up like Auri's. As we did yesterday, Hemlock led the way and Nerissa followed us. It astonished me how many miles of forest we were covering: it seemed endless.

"Three days total, yes?" I asked Nerissa. Her skirt was slightly torn from the branches.

"Yes."

"We'll get there tomorrow?"

"Yes."

I nodded and continued walking. To my disappointment, Auri didn't trip again, so I couldn't lend her an arm.

There was something odd about the forest. Parts of it appeared to be dying, withering away. Some of the evergreen trees were turning brown, needles dropping to the ground and creating a carpet that muffled our footsteps. There were dry, brittle leaves everywhere I looked. It was fall, yes, but this seemed more unnatural to me. I didn't hear as much wildlife as I would have expected for the wilderness, either. Granted, Auri and I were making about as much noise as a herd of buffalo, so that could account for the absence of creatures. But wouldn't there be a few squirrels out here, at least? Were there even squirrels around here?

I asked Auri, "Do you think they have squirrels in Feylinn?"

She snorted. "They're probably feathered."

Picturing a feathered squirrel made me giggle.

The forest floor was giving me a heap of difficulties. Normally when I walked, I had to step over lines in the sidewalk with my right foot. Here, that translated into stepping over branches. There were so many branches, however, that I developed a kind of halting walk, trying to position my feet just right. It slowed me down and didn't help my mental state at all. It also felt like everyone was staring at me, even though I knew from experience that nobody could tell I had OCD unless I told them.

My mental illness was always there, but it kicked up a notch when I was under stress. The last week had been the most stressful period of my life, and my OCD had reacted to that. I knew it was irrational, but I couldn't stop tapping every third tree we passed, kicking rocks with my left foot, and attempting to step over the sticks. Still, nothing felt *right*, and I could tell I was edging perilously close to a panic attack.

Then Hemlock stopped in their tracks and held out a long, willowy arm to stop us. Auri halted, and I bumped into her. "Nerissa," Hemlock said, "come advise."

Nerissa pushed her way through. Her hair flicked my shoulder as she passed. She came to Hemlock's side, and the two of them stared at what, as far as I could tell, was a perfectly ordinary grove in the forest.

"It's a Wasteland," whispered Nerissa.

Auri and I exchanged glances. It was decidedly empty, but I didn't see the cause for concern. I tapped my foot nervously, taking deep breaths to try and stave off the panic.

"There is no way around," said Hemlock. "Just move quickly." They started forward, entering the grove with no catastrophe.

"Come, girls," said Nerissa. She pushed us forward.

I stepped through the trees and gasped. The forest was dying. There were patches where the trees were withering away, and places where they had shriveled into ash. It looked like a wildfire had touched down here, but only in this clearing. And the second I stepped over the divide, all of my anxiety stopped.

It was like someone had poured ice-cold water over the anxious part of my brain and frozen all the thoughts away. I had never felt this peaceful in my life, never had a memory of living so completely without anxiety. I looked to Auri to see if she felt it, but she didn't show any signs of noticing. Well, as far as I knew, she didn't have a mental illness. Maybe it was just having this effect on me because of my OCD. But how was it happening? And how could I stay here forever, where my mind was quiet and I felt right in my body?

It lasted for about five minutes until we exited the other side: like a clear line had been drawn between the living and the dead.

"What was that?" I asked Nerissa as soon as I caught up to her.

"That was a Wasteland," she said. "For the last hundred years, they've been spreading. They're killing Feylinn."

How could the best anti-anxiety meds in the world be killing Feylinn? I opened my mouth to ask for more explanation, but Nerissa cut me off. "Just keep going, Cat. We don't have time for questions."

I still had plenty of them.

Chapter 23
Auri

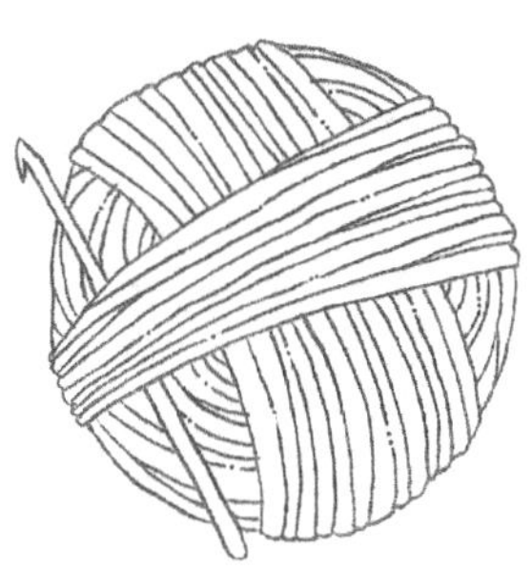

"Sometimes humans end up in the faerie realm by mistake. It does not end well for them. Humans are trespassers to the faeries and they will be treated as such. It is not a hospitable world."

- *The Modern Manual of Faeries by Eleanor Bishop*

It was late afternoon, and I was still puzzling over the Wasteland.

Cat had her hands stuffed into her pockets and was gazing at the forest around her as she walked. Her white peasant blouse was smeared with a bit of mud and grass stains, covering some of the embroidered flowers on the bottom.

"Hey, Cat."

She looked at me, tilted her head. "Hey."

"How are you holding up?"

She gave a sort of half smile, and winced. "Um. I'm fine." I felt a pang of guilt for having her be involved in this. If I hadn't solicited her help...

"Auri. I'm fine," she said, as if she could hear my inner critic. "My feet hurt a little, but what can you do?" She scuffed her foot along the ground, kicking a rock. We both looked down at her green Converse high-tops, covered in mud and dirt.

This is all my fault.

We were silent. For a minute, all I could hear were leaves crunching beneath my feet. It felt like all that existed was forest, spanning forever in all directions, a universe of trees.

"Auri. Are *you* okay?"

Despite her predicament, despite the pain she must be in, despite the fact that I was the one who had gotten us into this situation, she was still checking on me. It made me want to cry. So instead I said, "Are you kidding? It's a beautiful day for a walk, don't you think?"

I didn't really want to be joking around. I didn't want to make light of the situation; I didn't have the energy. So I was glad when Cat ignored my attempt at cheering us up. She met my eyes.

"Hey," she said. "Nothing's going to make this better."

We considered this statement for a minute. Nerissa slowed a little, as if she was curious to hear what we said next.

"So what do we do from here?" I asked.

The remark hung in the air like Cat's previous statement. It was like time slowed out here. There was something beautiful about two equally despondent people acknowledging their shared misery. When you know you're in an awful situation, where do you go from there?

Cat didn't try to answer. Instead she asked a question. "What do you miss most?"

"From home?"

It made me feel like crying just thinking about it. I could see it now: walking through the front door, being accosted by the aroma of my mom's carrot soup—when she had time to make it—dumping my purse on the coffee table and flopping down for an evening of gossip with Aidyn. It was August. I should have been getting ready for my first year of community college classes and enjoying the last few weeks of summer.

I didn't know how to describe it. You don't know how much you'll miss something until you think it's gone forever.

My chest felt tight. I knew there were tears running down my cheeks. I felt Cat's hand on my shoulder, and it was harder to breathe.

"Everything," I said. Because I was miserable and pathetic and melodramatic.

She stopped in her tracks, put her other hand on my other shoulder, and pulled me into a hug. She was significantly taller than me and my head rested perfectly on her chest. I could feel her shoulders shaking; she was crying too. I wrapped my arms around her and squeezed, probably tighter than a normal person does in a hug. I didn't know what the Fae thought, but I really couldn't have cared less. For the moment, it was just Cat and me holding each other in the middle of a forest, who knew how many miles away from home, the only thing each other had.

After a minute, I could feel my sobs subsiding. I kept clinging to Cat, unable or unwilling to let go. She seemed to be in no hurry either. My heart rate refused to slow down. I heard her sniff, take a shuddering breath, and relax a little.

"I'm sorry," I whispered.

"Don't be," she said. "I need you."

"This is all my fault." I wasn't just apologizing for crying into her shoulder.

"Auri. Will you please shut up and stop blaming yourself."

I lifted up my head, looking at her as well as I could from this angle. Her eyes were bright with intensity. "You didn't get us into this. It was Nerissa's fault."

"But if you hadn't met me, then—"

"I'm glad I met you. Despite all this." She pushed me back at arm's length to stare me down. She had tears in her eyes too. "Even knowing all this, I would still have met you, okay? I would do it again."

"Why?" Why would she do this for me, a girl she only knew in passing?

"Because I care."

I cared about her, too. With an intensity that scared me a little. "How are you so *calm*?" I asked.

She laughed incredulously. "Do you actually think that about me?"

"You just seem so…unflappable."

"My God, Auri, you have no idea. Can I tell you something?" I nodded. She bit her lip, dropped her gaze to the ground, and said, "I have really bad OCD. I'm not calm at all. I'm a mess inside, all the time. I don't even know what calm feels like."

I had never met anyone with OCD before. I didn't even really know what it was aside from being some kind of anxiety. "I didn't know," I said. "You really do seem so calm to me."

"It's not something I tell a lot of people."

"Thank you for sharing that with me," I said, trying to catch her eyes. "You don't have to be embarrassed. It's brave of you, telling me that."

Her eyes flicked up for a split second. "I'm the furthest thing from brave."

"I don't know what OCD is like, but I know you have to be strong to fight it. That seems pretty brave to me."

Her lip trembled. "Nobody's ever said that before."

"Well, they should." What was this rush of protective feeling that washed over me? "Maybe you can tell me about it sometime. If you want to. If you ever need someone to talk to."

"Nobody's ever asked before."

"Then you need to get a better group of friends, because you deserve people who care."

"I'm almost out of medication, and I'm so scared," she said quietly. "I only have a few pills left."

"Shit. How many?"

"Three. I counted this morning."

I couldn't imagine how scary that felt. "We're going to get out of this," I said, "and you'll be home again before you even run out of pills."

There was no way I could back up what I was saying, but

she took the comfort I was offering. "I would still do it again, you know."

"Do what again?"

"Come here with you." She blinked. "I'm glad I met you."

I felt a rush of warmth. Embarrassed, I looked down at my sandals. "I'm glad I met you too," I managed. My gaze flicked up, and I met her eyes, which were a beautiful, deep brown. They were fixed so intently on me that I blushed and pulled away.

Her arms dropped to her sides. I smiled at her, a little embarrassed.

I felt a sharp tap on my back. Whipping my head around, I saw Hemlock looking down at me. Maybe it was my imagination, but I thought I detected sympathy in their eyes. "We need to keep moving," they said, voice low.

"Sorry," I replied, taking a step away hastily. A root chose that moment to wrap around my ankle and trip me. I let out an undignified squawk and flailed my arms, whapping the nymph in the arm as I struggled to regain my footing.

Cat's laugh was the most welcome noise in the world. It made the disapproving scowl from Nerissa worth it.

Chapter 24
Cat

"Faeries value the natural arts, weaving their own fabric from handspun yarn gathered from their own animals. You will not find factories or assembly lines in the realm of the faeries. They are connected to the earth in a way we have long forgotten. If you wish to reconnect with your own magic, take up a needle art and see if you don't feel more grounded in a few months."

- The Modern Manual of Faeries by Eleanor Bishop

I'D TOLD HER, AND NOTHING BAD HAD HAPPENED. THE world hadn't ended. She wasn't looking at me differently, except maybe with a little bit more…respect? That wasn't the reaction I expected to get when I told someone about being mentally ill.

It was just like Stephen had said. I remembered that conversation, three or so years ago, when I was freaking out at him as I often did. He had leaned forward in his armchair, resting his broad forearms on his thighs, and listened as I poured out my stream of anxieties from the past two weeks. Mom had called, and I had overheard the phone call even though Grandma shooed me from the room. Just from hearing Grandma's side of the conversation, I knew Mom was expressing her doubts that I even had a mental illness and that I was just being particular. Even though I knew she was wrong, it still felt so icky to be doubted that I was having a hard time processing it.

"I just want to be normal," I confessed to Stephen. "I mean, it *is* just all in my head."

"That's because it's a mental illness, Cat," he said after a moment's pause. "Let's try to reframe that thought."

I had had a lot of practice at this since I'd been seeing him for a few years already. Whenever I had an intrusive thought, there were techniques I could use to reframe it as an alternative thought. "I mean, I'm not wrong. It *is* in my head."

"Okay. What would you say to your friend if they told you that?"

I always pictured Grandma when we did this "what if it was your friend" exercise. "Uh, I don't know. I would tell her that it's still valid even if it's in her head, I guess."

"Would you tell her that it's her fault for not getting better?"

I flinched. "Of course not."

"Right. So you don't need to be saying that to yourself."

I knew he was right. I would never be as mean to other people as I was to myself. "It's so hard to internalize that, though."

"It can still be true even if you don't feel like it's true."

We had talked about this a lot, how just because you

feel something doesn't mean it's true. *Feeling is not fact.* I'd written it on Post-It notes stuck all over the house. So when I had a panic attack and felt like I was going to die because the tag on my shirt was itching me, even though I felt like I was dying, I wasn't actually. Stephen liked to say that my brain had a trigger-happy panic button. While most people stayed calm unless something really scary was happening, just a small incident was enough to push the panic button in my brain and send me into a meltdown. When this happened, it was extremely hard to calm down again.

I had tried a bunch of different pills but nothing had really worked yet, so it was just a matter of riding out the storm until I could breathe again. Usually Grandma was there to talk me down. I hated having panic attacks in front of other people.

Stephen and I had talked about telling other people I had OCD, but I never actually did it. It was scarier than coming out as a lesbian, in some ways. Homophobia is real, and it's terrible, but at least being a lesbian is easy to understand: you're a girl who likes girls. Most people don't know what the hell OCD actually is. They think it's just being particular and liking to color-code your pencils. They don't know about the debilitating intrusive thoughts, the ones about hurting your family or jumping off a bridge or punching a hole in the wall, the thoughts you *hate* having but can't get rid of. And if you tell them about it, they look at you like you're crazy or dangerous. So you go through life trying to hide this disorder and thinking nobody will ever understand.

And then you meet someone like Auri.

My crush had intensified in the past half hour, and I could barely look at her without blushing. Thanks to my pale skin, my embarrassment was always extremely visible, especially when it matched the dark red of my hair. There was no way she didn't know that I was crushing on her. But she was straight. Right? It seemed like all the cute girls were either in a relationship or straight.

As if she could sense my thoughts, she looked at me through a curtain of dark blonde hair. "Can I ask you a question?" she said.

She can hear my thoughts, the paranoid part of my brain whispered.

That's ridiculous. She doesn't know what I was thinking, I hissed back. Even though she was magic, she couldn't read my mind. Right?

"Sorry, that sounded ominous," she quickly continued after I hadn't responded. "I was just wondering if there was anything I could do to help with your anxiety. Like, seeing as this whole trip is my fault and all."

Nobody had ever asked that before. Nobody besides Grandma. I couldn't believe what I was hearing.

I told her as much. "Nobody but Grandma has ever asked me that before."

"Are you serious?"

"Yeah."

"I'm not trying to pry, or anything. I just wondered…"

"You're not prying. It means a lot that you asked."

A quick smile from her, a little nervous.

"I guess…you're doing it already. Just checking in with me and asking how I'm doing."

"Oh, good. But that's just what a friend does."

We're friends! my stomach announced with a flip.

"Maybe I've never had a friend like you before, then," I admitted.

"Maybe I haven't either." Her voice was low. Could it be that she had experienced the same loneliness I had? How could a girl like her be lacking for friends?

"That is so hard for me to believe," I said. "How do people not see what a catch you are?" Then, of course, I was mortified because it showed *way* too much of my feelings for her. And it made her blush.

"That's sweet, but I'm not that special."

"Are you kidding? You're one of the kindest people I've ever met." There was no heterosexual way for me to tell her just how gorgeous she was.

"This isn't about me," she said, obviously flustered. "I just want to know how I can best help you. I don't know much about OCD."

Right, back to the topic at hand, not about how her chin-length hair curls in the cutest way around her heart-shaped face, or the way she bites her lip when she's thinking hard. OCD. Focus, Cat.

"It's not about being clean or tidy," I said. "I don't feel the need to wash my hands all the time."

"Okay. I figured there was more to it than that."

"It's like…" I stopped, searching my mind for a way I could explain it to somebody who didn't have it. How to explain that gnawing, guilty, awful sensation of having an obsession bouncing around your head? Then it hit me. The perfect example was right next to me. "The shawl!" I said. "It's like the shawl. How does it feel when you think about it?"

She thought for a minute, clearly unsure where I was going with this but willing to humor me. "It's like I can't stop thinking about it. It takes over my mind. Like, I literally cannot do anything but crochet it."

"That's it exactly," I said. "The shawl is the obsession. Crocheting the shawl is the compulsion."

"Ohh," she said slowly. "I think I understand. So you have a thought…"

"Yeah. The obsession."

"…and you have to act on the thought?"

"Well, it *feels* like you have to. But yeah. That's the compulsion."

"That totally sucks," she said. "Do you mind sharing… you don't have to. What sorts of things do you obsess about?"

"I don't really tell anybody that," I admitted. "It's too hard to say out loud." She nodded. I continued, "That's what nobody gets right about OCD. They think it's all cleaning or handwashing or whatever, when really it's the intrusive thoughts." Auri was listening quietly. "The ones that show up in your head without you inviting them in. Terrible stuff, like hurting the people you love, or hurting yourself, or shouting a swear word at the top of your lungs…Just shit like that, and you can't make them go away, and they just won't leave."

"Damn."

"My therapist says that everybody has them. Intrusive thoughts, that is." I twisted my fingers together. "But people with OCD…their brain can't filter out the intrusive thoughts like people without OCD. So we fixate on them. And we do compulsions to make them go away."

She blinked. "Like rituals and stuff?"

"Yeah," I said, surprised by her insight. "Like, knocking on wood or stepping on all the sidewalk cracks or…I dunno, everybody is different. Some people pray a lot. And yeah, some people wash their hands. I mean, you saw the hand sanitizer in my backpack."

"That sounds awful, Cat."

"I mean, yeah. It's pretty much hell sometimes." Had I shared too much with her? No, she was looking at me with sympathy, not pity. "But you learn to deal with it, you know? Everybody has their own shit to deal with."

"That's the truth," she whispered. "Thank you for sharing that with me. I want to learn more about it so I can be here for you."

And now she was making me tear up. "That means a lot," I said, blinking hard to make the tears go away.

"I'm here. And I'm going to stay. You're not alone, not in any of this," she said earnestly. "I can't imagine what you're going through without your grandma. But I am not going anywhere. You have me now, and my family, and we're not going to let anything bad happen to you. Okay?"

I wiped my cheeks, unable to get any words out. But it turned out I didn't have to, because Auri brushed a tear from my cheek and pulled me into a hug.

Chapter 25
Auri

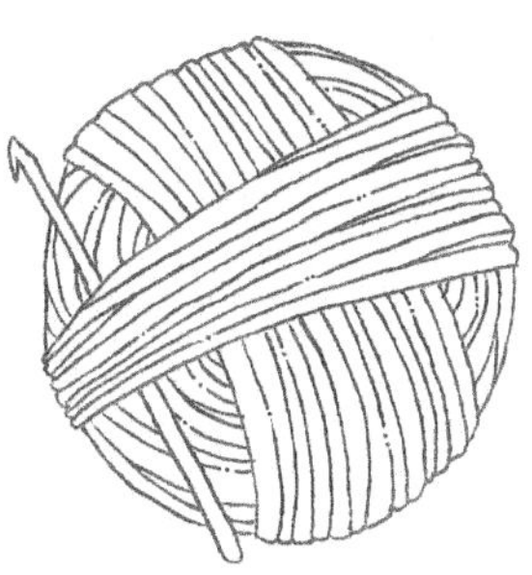

"A simple protection spell to wear around your neck when you wish to ward against magic: Combine dried marigold, dried rosemary, three red berries (it does not matter which kind, as long as they are red), a small chip of your birthstone, a drop of your blood pricked with a silver needle, and a dried flower that was picked in the moonlight in a small jar. Carry with you or wear around your neck."

- The Modern Manual of Faeries by Eleanor Bishop

I HAD NO IDEA EXACTLY WHAT CAT WAS GOING THROUGH, the sort of things she dealt with every day. How ridiculous that the crochet shawl was doing pretty much the exact thing to me. Only we were looking for a cure for the cursed shawl. Was there a cure for OCD? From what I knew, you couldn't really cure mental illnesses like you could some physical ones…you just had to live with them.

It just went to show you never knew what was going on inside somebody's head. And that just because something was invisible didn't mean it wasn't real. Sometimes the worst enemies are inside our heads.

As we walked deeper into the forest, the air started to feel more humid. We encountered more puddles and swampy patches of ground. My hair clung to my face and neck and it felt like my feet were developing their own ecosystem of mold.

Some of my family lived in southern California, and visiting them just cemented my preference for the weather of the Pacific Northwest. I couldn't get behind feeling hot all the time. In addition to making me super thirsty, it also made me feel tired more quickly. I much preferred the cold, rainy weather of Washington, even though other people thought it was depressing. So I felt as out of place here as a polar bear in the desert.

Both Cat and I were showing signs of dehydration; she kept applying lip balm and my tongue was so dry I was having a hard time swallowing. After about an hour of this, Hemlock took notice and stopped to offer us a drink from their waterskin. Until now, I had no idea what those were; turns out they were a waterproof pouch used to store clean water. You learn something new every day. The water was lukewarm and tasted odd, but it was clean, and when you're that thirsty, you don't complain.

After a few more hours of walking, I fell behind Cat in a particularly slick section of forest. She forged on ahead, agile and surefooted. I didn't think she meant to leave me in her dust, but I was having a much harder time than she was navigating the forest, which by this point felt much more like a swamp. I stepped over a clump of tall grass and put my foot—*splat!*—in a deep hole filled with mud.

"Eep!" I exclaimed. The mud squelched around my foot and pulled at me. I took another step forward out of surprise, but the mud refused to relinquish its grasp on me. I pitched forward, hands going into the glop, but I caught myself before I fell in completely.

It pulled at me, tugging me down into the airless depths. Was it quicksand? "Help!"

I felt the faintest whisper of a touch on my ankle, like dozens of little fingers wrapping around me and dragging me down. What kinds of creatures could be lurking down in the swamp?

"Hold on, Auri!" called Cat. She ran toward me as well as she could in the mud. I called for her to stop; it would do no good if she joined me in the quicksand.

Then a pair of strong hands wrapped around my upper arms and hoisted me out of the mud. Hemlock set me back on my feet on a dry patch of land.

I wheezed, shaking my hands to free them of the mud and sending splatters of mud every which way. "Thank you," I sputtered. "I'm sorry."

"Are you all right? The kelpies can be tricky." They looked at me intently.

"I'm fine," I said, still winded. "Kelpies?"

Cat and Nerissa joined us. "Hemlock, what happened?"

"Kelpies," said Hemlock. Seeing my confused expression, they added, "Creatures from the Boglands."

Finally, a piece of information! "Boglands?" I asked, trying to not sound too eager. I didn't want to scare them from telling us more.

"It doesn't hurt for her to know where we are," said Hemlock to Nerissa. "Auri, you saw the Well. We just finished the first leg of our journey, through southern Briarwood Forest. Now you see the Boglands. That means we're getting close to the Aethelney." A slight inclination of their head. "You've already made the acquaintance of a kelpie."

"Is that what pulled me in?" I asked.

They nodded once. Then they walked the few steps to the mud pit where I had fallen. Crouching down gracefully, they plunged their hand into the mud, wrestled around for a minute, and retrieved a handful of brown gunk.

I recoiled slightly as Hemlock extended their hand to me. "Look," they said. Hesitantly I peered closer and gaped as I saw a tiny, blob-shaped creature emerge from between their fingers. It looked like a little armadillo, but squishier and with a distinctly annoyed expression, like a dog that had been disturbed from its sleep.

Cat made a sound of surprise. "That's a kelpie?"

"They're everywhere." Hemlock sounded accustomed to them, sort of like how I would talk about a mosquito or fly. "We do not usually spend much time in the Boglands. I prefer a drier climate."

"I'm with you," I said under my breath. Maybe the tree nymphs would like the Pacific Northwest. Come to think of it, who was to say that the dense Washington forest didn't harbor a tree nymph or two? Had I ever really stopped to look?

"Are they dangerous?" said Cat, who was watching the kelpie with great interest. Her hand hovered in midair like she wanted to pet it. The kelpie wriggled in Hemlock's grasp, extending tiny paws in an attempt to get free.

"Not really," said Hemlock. "Just a nuisance. They can cause difficulties like your friend experienced, though. They do like to trip unwitting travelers." They let the kelpie crawl into their other hand.

Cat tentatively stroked the kelpie's back. It twitched and turned around in a circle. Hemlock kept their other hand over it to prevent it from getting free. "So cool," Cat murmured.

I wondered what Aidyn would make of this. The kelpie was one of the strangest things I had ever seen—like a blobfish out of water.

Nerissa was at my side; I hadn't heard her approach. That faerie was scarily quiet. "Put the kelpie back," she said. "Now is not the time to play with the animals."

"Very well," said Hemlock. They held out the kelpie for Cat to say goodbye. Cat patted it gently on the back and stepped back to allow Hemlock to deposit the kelpie back in the mud. It disappeared under the surface with a small splash, displacing some of the swamp as it burrowed to wherever it lived.

A splatter of mud hit Nerissa on the cheekbone, and I

couldn't hide my smirk. She wiped it off with the corner of her sleeve, icy rage filling her eyes.

"That was so cool," confessed Cat as we continued along, even though she was obsessively wiping her hands on her jeans. "I feel like I'm on the Discovery Channel."

That was such a Cat thing to say that it made me smile. I imagined movie night with her and Aidyn, watching nature documentaries on the couch while I crocheted. I was in awe of these creatures myself; who wouldn't be? What kind of a world had we landed in?

Cat picked at the mud on her palm before trying to wipe it on her jeans. But the mud was stubborn and it refused to yield. I could see the panic growing on her face. I pulled her hand into mine, giving it a squeeze that I hoped was reassuring, and she smiled at me gratefully. There was mud under her fingernails, but I didn't care if I got it on my hands. If I could help her stop worrying about the mud on her hands, then I didn't care at all.

Chapter 26
Cat

"The myth that faeries cannot cross running water is just that—a myth. There is plenty of running water in the faerie realm and they can cross it just as easily as humans can."

- The Modern Manual of Faeries by Eleanor Bishop

WE CONTINUED THROUGH THE BOGLANDS FOR THE REST of the afternoon. Auri and I tried hard not to step on any more kelpies, but I wouldn't have minded the chance to pick up another one. They were cute, like little muddy guinea pigs.

I took a bite of my granola bar and passed the rest to Auri. Hemlock and Nerissa were talking up ahead. I caught a small drift of their conversation and heard them mention "the girls." Auri and I looked at each other, then sneakily began to close the gap between us and them to try and listen further.

Hemlock was saying, in their soft voice, "…drop the girl at Northpass and continue on from there."

"I don't see the logic in that," said Nerissa. "I'm sure Elide will want to see the human."

They were talking about me. Fear surged up inside me.

"You didn't intend to bring her along in the first place, am I correct?" Nerissa huffed out an affirmative answer, clearly annoyed that Hemlock had pointed it out. "Then why should you bother bringing her to the castle?"

"For the very reason that I did not intend to bring her along," said Nerissa. She spoke with a long-suffering air. "It was unexpected. She was not part of the original plan. Elide will not want anything to throw a wrench into her plans."

"A wrench?" Hemlock stepped gracefully over a log, leafy tunic swaying.

"A stupid human expression." She shook her head. "It seems I am beginning to pick up expressions from Terrin."

Nerissa glanced over her shoulder and noticed me and Auri. We immediately snapped our heads to look at each other and acted like we were deep in conversation. She merely said, "Well, what are you two waiting for? Keep up the pace."

"Cat?" Auri said in a low voice to me. "Which one of us are they talking about?"

I tilted my head. "You know you're the one with pointed ears. I'm pretty damn sure she means me."

Auri winced and put a hand to her ear, the pointed tip hiding beneath her tangled hair. She looked a little self-conscious. "You're saying I'm Fae?"

She looked like she wanted confirmation, or to be reassured that she wasn't going insane. I wasn't the best candidate for that second one, having a tenuous enough grasp on my own sanity on any given day. But all signs pointed to Auri having some sort of Fae heritage.

"Not necessarily all Fae," I replied, "but I am saying you might not be one hundred percent human."

Auri wiped her forehead with the back of her hand. A sheen of sweat glistened on her face. I could feel myself sweating just as intensely. "My brother always called me a weirdo," she joked, "but this is taking it to a whole new level."

Nerissa was hanging back, almost like she was listening to us now. I ignored her. "You think I can do any fancy magic tricks?" continued Auri

"I think," I said, quietly so Nerissa couldn't hear me, "that you might want to try."

It was crazy to think that Auri might possess some sort of magic. But if so, we stood a much better chance of getting out of this alive.

"The closest I've ever gotten to otherworldly activity is when Aidyn and I snuck a Ouija board into the basement for a midnight séance," said Auri.

"Oh? How'd that go?" I smirked.

"It ended with me bursting into tears and him lighting the carpet on fire by mistake. My mom took away the Ouija board and grounded us for two weeks," said Auri. She laughed. "Later that week, I found *her* holding a séance with the very same board. She denied everything."

"Grandma hated Ouija boards. Said it was commercialized magic and that if you really wanted to contact somebody, you had to do it more authentically."

"Oh yeah? How would she suggest that?

"It sounds silly."

"Try me. I liked your grandma. I would listen to her."

I appreciated somebody besides me acknowledging the loss. It helped to hear that other people had liked Grandma too. "Every full moon we went into our backyard and left offerings for the faeries. Once I made oatmeal and raisin cookies for them and left it under our big oak tree in back. The next day they were gone. I always thought it was Grandma who ate them, or a bird that flew into the yard, but now I'm not so sure."

"Honestly, she might have a point," mused Auri. "I've seen so many things here that I thought didn't exist. But maybe magic has always existed, and it's just our limited human experience that means we don't see it."

I thought I saw a faerie once, when I was young—a brief flash of a beautiful woman with long pink hair and pointed ears, spotted by the side of the road when I was walking to the bus stop at an ungodly hour. The witching hour, Grandma called it, when both good and evil came out to play. I had always believed her, because Grandma was perceptive and honest and because I wanted to believe.

Auri went into a meditative state for the next half hour or so. I guessed she was trying to tune into her hypothetical magic. I didn't detect anything, and after a while she sighed, discouraged.

"Cat," she whispered, "got any tips?"

I was French braiding my hair so it would stop getting in my face and bugging me. "Tips for what?"

Auri wiggled her fingers in front of my face and made a scary expression. "Magic."

"Ah. I don't know." I thought for a minute. "I guess… There's something Grandma used to say. She called it 'magical thinking.'"

Auri was listening intently.

"If you see everything through a magical lens, eventually the magic will come to you," I said. "That's what Grandma believed. And so do I." I snapped the ponytail holder into place around my hair and let my hands drop to my sides, not bothering to pick out the leaves and pine needles matted into my hair.

"Hmm. That makes sense."

"I don't know if it's true or not. But maybe it could help." I paused, thinking. "How did you come by your Fae ancestry? Could you be adopted?"

"I mean, I really don't think so," she told me. "My parents weren't the type to hide something like that from me. Not to mention that I look exactly like my mom and Aidyn." Auri had a distinctly heart-shaped face and dimples on either side of her smile, the kind that would be instantly recognizable on a family member. "So I would rule that out."

"There goes that theory," I said. "Maybe somebody further up the line was Fae. Or made their way into Feylinn."

"You think my great-grandmother or somebody was from here?" The ground was starting to slope downhill, and I had to concentrate even harder to keep from slipping. It wasn't very muddy now but it did seem like we were making our way toward some source of water.

"I didn't say that. Not necessarily," I interjected. "But, I mean, *we're* here. She could have stumbled upon it by accident and really got to know the inhabitants. Really familiar, if you get my drift." Alluding to sex made my face grow warm, because of course an image of Auri drifted into my mind while I was talking.

"Ah." Auri nodded. "You're saying one of my great-grandparents could've been from here? How do you suppose they would have gotten back to Terrin then?"

I shrugged. "I don't know. It's just a theory."

"Girls," called Nerissa. "Hurry along." She hadn't spoken to us in hours, not since the kelpie incident. I perked up, wondering what she was on about. "We need to reach the Aethelney River in the next hour if we're going to cross safely tonight."

"Cross a river?" I asked, just as Hemlock blurted out: "You're not suggesting that we cross *today*, Nerissa?"

"Yes to both of you."

"That's ridiculous," said Hemlock. "You can't expect to cross safely today. The current—"

"I promised Elide that I would deliver the girl promptly," said Nerissa, "and that's exactly what I plan to do."

Hemlock said: "You would risk their lives? And ours?" Their voice, though usually soft and melodious, sounded distressed.

"It's a risk worth taking," said Nerissa firmly. "Do you wish to keep Elide waiting?"

"An extra day will not make that much difference."

Hemlock towered above Nerissa, and I was impressed that she didn't flinch at the disapproval in their voice. I would have been very intimidated in her place. "We can get word to her. Surely she will understand when she finds out why you were delayed."

Nerissa was walking faster, holding her dress up mid-calf to keep it above the grass and branches on the ground. I struggled to keep up with them. It was like they had forgotten we were there, they were so absorbed in their conversation. "We will not have to explain at all," she said. "If we cross the river today, we can make it to the palace at daybreak tomorrow."

"You would discount the current?" Hemlock kept up easily with Nerissa. If I was braver, I would have grabbed Auri and slipped away into the forest, but I didn't trust the fact that the Fae probably had supersonic hearing and would catch us in no time.

"It's much safer to cross earlier in the day," said Hemlock.

"You tell me what I already know," said Nerissa. "Stop worrying. I will personally ensure our safety. Do you think you are incapable of crossing a simple river?"

"I would not call it that," muttered Hemlock.

"Oh, come now," Nerissa said. "I would not have believed it; a tree nymph afraid? I suppose your lot just like to retreat back into their bark at the first glimpse of danger." She tugged her skirt over a fallen log. The woven green fabric snagged a little but pulled away when she yanked on it, leaving a few threads in its wake.

"You know that to be untrue," said Hemlock. "You insult my kind?"

"No, I do not," admitted Nerissa grudgingly. "Elide and I are very grateful for your assistance. I merely scoff at your inability to calculate risks."

"I would call it an unwise decision, myself," offered Hemlock.

"When you agreed to this mission, you accepted that I was in charge," said Nerissa. "You will obey my orders or I will report your negligence to Elide."

Hemlock fell back a step.

"Don't say that I did not warn you," said Hemlock, their voice respectful but clearly disapproving.

Auri and I exchanged glances. I tied my sweater a little more tightly around my waist, then reached down for another berry out of the pouch. If we were going to cross a life-threatening river, I needed my energy.

Hemlock fell back to walk next to Cat and me.

"What's going on?" I asked them.

"We're crossing the Aethelney River. Extremely dangerous, and I advised against crossing tonight."

"Well," said Auri, "that sounds promising."

"You have a boat or something?" I asked. "Tell me we're not going to kayak across."

"I'm not sure what that is," said Hemlock. I let out a breath—so we weren't going to boat across a crazily rapid river. Then they said: "We have different boats here than you are used to."

"We're taking a boat?"

"I am sure we will be fine." They sounded unconvinced. Well, after their argument with Nerissa, I already knew they weren't filled with confidence. "I have made the crossing several times. It is difficult, but not impossible."

"But you were telling Nerissa…"

"That it is easier earlier in the day. Yes." They pressed their lips together in a tight line.

"Because it's lighter? Easier to see?" Auri guessed.

"In a way," said Hemlock. "No, you would not be familiar with this, I suppose."

Nerissa called back to us. "Hemlock, I see you are enjoying chatting with the captives."

"I am merely familiarizing them with the routine." Hemlock sounded like they were barely restraining themself from snapping at Nerissa, which, from my impression of the nymphs thus far, seemed rather unlike them.

"If you are doing that, you may as well inform them about the population," said Nerissa. "We should be there within the hour. Make sure they know the protocol."

Protocol? Population? What kind of a river was this?

The sky was starting to darken, the sun slipping down between the trees and lengthening the shadows. I quickened my pace, along with the rest of my companions. I would take Hemlock's word for it that I didn't want to be on the Aethelney River after sunset.

Hemlock sighed. "Auri, Cat, you already met the kelpie. There are other creatures out here that are…less hospitable."

A muscle jumped in Cat's jaw. "Go on."

"You do not have kelpies in Terrin, no?" I shook my head. "I am guessing that you do not have sirens, either."

"Oh no," said Cat. "Are you saying that…"

Hemlock nodded. "I'm afraid so. And they come out after dark."

Chapter 27
Auri

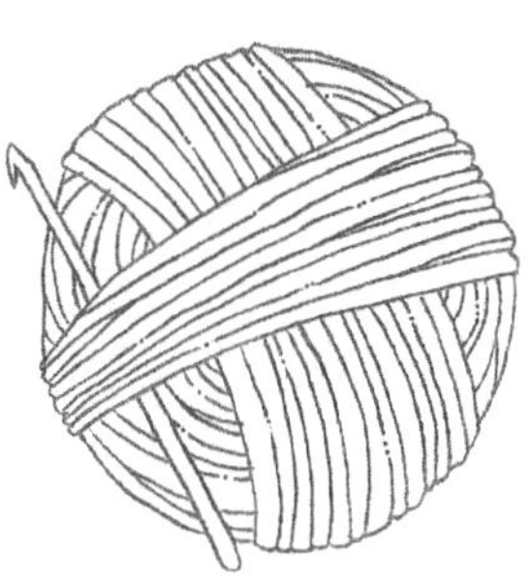

"Most mythologies are based on reality. Humans simply aren't creative enough to invent these things. If you hear about something over and over from many different cultures, odds are that it exists, so keep your eyes out."

- The Modern Manual of Faeries by Eleanor Bishop

Sirens. Just what we needed.

Having read my fair share of mythology, I was familiar with the myth. "Sirens are the ones who sing sailors to their death, aren't they?"

"That is correct."

Nerissa was scrounging around in the pocket of her dress. She turned to me, holding a pair of earplugs. "Auri, are you attracted to women?"

"What?" I must've heard her wrong.

"Do you like girls? I need to know if you'll be attracted to the siren's song."

Oh. Way to come right out with the question. "Um, no. I mean, I've had a boyfriend." Based on past experience,

I didn't think I would be drawn to the sirens. "Does that mean I don't need the earplugs?"

"That's right," said Nerissa. "Remember those stories about the sailors? Most of them were crazy over women."

Hemlock declined the earplugs. When they saw me looking, they said, "Many of us tree nymphs are solitary creatures. We don't form relationships like you do."

"Fair enough," I said. "Sometimes I think it's more trouble than it's worth."

When I turned around, I saw Cat stuffing a pair of earplugs into her ears. I paused, not knowing what to say. She saw me looking and dropped her gaze. "Are you gonna be okay?" I asked her. "I don't want to lose you to the sirens." I smiled at her, trying to convey that I would like her no matter what. But now my mind was flashing to us holding hands in the forest, curling up next to each other at night. Had it meant something more?

"I'll be fine. Worst case scenario, you pull me back into the canoe."

"I don't think it works that way," I said. "Can you swim very well?"

I pictured myself going overboard, dragged beneath the rushing water by slimy siren hands and held underwater. I imagined the breath being sucked from me and ice-cold water pouring into my lungs, choking to death right there in the Aethelney River. I had taken swimming lessons for most of my childhood, but what use was that against whitewater rapids and a mob of seductive sirens? Come to think of it, they wouldn't even have to seduce us. They could just push the boat over and let the water do its trick, no need to overexert themselves or use any fancy, magical methods.

"I'll be fine," she said, and left it at that.

For reasons I couldn't quite explain, even to myself, I kept sneaking glances over at Cat. She was gazing at the ground and didn't see me, or at least I hoped that was the case, because she would probably ask why I was staring. She had gone quiet since her remark about the sirens. I didn't know what to say to open up conversation again between us. She had been pushed into sharing that information with me—that she was into girls—and I felt like I had overstepped a boundary. I hated Nerissa for forcing us into this situation. The thought of losing my bond with Cat made me feel sick. It scared me a little, how strongly I felt.

We heard a faint rushing of water as we continued our fast-paced hike through the forest. Normally this would have filled me with excitement, because it meant a chance to wash off and have a refreshing drink of water. Now a tingle of dread began in the pit of my stomach. We were racing the sun as it continued its descent towards the river. I wanted to scream at the Fae to walk *faster;* maybe *they* were used to dealing with hazardous, magical creatures, but Cat and I were most certainly not, and I would appreciate it if they didn't take liberties with our lives. But I refrained from saying this.

"Come on," said Nerissa. "Nearly there."

Just a few dozen yards, and then I saw it. The Aethelney River lay directly ahead, sprawling out in dark blue waves topped with white foam. It was so much wider than I had expected. I could make out the other side, but just barely—no more than a faint line in the distance, obscured by the white-crested waves. There were large rocks sprinkled throughout the water, posing an extra danger, as if the sirens and rapids weren't enough.

We approached the shore. The woods fell away abruptly, leaving me with a clear view down each side of the river. All I could see were trees along both sides, just trees for miles and miles. It made me feel small, an insignificant speck in the Fae universe. Pebbles crunched beneath my feet and I stumbled a little. It was hard to walk fast over the rocky beach.

"Where's the boat?" Cat sounded like she was starting to panic. I was with her. What, were we supposed to swim across the river? She tapped her foot repeatedly on the rocks.

Hemlock walked on ahead of us, going a stone's throw down the river to a cluster of three huge boulders. I heard a scraping, thumping sound and saw them dragging a long, skinny boat with several seats.

It was not a vessel that I felt comfortable crossing a small ocean with.

"That looks promising," I said sarcastically.

"Hush, Auri," snapped Nerissa. "We're going to get across this river before dark."

"Nerissa, it is dusk already," said Hemlock quickly. "We can wait until the morning dawn and then proceed to the other side, it really will not—"

"Hemlock, I have made my orders clear. Are you going against me?"

Hemlock closed their mouth and straightened up proudly. "I am merely giving my advice, Nerissa. If I remember correctly, that is why you requested my services."

Nerissa took a deep breath. I saw her fidgeting with the sides of her skirt, which was my first indication that she might be apprehensive. It was an oddly human thing for her to do. "I know the dangers," she admitted. "But I cannot afford to keep Elide waiting any longer than she has been already."

"And you will not have to," said Hemlock. "But please do not make the girls risk their lives."

"You are more than capable of transporting us the rest of the way to the castle," said Nerissa. She balled up her skirt in her hand and released it.

"But—"

"Hemlock, it seems to me that you are letting your feelings interfere with my orders." Nerissa looked intently at the nymph, and Hemlock seemed to shrink. "I thought I had made it clear that we would be crossing *tonight*."

Hemlock remained silent. I could tell Nerissa's words had hurt them, and I felt a pang of sympathy for the nymph. They were at Nerissa's mercy just as much as we were.

Hemlock dragged the canoe to the riverbank, lips pressed together in a tight line of worry. I was impressed by how easily they drew the canoe along the pebbly beach, like it took no more effort than carrying a handbag. How strong exactly *were* the nymphs? The canoe looked heavy enough to require at least two humans to pull it along.

"I hope there is enough room for all of us in there," said Nerissa, pitching her voice a little higher. If I didn't know better, I would have said she was making light of the situation, trying to make a joke.

"Just enough." Hemlock did not return the humor. They let the rope tied to the canoe fall to the ground and pushed it closer to the water. "We had best hurry."

The trees were in shadow now, the sun barely a sliver of burning red against the silvery green background of the forest and water. I gazed across the river and thought I could make out a splash of something ominous out there in the rapids. What was lurking out there, waiting for stupid travelers like ourselves to cross into their territory?

"Quickly, in, in," urged Nerissa, pushing me toward the canoe.

I scrambled over the side, plunging my foot into the river as I did so. The freezing cold water sent a shock through my body. The canoe rocked dangerously from side to side as I looked apprehensively at the river and pictured the canoe rocking when we were out in the middle of the water, no pebbles to catch us if we fell out, just the icy embrace of sirens.

I offered Cat my hand for her to climb in. She took it, sending another tingle through my body, and crashed down next to me on the thin, wooden bench. She gripped my hand, and I was sure she could feel my pulse pounding a thousand beats a minute in anticipation of the journey.

Nerissa climbed in behind us. I turned around to watch, craning dangerously in my seat. The canoe shot forward as Hemlock pushed us into the water, and then they jumped in themself, their lanky yet sturdy form balancing out the canoe on the other end. A wave splashed over the side, and I jerked away from it, bumping into Cat's side.

"It's okay," she said, voice loud due to her earplugs and clearly terrified.

Hemlock unearthed a canoe paddle from the front of the boat. Plunging it into the water, they started drawing the boat through the water with quick, deft strokes. Cat entwined her fingers with mine and I rubbed my thumb over the back of her hand, marveling at the feel of the delicate bones beneath her skin, strong and fragile at the same time.

The waves crashed over the rocks and the spray hit my face, getting in my eyes and mouth. The current was pulling us down the river and away from the shore. Hemlock had to work even harder to keep us progressing forward toward the opposite shore, but the water was pulling us away.

"Go!" Nerissa called. "You have to move faster!"

My heart was in my mouth. All I could see was the canoe tipping over and spilling us all right into the jaws of death.

The sun slipped below the horizon. I couldn't see the moon, just a vast expanse of sky. It wasn't dark enough yet for the stars to come out, but I could see a couple sprinkled against the grayish sky. The trees on the other side of the river seemed so small, like they were taunting us. It seemed like we were caught in a time loop, unable to move from the middle of the river, stuck here forever.

But then suddenly we were moving, and I could see us progressing, avoiding all the jagged boulders and whirlpools and small waterfalls threatening to pitch us over. It seemed like we might actually make it, and I could feel Cat squeezing my hand like there was no tomorrow, and when we reached the other side I was going to throw my arms around her and never let go. We could do it. We could make it.

And then I heard it.

A long note of music that seemed to pierce straight through my heart. I had never heard anything like it before; there were no words to describe it. Like molten lava, filling my body with warmth.

Behind me, Nerissa and Hemlock exchanged worried glances, but it meant nothing to me. The music was like nothing I had ever experienced. It was a high, warbling note, like spun silver, pure and beautiful. I looked around to see where it was coming from; it seemed like it was emerging from the river itself.

Nerissa was saying something insistently, but I couldn't figure out what Hemlock was replying; my only concern was the music.

Then I forgot my companions' names. I forgot my own. There was a person on the cluster of rocks nearby, a few hundred feet to our left. It was the most hauntingly beautiful woman I had ever seen in my life. She was draped in greenish-blue silks, like they had been woven from the mossy riverbanks themselves, and her skin shone iridescent. Her hair was long and luminous and flung over one shoulder carelessly, and my fingers itched to run through it, to smooth out that one strand that stuck out from the others.

Her eyes met mine, and I could have melted. I was instantly filled with longing: it felt like she was singing *just for me.*

I would have done anything to keep listening to that perfect note of music. Then she started to sing for real; ethereal, resonant sounds that echoed off the water and seemed to reside in every wave. I was standing up. I didn't remember getting to my feet, but every fiber in my body was pulling me toward the woman. I would die if I didn't get there. She was the only thing that could save me. It was like she was at the center of a black hole and I was the hapless planet hurtling toward destruction.

Then I became aware that there were more of these creatures. The water was positively teeming with them. They gathered by the rocks, singing, looking at me, drawing me in. I could hear them calling my name, and it had never sounded so beautiful as it did on their lips. Something clamped around my wrist, clawing its way up my arm, trying to prevent me from joining the sirens. But nothing could stop me.

Their voices slipped their way into my head, filling my entire skull with resonant sound. I ripped my arm free from its restraints and let myself fall, wanting nothing more than to join them and be one with that beautiful song. I would swim to them. I had no plan other than the fact that I could not bear to be so far away from them.

Then I hit the river, smacking hard into the surface of the water and hitting my head against the canoe. The spell broke. Water flooded into my sinuses and I coughed and sputtered, trying to keep my head above water. The current yanked me away from the boat. Cat was screaming my name, leaning precariously out of the canoe and reaching for me. I stretched out a hand, straining desperately to connect with hers.

The sirens continued singing, but the sound of the water drowned them out. The spell had been broken when I had flung myself into the water. They had accomplished their mission. Now all they needed to do was collect their prize. I screamed as I felt something wrap around my ankle, but it was just a piece of seaweed or something, and I continued to frantically tread water. I had to make it back to the canoe. Then I could plug my ears and we could make it to shore.

"Auri! Swim!"

Hemlock was turning the canoe around, coming back for me. Nerissa looked absolutely frantic. What would she tell Elide if she lost her prisoner? Cat was screaming her head off, yelling at them to hurry, paddle faster, get the canoe over to me *now*, and I just needed to keep my head above water—

And then something yanked me hard by the ankles and pulled me down into the depths of the river. I knew at that moment that there was absolutely nothing that anyone could do. There were some advantages sirens had over tree nymphs, and the ability to navigate the river was one of them.

I caught one last glimpse of the canoe rocking back and forth in the rapids, Cat screaming my name.

Then my head was underwater and my eyes were burning with the sting of the river water. I'd had the sense to suck in one last breath before I went under, and my lungs throbbed with the pressure. I kicked as hard as I could, but my captor was too strong. I thrashed my arms wildly, trying to pull myself through the water, but only connected with more resistance.

There were more sirens swarming around me. Their long, spindly fingers closed around my limbs, dragging me down, down into the river. How deep was it? They would certainly bring me all the way to the bottom. After all the air had disappeared from my lungs, what would they do? Display my body as some sort of trophy? What joy could they possibly get from this?

Their exquisite faces were menacing, eyes set unnaturally far apart and wide in their blueish faces. I clawed at the hands on my arms, thrashed about madly. My heart was pounding out of my chest.

I was going to die here, choking on river water, in a siren's embrace.

And there was nothing I could do about it.

A wave of complete acceptance flooded through me. I stopped struggling and basked for a moment in the absolute calmness. My lungs screamed for air, and I knew it would be only moments now.

Then a wave of frigid sensation shot through my limbs. My whole body had been electrified. It felt fiery hot but icy cold at the same time, and I thought my veins would split apart from the feeling. The sirens fell away as though something had hit them with a lightning bolt. I needed air, that was all I could think of, and I struggled up through the water, swimming frantically. Something tangled around my legs, but it didn't slow me down, and I ignored it as I pushed myself desperately toward the surface, lungs burning desperately for air—

My head broke the surface and I gasped in a breath, inhaling the spray of water that broke off the waves.

Chapter 28
Cat

"Human-faerie relationships have happened. Of course they have. If they result in children, that child will not live an easy life, but it has happened before and will happen again. Love isn't limited by such things."

- The Modern Manual of Faeries by Eleanor Bishop

TERROR FILLED ME LIKE NOTHING I HAD EXPERIENCED before. Nerissa had to forcibly restrain me from jumping into the water after Auri. I was hyperventilating, trying to break free, but Nerissa used some sort of magic to keep me restrained.

When Auri's head broke the surface of the river, relief flooded through me, but she wasn't out of the woods yet—or the river, as it were. "Let go of me!" I screamed at Nerissa, and she relaxed her grip just enough for me to break loose. I plunged over the side of the boat and into the churning water. My earplugs fell out as I did so, but I was past caring. The sirens had already done their damage.

"No! Cat!" Auri yelled. "Get back in!"

I swam to her, breaking through the waves, and flung my arms around her right there and then. We tumbled underwater for a second and emerged sputtering. "Auri! I thought you were—"

"I know," she said, and her face reflected my own panic. I really, truly thought I had lost her.

I made a noise that was half laugh, half sob. "You just dove right into the water. It was like you weren't yourself! I tried to stop you, but it was like you were possessed, I couldn't—"

"I know. Cat. It's not your fault." She accidentally kicked one of my legs while treading water. A wave broke near us and soaked us even more.

"Girls! Here!" Hemlock smacked my shoulder with the canoe paddle, signaling for me to grab hold. I held onto it and wrapped my other arm around Auri, and she gripped me tightly as Hemlock tugged us toward the boat. I got my upper half over the side and tipped over into the wooden bottom, sending us rocking and threatening to plunge us all right back into the Aethelney River, but Hemlock deftly shifted their weight to counterbalance us. Nerissa was screaming at us, something about how could we be so reckless, but I paid absolutely no attention to her until I had safely pulled Auri in beside me.

We lay there on the bottom of the boat, wheezing and gasping for breath.

"What's the matter with you, Auri?" exclaimed Nerissa. "You couldn't just put in a pair of earplugs, now could you?"

"Leave her be!" I said, coming to her defense. My own

earplugs were at the bottom of the river by now, but something told me the sirens wouldn't attack us again after what had happened. "She didn't know! You think Auri would have flung herself into the river if she'd been in her right mind? They cast a spell, the sirens. They make you lose yourself!"

I had heard a little of their song myself, a distant strain through the earplugs, and so I understood a little of the feeling. Without the earplugs, I wouldn't have stood a chance.

"We almost lost you!" Nerissa was filled with anger the strength of a firecracker. "What would I do if you had drowned, Auri? How would I explain that one to Elide?"

As she screamed at her, Hemlock navigated the river with incredible speed, taking us to shore faster than before.

Auri shivered violently next to me as my own body was racked with chills. We clung to each other as the rapids crashed against the sides of the boat, splashing everyone on board, but I was so thoroughly soaked that I barely noticed. I hardly dared to move. All I could think about was how close I had come to losing Auri without telling her how I felt. But unlike with Grandma, I still had a chance to tell Auri. A second chance.

The waves changed, moving with us instead of against us, propelling us toward the shore. I sat up, watching the beach rush closer. The trees swayed in the wind, and though the gusts were inaudible over the rushing of the river. Then, with an emphatic scraping sound, the canoe ran aground on the shore, jolting us forward.

Hemlock leapt out, alighting upon the shore, and quickly pulled the canoe up and out of the water. With minimal effort they heaved the canoe along the beach a few yards. I wanted to get out and help, sure that my added body weight didn't make the job easier, but I found myself unable to move. I didn't want to process everything that had happened. My limbs felt like they were frozen in place.

"Get out," said Nerissa. She jumped out of the canoe and started wringing out her sopping wet skirt. I felt a flash of victory—at least she was in discomfort now, too.

I followed her. It was impossible for me to be any colder than I was already. Auri, however, stayed frozen in the bottom of the boat, looking at me as if through a mist.

"Auri," I said. She blinked slowly at me. I lifted her up by the arm, helping her swing her leg over the side of the boat and totter onto the shore. Her legs refused to hold her up. "Can you hear me?"

"Mm-hmm." She didn't meet my eyes.

"You're going to be okay, you hear me?" My voice was edged with panic. "You're okay, we're okay. You just need to warm up and you'll be okay."

"I'm okay," Auri said. She sounded drained beyond belief. I slid my hand into hers. "Something happened, Cat. I don't know how I got away."

I stared at her. "It doesn't matter. You're fine now." I started to walk away from the water, heading toward the shelter of the woods, pulling her along with me. "You're okay." The word *okay* no longer sounded like a word. Behind us, Hemlock was shouting something at Nerissa.

"No," she said, "it's bothering me. You didn't see what I did."

The pebbles crunched under our feet. My waterlogged socks were suctioned to my feet, and part of my mind was freaking out over it, but I managed to shove it to the back. I reached up with the hand that wasn't holding Auri's to wring out some of my hair, spraying water droplets onto my already soaking-wet shirt. My sweater had fallen off in the struggle and was now somewhere at the bottom of the Aethelney River. Another piece of Grandma I would never get back. I hoped the sirens would at least appreciate the hand-knitted cables.

"I think I might know," I said slowly. I didn't want to freak her out, but I also thought I understood her panic.

"Could you see what was happening underwater?"

"No," I said, trying not to think about Auri being pulled down into the water. "But at the end…I think you used magic to get away, didn't you?"

Auri paled. I caught her as she started to slump down. "It sounds crazy."

"I know a thing or two about crazy."

She breathed an incredulous laugh. "It was magic."

She fell silent. So did I. Glancing across the beach, I saw that Nerissa was still occupied with the canoe, stashing it in the safety of the trees, probably tying it to a rock somewhere.

"I mean, it's hard to tell exactly what happened, but they pulled me down, and I knew for certain…I thought I was going to die." The explanation suddenly rushed out of her in a flurry, like she was trying to convince me she wasn't crazy, despite my reassurance. "Then I felt this surge of energy go through my entire body. Like I'd been struck by lightning. And it was like something yanked them away."

"By what?" I asked. Auri didn't sound disbelieving anymore. She just sounded tired and scared, and like she wanted this whole thing to be over.

"I don't really know. I think somehow I manipulated the plants in the river. They somehow sprung to my rescue and wrapped around the sirens' legs to pull them away…it was like they came to my aid."

"That *is* crazy," I said.

"I told you."

"I'm teasing. That's amazing." And I meant it.

"I don't know for sure. It all happened so quickly." She paused. "But I don't know how else to explain it."

"Do you think you could do it again?"

"I don't know."

We were back in the forest, stepping below the verdant curtain of trees. It was a relief to leave the open banks of the Aethelney behind and retreat below the canopy. The forest even seemed to muffle the noise of the river, giving an impression of peace. I couldn't see the guards from here. Part of me wanted to bolt, but they would certainly catch us before we could go any distance at all, and we were too exhausted for that anyway. We sank to the ground right there, sitting on a curved log that had a cushion of moss.

I wrapped my arm around her waist, pulling her in close. She was shivering uncontrollably. I rubbed her shoulder, wishing for a blanket.

In the distance, I heard the scrape of the canoe along the rocks, and Nerissa screaming instructions at Hemlock. I tuned her out, instead focusing on the quiet murmur of the forest, the hum of waves in the background. My own stomach was twisting. There was something I needed to know, something hanging unspoken between us.

"Why didn't you ask for earplugs?" I asked.

Auri stiffened, and I immediately regretted asking.

"I…don't know. I didn't think I would need them," she said helplessly. She lifted her head from my shoulder and met my gaze. Her closeness was distracting; I had a hard time focusing on what she was saying.

"You didn't think you would be affected by the sirens," I said. *But you were.*

"But I was." She nodded, percolating on this for a minute. "I've never said this before, but I've been thinking about it for a while. Wondering." She took a breath, working up the nerve. "After what just happened, I guess there's no denying that I'm bisexual." She let out a small laugh.

"Pretty dramatic realization," I said, giving a half smile myself. "That takes the cake. I've known I was gay my whole life. I just don't tell many people."

"I'm sorry you were forced into revealing it now," Auri said.

"I guess the sirens outed me."

Auri snorted. She intertwined our fingers and gave my hand a squeeze. "You know nothing will change how I feel about you."

How *did* she feel? She had been nothing but mixed signals…and now that I knew she *did* like girls, could it be possible that she returned my sentiments?

"When you dove out of the boat," I said, "it was like you weren't yourself at all. You were in a trance. I don't think I've ever been so scared in my life."

Auri kept quiet, no doubt remembering that moment herself.

"I honestly thought I was going to die," she said.

"I thought so too," I agreed. "I really did."

She squeezed my hand again. I hadn't realized I was shaking.

"I thought I had lost you," I said, suddenly overwhelmed with pain even though she was right in front of me. I couldn't go through the pain of losing someone again. Not when I had finally grown close to someone other than Grandma.

"But you didn't. I'm fine, Cat, I'm right here." Auri moved a little nearer, and I was suddenly hit by her closeness, flooding me with a wave of dizziness. It was hard to breathe.

There were only inches between us. It was the easiest thing in the world to close the space. I leaned closer, feeling her breath on my cheek, and I did what I had wanted to do for months and finally kissed her.

Chapter 29
Auri

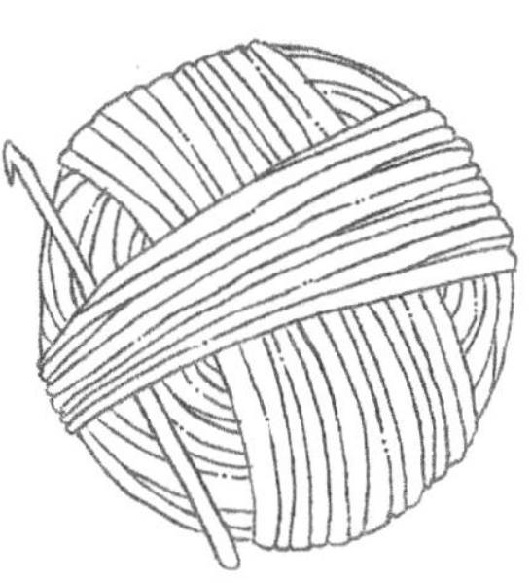

"Every faerie has the ability to do magic. Some have stronger magic than others, but all can perform even a little bit, if it's just drawing moisture from a leaf or creating a small bit of a breeze. Every faerie has a different kind of magic."

- The Modern Manual of Faeries by Eleanor Bishop

SHE LEANED IN AND OUR NOSES BRUSHED AND THEN I WAS kissing her, her lips warm against mine. I could taste her vanilla Chapstick. Then she was pulling away, leaving me with my eyes closed and heart pounding a thousand beats a minute.

"I'm sorry," said Cat, misreading my silence as disapproval. "I just thought…"

I placed a hand gently behind her head and leaned in, thinking it was better, in this situation, to have no talking at all be the answer. Then I wasn't thinking at all, lost in the feeling of her skin and hair and lips, so perfectly soft. I pulled away, our forcheads pressed together and breath mingling, her gaze fixed intently on me.

"Don't apologize," I whispered.

Her eyelashes fluttered. My own breathing refused to slow down, and my hand was shaking. Then Cat sat up with a start. "Holy shit," she exclaimed, "look!"

Had I done something glaringly wrong? I looked to where she was gesturing. There was a thick clump of bushes directly behind the log we were sitting on, and as I watched, one of the vines slowly twined its way around Cat's arm in an embrace. My mouth fell open in astonishment; I could barely believe what I was seeing. Could it be some sort of sentient Fae plant? But none of the vines were making a beeline for me; they were just gently twining themselves around Cat's hand, and now a smaller vine was wrapping almost shyly around her pointer finger, like a little kid clinging to a parent's finger.

"Why..." I said, at a loss for words.

"I think we solved the mystery of your magic," she said, with a big smile on her face. "I think that's all you, Auri."

"Well." A flush spread through my face. Cat was looking at me so proudly, like she had the utmost faith in me. It did make sense, though. When I was underwater, I was thinking about absolutely nothing except my impending death, and it was as if my subconscious had forced the river plants to save me from the sirens. It was the adrenaline that had done it, that had caused the magic to shoot through me. Cat had definitely triggered a similar level of adrenaline. The plants had followed my subconscious and basically mirrored my affection toward her.

"If it's all the same, next time I have to use magic, I think I'd prefer kissing you to fighting off sirens," I said, making her blush.

"That's good to hear," she said.

The plant slowed its progress up Cat's arm. I reached down to gently untangle it as I heard the Fae approaching. Cat and I hadn't been sitting here that long, but I felt like Nerissa would be able to tell everything that had just happened from one look at my face. Aidyn certainly would have been able to. I never had been much good at keeping secrets.

Well, the magic was the only important secret to keep here. I didn't care if anyone saw me with Cat. I wasn't ashamed. But I didn't want to put her in danger by getting close to her. Or by letting anyone else see how much she meant to me.

It was no surprise that my thoughts were all over the place for the rest of the evening. Nerissa and Hemlock joined us in the shelter of the trees and led us further from the roar of the river. I had horrible visions of the sirens crawling out of the river and slithering after us. For a while I could have sworn I saw their glinting eyes peeking out between ferns and hedges. But we walked for at least fifteen minutes, and something told me that they wouldn't go too far from their river. Sirens were, after all, creatures of the water.

We slunk along in the forest, Nerissa pulling up the rear and Hemlock striding in front of us. Well, they were slinking, anyway—I was crashing through the leaves and branches as usual. Walking through the woods was hard enough in broad daylight; now it was after dark and I was still reeling.

What *had* just happened? It had all transpired so quickly. I would have put it down to just pure relief that I was all right…but that didn't explain the way Cat had looked at me. It didn't explain the rush of butterflies as she had leaned in closer to me, our noses brushing and her constellation of freckles impossibly close. This had been brewing for a while, but I had been too distracted to realize it.

I had never really been in a relationship before, not a serious one. My most memorable romantic experience was an incredibly awkward trip to the ice cream parlor with a boy from math class in my junior year of high school. I was not at my best in my junior year of high school. I don't think anyone is. It culminated in him trying to kiss me and me upending my hot fudge brownie sundae all over my pants. I didn't leave the house for the rest of the weekend, trying to drown my embarrassment in yet more ice cream sundaes.

But in the short time I had known Cat, I had come to care about her more than I could have imagined. I felt closer to her than I had to any of my friends in what felt like forever. I couldn't imagine anything happening to her… and even knowing everything that would happen, if I had the choice, I couldn't imagine *not* picking up the Briars and Roses Shawl. It was simultaneously the best and worst thing that had ever happened to me.

For a person who never really had anything remarkable happen in her life, I sure was pulling out all the stops now.

I had been passing off Cat's affection as just a friendly gesture for all this time…now I knew it definitely wasn't just a friendly gesture. She meant it as something more. Maybe that would be obvious to a smarter person, but I didn't have much experience at all with this sort of thing. And until this point, I had never crushed on a girl. Did I actually *like* her? Or was I just scared and lonely and seeking comfort? I cared about her deeply, but was that in a friendly way or something more? The butterflies didn't have to mean anything. They could just be nerves. I couldn't bear to mess this up and ruin our friendship.

Was this really a good time to start being *more* than friends?

I still hadn't told her about her grandma's suicide note. What kind of a person did that make me? Lying to her, even by omission, filled me with sickening guilt.

Cat rubbed her thumb across the back of my hand. A shiver ran up my spine. I squeezed her hand once and pulled my hand away, feeling terrible as I did it, but I tried to brush it off as just me tripping over yet another log.

"You all right?" she asked, and I couldn't tell if she was referring to me tripping or to what had transpired a mere twenty minutes ago.

All I could do was say, "Yeah. I'm fine." What could I tell her? This was my own problem, something I had to sort out on my own. I didn't need to drag her into it.

My eyes widened as I took in our surroundings. Up ahead there was an enormous stone building. *The castle?* I wondered, dread creeping through me. But it didn't seem big enough to be a castle.

Hemlock brought the group to a stop and called Nerissa up to the front. The two consulted for a minute, and I could just barely overhear their conversation.

"Northpass," said Hemlock.

"Excellent. We've made wonderful time."

"You want to drop her off here, then, and proceed?"

"That's correct."

My heart beat faster. They surely couldn't mean what I thought they did. But then Hemlock strode over to Cat, whose eyes were wide with fear. "No," I said.

"This is where you part ways," said Nerissa, standing with her arms crossed.

"No, you can't." I took hold of Cat's other arm as if preparing to engage in a game of tug-of-war with her in the middle.

"We have no need of her," she said, "only you. Would you rather I killed her?"

"No!"

"What is this place?" asked Cat, doing her best to extricate herself from Hemlock's grasp.

"Northpass Farm," explained Hemlock. "It's where most

servants are trained, the ones you'll see around the palace, Auri. They always need more workers. Your friend will be safe here." It was the most words I had heard at one time from the nymph.

I was not reassured.

"You're not taking her," I protested. I pushed Hemlock's chest as hard as I could, but it was like attempting to push, well, a tree. I could have sworn they were rooted into the ground. "Please."

"I'm sorry," said the nymph, sincerity in their voice.

Then Nerissa's hands latched onto my shoulders. I screamed, stomped on her foot, and jerked my head back to smash her nose. She fielded all my attacks, and I reached down deep inside me to access my magic. But before I could draw from the power, Nerissa held out her own hand, pointing her index finger right at Cat's heart.

"I'll make this very simple," she said. "If you protest, your friend dies."

I had seen enough of Nerissa's power to know she was more than capable of it. I slowly let my hands drop. I had never felt so helpless.

"Please don't hurt her," I whispered.

Cat hadn't even been struggling. Had she given up? Nerissa released me, and I ran to Cat. "I'm sorry," I told her.

"It's not your fault."

"It is."

"You can't do anything about it. Please take care of yourself."

Would I ever see her again? I had to tell her about the note. If I never got the chance, it would be all my fault, and she deserved to know.

"Listen, I need to tell you something," I said.

But Hemlock was already pulling her away. I tried to follow, but Nerissa shot me one look and I knew Cat's life was in my hands. I watched her go, my eyes filling with tears. It was my fault, and she was gone.

Chapter 30
Cat

"Putting a line of salt along your windowsill is a good way to stop unsavory faeries from creeping in during the night. However, it is also a good way to attract ants, so you may have to choose the lesser of two evils after a while."

- The Modern Manual of Faeries by Eleanor Bishop

DISPOSABLE. THE WORD RANG IN MY HEAD AS HEMLOCK led me away. Here I was, being abandoned yet again. *Nobody wants you,* my thoughts informed me. *Even in another world, you're disposable. There's no world where you fit in.*

I blinked back the tears and focused on what lay ahead. As we drew closer, the building looked less impressive and distinctly more dilapidated. There was a stable outside, and a few faeries walked quickly by, likely on their way to clean out the stalls. I shuddered at the thought and hoped that task wouldn't fall to me. The building itself was two stories tall, made of stones that looked like they'd been dragged from the riverbank. It gave a mismatched vibe. Limp curtains hung from the windows in front, and the door was starting to mildew. I held my breath as Hemlock knocked on the door.

I heard shouting and footsteps from inside, and braced myself as the door opened. A woman with pale skin and a navy blue dress peered out at us. Her dark hair was slicked back into a bun from which a few tendrils had escaped. She had elegantly pointed ears. She waited expectantly.

"A delivery," said Hemlock.

"Ah," said the woman, "we are not expecting any deliveries."

Hemlock inclined their head. "I apologize for the inconvenience, but it was unavoidable."

The woman pursed her lips. "I suppose we could always use another set of hands. What bloodline is this one?"

"She's a human," said Hemlock, lowering their voice.

The woman's eyes widened. "A human? But how did she…"

Hemlock interrupted. "Nerissa of the Nyfain is on her way to Windermere to meet with the queen. This girl was along for the ride."

I would give just about anything for a map so I could figure out where the hell I was.

The woman looked from me to Hemlock. She yanked my hair away from my head and pulled at my ear. Startled, I jerked away. "Interesting," she said. "Well, we can put her to work."

"Thank you," said Hemlock.

I gave the nymph a pleading look. They merely shook their head, gave my shoulder a squeeze, and walked away. I strained my eyes, but I couldn't even see Auri in the distance. I hadn't gotten the chance to say goodbye. And right after I had finally told her how I felt about her.

The woman snapped her fingers. "I'm Edelkiasha," she said. "You may call me Edel, it works as well as anything. Your name?"

Grandma had taught me well enough to know you should never give a faerie your real name. I was willing to bet anything that Edelkiasha wasn't her complete given name. "Natasha," I said. My mom's name, as a tiny bit of revenge.

"Too long. How does Nat sound?" She didn't wait for a response. "I'll put you in the kitchens, we could use help there." She regarded me with mild interest. "Never had a human here before." She didn't seem fazed by it.

I followed her through a long hallway lined with doors. Edel noticed me looking. "Sleeping quarters," she said. "You'll be boarding with the other ladies. The kitchen's this way. Stables outside. Nothing exciting around here, but it does the job."

She pushed through a door at the end of the hallway, and we emerged into a dimly lit kitchen. It was about twice as big as my and Grandma's entire house. There were wood-burning stoves and a large stone counter in the middle of the room. A cauldron bubbled with a mysterious orange substance that smelled so good my mouth watered. Pots and pans clattered. The room was swarming with faeries.

"You can be a dishwasher for now," said Edel. "Jack will get you started." She waved me over to the side of the room, where a monumental stack of dishes waited. My heart sank. Not at the thought of dishes—I had washed more than my share at home—but at the thought of being stuck here.

Edel called to someone, and a young boy bounded over. He looked to be no older than ten with pale skin and blond hair so light it was nearly white. "This is Nat," she told him. "Nat, this is Jack."

"Pleased to meet you," I said. He looked like a sweet little kid, too young to be stuck in a place like this.

"You're new here," he observed. "Don't worry, dishwashing is easy." He grinned, revealing a missing tooth.

Edel left us to the dishes. There was no running water, only a bucket of water that would have to be replaced at regular intervals. I saw a few faeries looking at me curiously, but they quickly returned to their work. I made sure my ears were covered by my hair so they wouldn't identify me as a human.

"I'll wash, you dry," instructed Jack. He was barely as tall as the cauldron.

I obeyed, drying the dishes as he handed them to me. "So you're training to be a servant?"

"Servant? Is that what they told you?" He laughed. "No, this is a camp for the troublemakers. A prison!"

Of course. Nerissa had just said that to comfort Auri. "So we're locked in, huh?"

"Yeah." He deftly chipped dried soup out of the bottom of a bowl. "There are ways around that, though. Don't tell anyone I said that."

"I won't." Maybe Jack could show me a way out of here. "Prison? What'd you do, steal a cookie?"

"Golden egg," he corrected me. "Turns out you don't want to annoy a giant. They got the giant under control, but they sent me here."

"Did you climb a beanstalk to get there?" I asked, astonished at the fairytale character right in front of me.

He rolled his eyes. "Think you're clever, do you? Of course I did."

I puzzled over this.

"Look, I can tell you're not from around here," said Jack finally, handing me a frying pan. "Where are you from, Nat?"

I felt silly mistrusting a child, but you never knew who was listening. "A long way away."

"What are you here for?"

"Offending a faerie."

He looked at me curiously. "Which one? There's a lot of Fae here."

Right, they were all Fae. Oops. Well, what's the worst that could happen? If I revealed a secret to him, maybe he would trust me. "I'm not," I said quietly, and tucked my hair quickly behind my ear.

His eyes widened. I let my hair fall back into place. "No wonder why they brought you to Northpass," he said incredulously. "Humans never set foot in Feylinn."

"I have a question," I said. "Why weren't you surprised when I asked you about the beanstalk? Is it that common a fact?"

He paused his chatter but kept scrubbing. "I guess I'm your tour guide then."

I gave him a small smile. Who better to get information from than a young child? Kids were talkative, sweet, and had no filter. They also were too young to be prejudiced against other people—not as much as adults were.

"Okay. Feylinn is also called the Land of Curses," Jack started. "It's a land where fairytales repeat themselves. A few humans have stumbled here before and gone home with a heap of tales. I'm not surprised you've heard of me." He extended his arms triumphantly.

"Jack and the Beanstalk."

"Yep. My family was starving, and we had to sell the cow. When I got offered those beans, I knew I was doomed to repeat the Jack story. It could be worse, though. Ever heard of Bluebeard?"

I grimaced.

Bluebeard was a tale about a woman who married a man with a blue beard (the names of these stories aren't very original). He gives her the keys to all the rooms in his mansion with the condition that she must never go into a particular room, then he leaves on a trip. Of course she goes into the room.

There, she finds the mutilated bodies of Bluebeard's past wives. Terrified, she drops the key and it lands in a puddle of blood, which refuses to wash out. She has to return the key to him, and when he sees the blood, he tries to kill her. She gets saved by her brothers or mother running in at the last minute in a typical deus ex machina. Not exactly a soothing bedtime story, but Grandma let me read the original Brothers Grimm and Perrault fairy tales for a reason: *It's not a pretty world out there, Cat, even if the Fae are pretty on the outside.*

"Is that…is that story real?"

"'Course it is. You think somebody could make that up?"

I didn't know. The mind has a way of running wild sometimes. "I guess I hoped so."

He shrugged. "Anyway, there has to be a certain balance of curses in the world, or Feylinn will die. It has to stay balanced, you know?"

I did understand, in a way. My own life had to have a certain balance to it.

"There has to be a balance of good and evil. That's what we're taught from birth. Good and evil. Otherwise…how much exploring have you done?"

"A bit," I said, thinking of our three-day trek through the forest.

"Then you saw the weird patches?"

"The Wastelands?"

"Yeah! Those."

They were the opposite of "weird." They marked the only peace I had felt in years. Was there something wrong with me to make me feel at home in these places, while others frowned upon them?

"Faeries were cursing each other from the beginning of days," he said, sounding like he was reciting from a textbook. "Eventually the first queen from the Pryderi bloodline got all the fighting to stop. Everybody was tired of it, anyway." It was such a little-kid way to tell history, which was exactly my speed at the moment. "It was all fine till about a hundred years ago. Then the world started dying, so we had to start cursing again. It's not working so well, though. Anyway, that's how I ended up here."

"What do you mean, dying?" I asked.

"Feylinn is dying," Jack said. "Mom says a big curse went wrong one day. Until it gets fixed, we're basically screwed." He shrugged and went back to washing dishes.

I was not content with this explanation, but I didn't want to interrogate the kid.

My arms were sore and aching when the dishes were finished. Since I'd traveled all night, Edel told me that I could rest for a few hours until lunch.

Exhausted, I followed her to the girls' dormitory, which was crowded with bunk beds, She assigned me the top bunk in the middle of the room: not my ideal situation, but I was too tired to care. I climbed the ladder and flopped onto the thin, rough mattress, completely drained in body and spirit.

Edel had confiscated most of the things in my backpack, but she let me keep Simon the sloth, so I curled up with him and tried not to cry. I wondered how Auri was doing. Had they reached the castle yet? What would Elide do to her? A tear slid down my cheek despite my best efforts, and I wiped it away angrily.

A big curse went wrong, Jack had said. What if the big curse related to Auri? I couldn't think of any fairytales involving magical crochet shawls, but maybe it was a variation of something. Rumplestiltskin, spinning straw into gold? Then it came to me: Sleeping Beauty. She had already pricked her finger on that too-sharp crochet hook. But if that was the case, why wasn't she in a coma?

I rolled over, trying to get comfortable without a pillow or blanket. There was one thing I didn't understand. Jack said their world was dying. But why? What curse had gone so wrong that it was killing an entire kingdom? In the history of Feylinn, there had to have been other curses that went wrong, yet they didn't have an impact.

So why this one?

Chapter 31
Auri

"Faeries are big on tradition. If you thought Thanksgiving dinner was rough because of family traditions that people just won't let go of, then the faerie world will come as a big shock to you."

- The Modern Manual of Faeries by Eleanor Bishop

I CRIED AS WE CONTINUED OUR QUEST THROUGH THE FOREST. I couldn't believe we had just left Cat behind. Nerissa told me that if I put one toe out of line, she would send word back to Northpass and Cat would be killed. So I stayed compliant, but I didn't stop thinking about how to get her out of there. Northpass looked like a prison.

We hadn't been walking an hour before we stumbled upon something strange. As we walked, we watched our surroundings change slightly, little by little: here was a boulder covered in moss, there I saw a random plank of wood discarded in the trees. There was a small pile of rocks in the trees a few dozen yards from us, like someone had been building something. But there was nobody out here, right? Nobody except us and…

"Whoa," I said. I came to an abrupt stop on the trail and Nerissa crashed into me, smashing her nose into the back of my neck.

"Watch it!" she snapped.

Right in front of us was an enormous stone tower, sort of like a water tower but built with rocks. It was made of intricate cobblestone patterns, stones of all shades of gray and pale blue and green, like they had been hauled from the river and transplanted into the middle of the forest. It was big enough for a person to spread out comfortably in it, and only about two stories tall, explaining why we hadn't spotted it earlier. All in all, I was amazed that a great big stone tower could be so perfectly camouflaged, but here it was, and we had barely noticed it from ten yards away.

"Classic," said Hemlock under their breath. "Nerissa, we can't walk away from this."

Nerissa swore.

"What is it?" I asked, still craning to see. I looked like a tourist ogling the skyscrapers.

"A classic Rapunzel curse," said Hemlock. "Auri, I believe it's meant for you."

I looked at them, confused.

"You're caught up in a fairytale," they explained. "You have to see it through to completion. Someone is at the top, and they need to be rescued. You're the chosen one."

A prophecy? Really? "How do you expect me to get up there?"

"For the love of…" said Nerissa.

"Be patient with her," said Hemlock, putting a hand on her arm. "Auri, don't you have this fairytale in Terrin?"

I nodded, running my hands over the smooth stone, visions of the sirens springing to mind. There was still beauty to the river, though, despite the fact that its inhabitants had tried to kill me. It was nice to be able to appreciate the stunning glamour of the rocks now, when my life wasn't in peril. It was like a thousand colors of beach glass all blended into one beautiful structure; I had never seen anything like it before. This was really my first glimpse at Fae architecture. If Windermere Castle was anything like this, I was sure it was a marvel.

Of course I knew what to do. How many fairytales had I read as a kid? How many times had Aidyn and I stayed up past our bedtimes watching Disney movies? There had to be some poor girl up there. While it was usually a prince who rescued Rapunzel, Feylinn apparently did not conform to gender roles.

Feeling like the world's biggest fool, I put my hands to my mouth like a megaphone and hollered, "Rapunzel, let down your hair!"

Nothing happened. I was mortified. I wondered if I could climb up somehow.

Then I heard it: a rattling noise from overhead, like somebody was pushing open a creaky cupboard.

So there *was* somebody up there! I was unsure whether or not to call out, not wanting to scare the girl, the Rapunzel being up there. And then a low voice, lower than I had expected, said: "Hello? Is that you, Mother?"

Call me stupid, but I usually thought of princesses as having high voices. Sort of squeaky. Maybe that was silly, because I certainly had an idea of faeries and then I found out that I was Fae, and I definitely didn't meet that definition. In any case, I decided not to answer, instead waiting for Rapunzel to make the next move.

"Just a moment," called the person, and then it happened just like I knew it would. A long, golden rope of hair dropped from overhead, spiraling through the crisp autumn air, and thunked against the stone exterior of the tower. The end of it brushed along the dirt, sure to be a pain to wash out later. How did you even wash hair this long? Wouldn't the split ends get out of control?

Stop asking stupid questions and climb already.

I slid my sandals off my feet. "Would you keep an eye on these for me?" I asked Hemlock, who nodded solemnly. No need to have them falling off while I climbed.

Okay. Here goes nothing. I twined the hair around my wrist, braced my feet on the side of the tower, and hoisted myself off the ground. I then began my ascent into the tower.

It wasn't as easy as it looked in the movies, though, and I began to question my own strength. If an old woman like the witch in Rapunzel could manage it, then why couldn't I? Probably because I had the upper body strength of a limp noodle. It was all those skipped gym classes as a child. I should have gone to gym instead of hiding out in the nurse's office, I thought, as every muscle in my body ached and screamed at me to get right back on the ground where I belonged. I was paying for it now. Gym karma, I supposed.

I developed a method: place one foot firmly into a foothold on the wall, put the other one up too, and then scoot my arms further up the hair. But it was harder than it sounded because the stone was slippery and uneven, which made it difficult to brace myself securely. There were no carabiners or trampolines waiting down below to catch me, nor did want to fall and squash anyone. (Well, maybe Nerissa.) So I had to content myself with trusting my own abilities, which did not fill me with confidence.

The higher I got, the greater the temptation was to look down. Granted, it actually wasn't *that* far to the ground, but it was far enough that I would certainly injure myself if I fell. And I couldn't exactly rush off to the hospital out here.

"Don't look down" was always the advice they gave you when you were rock climbing or on a ski lift or something. And while I wouldn't say I was afraid of heights exactly, I did have a healthy respect for them, or rather a healthy respect for my body staying in one piece. Climbing up a *head of hair* was not on my list of safe and reasonable activities for an afternoon in the forest.

The hair was actually pretty gross, too. In the movies you watch about Rapunzel, she doesn't have split ends or greasy hair or anything, because how disgusting would that be? Her hair is always flawless, perfectly coiffed and gleaming to perfection, with nary a speck of dirt in sight. However, in real life, this Rapunzel's hair was tangled up and matted. I was sure my hair would look the same way if I let it get that long; it was annoying enough to wash and brush it chin-length as it was now. Some strands of hair were coming off in my hands as I climbed up this rope of hair, and it was coarse and dry like a broom.

This chick needs some deep conditioner. Maybe we can take her to a hair salon when we get back home. Not that we were bringing a random Rapunzel back to Terrin, but she could really do with a trip to the spa.

I was exhausted, my arms begging me to stop and take a break. I looked down despite myself and felt a little dizzy seeing the ground a couple stories below. But I was almost at the top.

I glanced up, straining the last few feet, and tossed my arm up to catch the edge of the ledge. I heaved myself over it, focusing on the tower just enough to make out the window through which I was climbing, framed by two small wooden doors that the owner could open and close to keep out bugs and random intruders such as myself.

I flopped over the edge and onto the floor, slumping down and catching my breath.

"You're not Mother!" a voice exclaimed.

I pushed myself up on one elbow and prayed I wouldn't get smacked in the head by a frying pan. Then I realized what I was seeing and my jaw dropped. Rapunzel was…a guy who looked like he was around my brother's age, maybe fifteen, sporting a green shirt with laces around the neck and a pair of pants the color of tree bark. He was barefoot, partially hidden behind a table, and from his head spilled the longest and snarliest mess of honey-blond hair I had ever seen.

"You're…" I said.

"You're…" he sputtered.

We stared at each other, neither of us knowing what to do. He had enormous blue eyes, the color of one of the stones in the tower itself. He looked like he had never seen somebody his own age before, which was maybe the case. Or maybe he hadn't ever been around a girl before. Maybe both.

"Please don't be scared," I said, trying to reassure him quickly. "I'm not going to hurt you. I just thought you might need help."

He was yanking up the tail of blond hair, coiling it at his feet. Then my hands were being clasped together with something, and he was shoving me against the wall near the window. I squeaked, afraid he was going to tip me out and let me fall to the hard forest floor. "I'm not here to hurt you!"

"Who are you?" he said. "Why are you here?"

"I'm…" What to tell him? I couldn't think of a cover story fast enough. There was probably no harm in telling him my name, anyway. "I'm Auri."

"What sort of a name is that?" He was gripping my wrists loosely enough that I probably could have broken away if I tried. But I would let him feel like he was in control right now, and maybe I could get an answer out of him that way.

"It's short for Aurora," I said defensively. He blinked at me. "Why, what's your name? And is that really what you want to ask somebody who broke into your tower?"

He looked astounded. I raised an eyebrow at him.

"How…how did you get here?" he asked. "There is not supposed to be anyone around for miles and miles. That's why…"

He reached up to smooth an unruly curl of blond hair. The hair was really disconcerting, and not because of his gender: it would be shocking on a girl too. There was simply so *much* of it! But this guy owned it, even if it did cause me to stare incredulously.

"That's why your mother locked you up here," I said, to finish his sentence. He looked too perplexed to continue.

"She is not my mother," he said. There was no emotion in his voice at that sentence. Well, his not-mother was lying to him. He wasn't miles and miles away from people. Northpass wasn't far away at all, and if I understood Nerissa correctly, we weren't far from Windermere Castle either.

He released my wrists but didn't step away. He looked so intently at me that it made me redden a little; it was like he had never seen another human before. Or Fae. Which probably he hadn't. If this was anything like the Rapunzel fairytales I was used to, he had been taken away as a baby and raised in captivity. It was incredibly sad; I had always thought the Rapunzel tale was tragic, but seeing a real person afflicted with it brought it to a whole different level.

Were *all* the fairytales things that had really happened?

Chapter 32
Cat

"A quick and easy way to protect yourself from the Fae is to turn an article of clothing inside out. Make a habit of wearing your undergarment inside out, or wear one sock inside out every day, and you will add an extra layer of protection to your everyday Fae wards."

- *The Modern Manual of Faeries by Eleanor Bishop*

EDEL LET ME SLEEP UNTIL LUNCHTIME, BUT I COULDN'T catch a wink. I simply lay there with my face buried in Simon the sloth until Edel threw open the door with a loud thud and ordered me to wake up. This did not lead to a particularly cheerful mood.

I stumbled into the bathroom to splash my face with icy water. My mouth tasted like something had died in it, so I brushed my teeth with a strange powder that smelled like lavender. What wouldn't I do for a tube of toothpaste? I would never feel properly clean again. I scowled through this routine and all the way to the kitchen. I worked through the rest of the afternoon and slept through the night.

"Hi, Nat!" said Jack, who had suddenly appeared at my side the next morning.

"Ugh," I said. "How are you this chipper?"

"I'm a morning person," he told me. "Mother hated it too." He tugged on my arm. "Here, I'll get you some carrot stew."

The mysterious orange substance turned out to be carrot stew and wasn't half bad. It filled me up and warmed me to the core. After I finished my breakfast and took one of my few remaining Lexapro, I had to admit that I did feel a little better. Jack polished off his bowl of porridge in two minutes flat and sat there until I had finished mine. Then he sprung to his feet. "I'm on stable duty today."

"Oh, that's neat," I said. "Do you like horses?"

He nodded enthusiastically. "They probably won't put you on stable duty yet. Go ask Edel what you're doing today."

I ambled over to the older faerie, who was sitting in the corner with her own bowl of porridge. She observed me. "Nat," she said. "Good first night?"

Cat, I thought. "Yes."

"You're used to walking about in the forest. Today you'll be collecting firewood." The panic must have shown on my face, because Edel added, "You won't be going alone. Lilac will be your companion." She nodded to the door. "You'd best get a move on. It'll take a good number of trips."

I bid goodbye to Jack. Edel told me to meet Lilac outside the door.

"Don't bother running," she said. "You'll be staying within our borders. If you cross the fence, we'll know."

I deflated inside. Of course there was security. This wouldn't be the way to freedom.

———————

Lilac was a faerie who looked like she was in her mid-thirties. But who knew how old or young she really was? I caught myself staring at her hair, which looked like actual lilacs growing out of her head. She had light brown skin and a round face with purple freckles sprinkled across her nose and upper cheeks. I caught the faint scent of flowers. She turned her head when she heard me. "Good morning."

"Hi," I said. "I'm Nat."

"You are joining me today?"

I nodded.

She stood from where she was slouching against the wall. She was tall, at least six feet, not what I would have expected from a faerie. That was when I realized I was thinking of faerie stereotypes, and how annoyed was I when people went by gay or OCD stereotypes? We ambled into the forest together, and I took pains to make sure I stepped evenly over the branches and sticks.

The house vanished from sight. I was too worn out to feel any anxiety over walking into the forest *again* with a stranger.

Lilac broke the silence. "I've been wanting to speak with you."

"Me?"

"I sensed your presence when you arrived here," she said. She studied me intently. "I knew it was a matter of time before we met. We have much to discuss."

"That's awfully cryptic," I told her. "How could you have sensed my presence?"

She held a branch aside for me. I ducked underneath. We reached a pile of firewood stacked under a thick cluster of pine trees, and Lilac stopped.

"I will not be cryptic," she said. "We cannot fix this with cryptic messages." She sighed. "I sensed your presence when you arrived in Feylinn because you are involved in a curse that I, too, am wrapped up in."

I tilted my head. "Curse?" Could she somehow know about the shawl?

"You did not come here alone," she said. "Who was your companion?"

Did I dare tell her? Grandma had warned me about not giving your real name to the Fae because they could use it to control you. As if she sensed my mistrust, she said: "I know there are two of you. I am not going to hurt you; I want to end this curse just as badly as you do."

"Auri," I said, against my better judgment. That wasn't her full given name, so she would be safe.

"Where is she now?"

"I don't know! They were headed to Windermere Castle when they left me here."

Lilac's face paled. "Then we don't have much time."

She paced around the stack of firewood. I didn't know

how long we had before Edel would expect us back. But I had a feeling Lilac was referring to something different. "Time? What do you mean?"

"Someone brought you here. Who?"

"A faerie named Nerissa. She wanted to bring Auri to someone named…" I cast back through my memories. "Elide, I think."

Lilac shook her head. "Of course she does. Tell me, Nat, why did Nerissa target you? Did you stumble across something in Terrin?"

I didn't ask how she knew I was from Terrin. Between my ears and her mysteriously "sensing" my presence, she had clearly figured it out. "No, you tell me something first. What curse are you involved in?"

She pressed her lips tightly together. "It was dozens and dozens of years ago. I stepped in to prevent a curse, and because of me, the designated recipient of the curse escaped into Terrin. She's been there ever since, and it's thrown our world into a terrible imbalance. Because of this, I was confined here, unable to age until the curse is completed."

"*What curse?*" I asked more insistently.

"A cursed shawl."

Chills crept up my spine, but somehow I had known from the beginning. "That's what Auri discovered," I said. "She came looking for answers, and Nerissa found her."

Lilac nodded slowly. "I thought as much. Nerissa brought her back to try and make things right."

"To save the world?" I asked.

"Yes. To save Feylinn."

"And how's she going to do that?"

"By completing the curse as it was originally intended," Lilac said. "What do you know about the shawl?"

"It killed my grandma," I said. I would never get used to the stab of pain when I said those words. "That's what I know about it."

Lilac pressed her lips together sympathetically. "Yes. That's how the curse ends. Anyone who begins work on that shawl will either finish it or die trying."

And Auri had tried. So what must Elide have planned?

"She's going to kill Auri," I whispered, tears springing to my eyes. "I can't leave her to die."

"It's impossible to leave here," said Lilac. "I have tried many times." She held her hands to the sides to show defeat. "My magic is limited here."

I slumped against a tree, mind working a thousand miles a minute as I tried to calculate a way out of here. I had to find a way to Auri's side. I had no plan, no powers, nothing at all, but I had to try.

"Please," I said. "You're the only hope I've got."

Lilac thought. "There is only one way I can imagine getting out of here." She picked up a handful of firewood. "My magic will return if I am doing something to remedy my wrongs. That is, the only way I can get us out of here is if I'm going to the original curse."

I got what she was saying. I scooped up some firewood myself, knowing we had to get back. "To finish things with the curse."

"That is correct."

"Which means Auri will die."

"I have always been opposed to the ideal of the Land of Curses," she said softly. "I do not believe we deserve to live in a constant state of good versus evil. I believe nobody should have to be evil if they don't wish to be." She pushed her way through the blanket of trees. "My role in the curse is to impede the evil one. Now that the curse has finally continued, I can reprise my role."

A sliver of hope surged up in me.

"We have to move quickly," she said. She dumped the firewood on the ground. "There is no time to waste."

Chapter 33
Auri

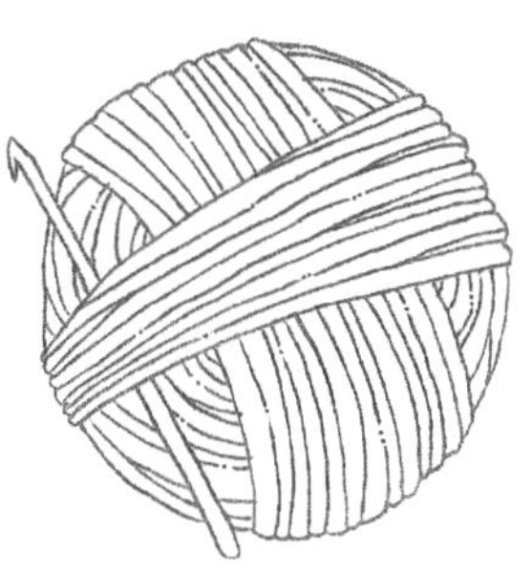

"There are several sorts of animals that appear in both worlds. The domestic housecat has always belonged to both worlds and can travel back and forth as it pleases, because neither the humans nor the faeries fully understand cats, no matter how long they have tried. Cats have a knack of getting in places they shouldn't, so is it any surprise that they find portals?"

- The Modern Manual of Faeries by Eleanor Bishop

RAPUNZEL BOY FINALLY RELAXED A SMIDGEN AFTER HE seemed to decide I was no threat. "My name is Basil," he said, toying with a section of his hair like he didn't know what to do with himself.

"Nice to meet you," I said. I rubbed my wrists, sore from being tied. "I'm sorry, but I'm a little confused. How did you end up here?"

"I suppose you have heard of the bloodline curse," Basil said, still fiddling with his hair. "Most everyone has."

"Bloodline curse?"

"Yes, of course," he said. "Have you not? Well, this one is a tradition."

"It's okay," I said. "I'm sorry. I know this is all a little sudden."

I stepped away from the window, unwilling to meet my death from a fall to the forest floor.

"Is your mother going to be back soon?" I asked. I glanced behind me out of the window, half expecting to see a black-robed witch in a pointed hat strolling along the trail.

Basil looked between me and the window. "Not until tomorrow, I would imagine."

This could have easily been a lie. But this was a boy who had little to no experience with the outside world. I would take my chances. Instead I looked at Basil. "Would you mind if I stayed for a bit, then?"

"Well…yes, I…I suppose that would be fine." He shifted from foot to foot, clearly unsure of what to do with himself.

I took a look around at the tower room. It was small, even smaller than my bedroom at home. There was a curtained section off in the back that probably held a bathroom of some sort. Had the Fae invented plumbing, or would I be stuck using a chamber pot when I finally made it to Windermere Castle? There was a small twin bed with elegant spiraled legs, a blanket tossed haphazardly over it like he had just woken up. Next to this was a sturdy wooden table with a few mismatched chairs. The floor of the room was made of cobblestone, which made the chair legs unsteady and caused the chairs to wobble back and forth.

There were a few paintings on the walls of flowers and trees and the forest. I looked around a little more and saw dried flowers hanging from the rafters, filling the air with a delicate, sweet scent. It was a good idea to have those hanging there, otherwise I could see the tower getting musty and stifling very quickly. It wasn't as dark as I would have expected for the inside of a tower. Basil had done a nice job filling it with life. Still, it had to get incredibly lonely living here. How many hours must he have spent bored out of his mind as he awaited his next visit from "Mother Gothel" or whichever fairytale character cared for him?

"Would you care to sit down?" offered Basil. He directed us to the small table, pulling out a chair for me. I sat down and scooted in a little, chair legs grating along the stone.

"It's simple, really," he said. "I'm of the Tressa bloodline, which makes me a recipient of the Rapunzel curse." He looked at my baffled expression. "You are, of course, familiar with the bloodline curses?"

"Not exactly," I said, hoping he would go on.

He was perched on the edge of his chair like a bird ready to take flight. "How is that possible?"

"Look," I said, "I'm not exactly from around here. In fact, I think I may be the victim of a curse myself. So how about you educate me on this bloodline stuff, and I can help get you out of here?"

"Please tell me where you are from," he said. He looked so innocent and scared, but genuinely curious. I was probably the first human he'd ever seen. So I told him the truth—that I was from Terrin—but that was all.

Basil had grown up hearing stories about humans just like we had heard stories about the Fae, but the difference was, human stories are even less pleasant than fairytales—which is saying something, if you've read the Grimm originals. When I asked him what he knew about humans, he said that humans were supposed to be bloodthirsty creatures that specialized in death and destruction. They didn't believe in magic *or* the Fae, and when witches had walked among them, they captured them and burned them alive. The human world was a place nobody wanted to end up. He had grown up hearing the stories and had accepted them as truth, as most Fae did, to the best of his knowledge. So they knew about humans, but most of them never had any interaction with us, and apparently had no desire to.

Well, I didn't really blame them. Some days I didn't much like humanity either.

"I'm not a bloodthirsty monster," I said. "Just so you know. Maybe a lot of humans are like that, but not all of us, Basil."

"I…would not have called you bloodthirsty," he said, and blushed to the roots of his hair.

Oh brother.

He rushed to continue. "In Feylinn," he said, "there can be no good without evil. We balance each other out. Everyone has a responsibility…to uphold their end of the deal, as it were."

"Good versus evil," I said. "How does that relate to you?"

"It's the curse," he explained. "Every bloodline has a curse they are known for. Do you know what a bloodline is?"

"Like a family?" I guessed. It sounded a lot less warm and fuzzy than the word "family," though. I couldn't imagine telling people I was going to spend the holidays with my bloodline, or having a "bloodline reunion."

"I suppose," he said. "Less loyalty, though, than I...than I think a family would have."

He hurried on before I could mangle the situation by going on about how sad that was. "Bloodlines can be traced back to the beginning of Feylinn. The Tressa bloodline is known for the tower curse. I see that you, too, have heard of it."

Rapunzel. That tale had made it to Terrin.

"I told you there always has to be a balance, yes?"

"Yeah," I said with a nod, "but I'm not sure exactly what you mean."

He tilted his head, thinking. "This is what we are taught from a young age. Mother tells me that all Fae know this. There are probably phrases like this in your human world, Terrin, right? Things you are so used to, you do not even stop to question them." He paused. "It goes like this: Everything has a role. And everything must play that role for Feylinn to survive. There can be no good without evil."

I didn't quite get what he was after. He saw my confusion. "It is difficult to explain...I suppose, if you have never heard it before..." He looked like was trying to find the right words.

"The fact is that there must *always* be…an equal balance of things, an equal balance of good and evil. Without evil curses pushing against good faeries fighting them, our world would cease to exist. It would…well, it would die."

I nodded slowly, the words sinking in. "There has to be a balance."

"Yes. Always." Basil looked at me. "If not, the balance is upset…have you seen the trees?"

"Hmm?" I looked, reflexively, out the window. The trees, in their dappled shades of greens and browns, swayed in the slight breeze. It had to be a really relaxing view to observe. I could probably have spent hours perched on the windowsill, dangling my feet over the edge and watching the sights of the forest, listening to the birds chirp and waiting for sights of other amazing magical creatures. "What about them?"

"They…they're starting, well, to die," Basil said quietly. He sounded resigned to the fact, like the way you would speak about a family member with a horrible, incurable disease. For him, the forest probably *was* like family. I thought about how I would feel if my home started dying.

"You mean because of the bloodlines? Are they not casting enough curses?"

"I do not know why," said Basil quietly, "but…it just, it seems that is the only thing that makes sense, that could explain it…" He paused. "Truth be told, I do not know why. It does not make any sense; I do not understand why the forest would suddenly start fading like this." He pushed his hands through his hair, pulling it away from the leg of the chair, where the golden curls had started to tangle.

"Do you think," I asked, "that has something to do with why Nerissa brought me here?"

It was slowly starting to click into place. Nobody had bothered to explain anything about Feylinn to us when we had first arrived here. But now that I was starting to get some of the backstory, things were falling into place. These were things that Fae children knew, things that should have been so obvious that I could put them together instantly. Now that Basil had explained about the bloodlines, I thought maybe that related to the reason for our capture, the reason Nerissa had brought us here.

"If I have Fae lineage," I said, putting a hand to my ear as to prove that it was still there and I was indeed some sort of faerie, "then I could be tied to the curses somehow. The shawl..."

An image of the shawl flitted into my mind, so strong it almost knocked me over. Then I had an awful realization. In my hurry to climb the tower, I had left the bag with the crochet shawl.

Dread coursed through my veins. It had taken me so long to crochet that much; I would never be able to do it again. It was looking more and more like the only way to break this curse was to finish crocheting the shawl, and if Nerissa undid all my progress, who knew what would happen?

Chapter 34
Cat

"Perhaps surprisingly, the common pigeon is Fae. It originated in the faerie realm and hopped over to the human one, then made itself at home. Pigeons are now one of the creatures that exist in both realms. They are quite adept at scavenging food which makes them a survivor anywhere."

- The Modern Manual of Faeries by Eleanor Bishop

WITH LILAC BESIDE ME, HER HAND ON MY SHOULDER, WE were able to walk directly through the barrier of magic keeping us prisoner.

It shimmered up ahead, barely perceptible, and we walked through without so much as a tickle.

"This feels so nice," said Lilac, a smile spreading across her face. Her strides lengthened until I was running to catch up with her. "A hundred years is too long to live in such a small place."

I looked over my shoulder, feeling a pang of sorrow over leaving Jack in that place. He was a young and innocent child, even if he had stolen from a giant; he didn't deserve to spend his whole life in Northpass.

"We need to make quick time to the palace," said Lilac. "Auri could already be there. We need to intercept her before she sees Elide."

I didn't want to ask what would happen if we failed to do so. "How far away is it?"

"Too far to walk," said Lilac. "We'll catch a carriage."

There were so many things wrong with this plan. March into the palace with a formerly imprisoned faerie and only my conviction that Feylinn was *not* dying, trying to save my friend?

"Okay," I said.

Lilac took us to a place called Falcon Crest. It was a small village close to Windermere, and we planned to catch a carriage the rest of the way to the palace. As Lilac explained it, although Feylinn was a large country, not much existed south of the Aethelney River—*except for the Well,* I thought. Most everything happened in the north, close to Windermere Castle, before the city gave way to the cold and foreboding Lenia Mountains. I could see them in the distance, tall enough to scrape the sky.

The city Lilac took me to was bustling. It was lined with shops selling everything you could imagine, from spinning wheels and potion supplies to sparkling tiaras and silken dresses. I stopped outside Harriet's Haberdashery to stare at the various sunhats and bonnets. One of my favorites had a few striped feathers artfully tucked into the wide blue ribbon. If we weren't in such a hurry, I would have stayed and looked, but Lilac pulled me away from the window.

Carriages were plowing down the street, and heaven help you if you stepped in their path: it looked like they would stop for nothing in their way. Lilac led me to a small wooden shelter where a bunch of other Fae were standing. "We wait here," she said.

"What, for the bus?"

She tilted her head. "For a carriage."

"You're kidding." There had to be a better way of emergency transportation than essentially taking the bus.

"Do not worry. It will be here shortly."

I tapped my foot, feeling the anxiety of running late. With every minute that passed, Auri was in more danger, and I found myself short of breath. I accidentally brushed against one of the Fae at the bus stop and apologized, backing up against the wall. It was a man wearing a dapper top hat and light blue coat, and he tipped his hat to me as I apologized.

Then a supersize carriage wobbled down the street, pulled by four beautiful, black horses. Lilac pushed my back to make me walk forward. I joined the throng of people heading for the carriage. It came to a stop. A footman leaped down and walked around to open the door, ushering the people inside. "Lilac," I said, tugging on her dress. "I don't have any money."

"Don't worry," she said.

When we got to the front of the line, the footman gave me a hand to help me into the carriage. I climbed inside. It was filled with plush red seats and had curtains hanging over the windows. It was altogether quite inviting. The seats were already half full and I slid into one near the front, shuffling over to the window seat.

Lilac joined me, and the carriage continued to fill up, offering the best opportunity for Fae-watching yet. They were wearing clothes of all designs and patterns, although long coats seemed to be in fashion—a Fae lady was sporting a particularly eye-catching peacock-blue one. It didn't seem like there were any limits on style, you just wore what you pleased, and it made me smile. I thought I looked out of place in jeans and a blouse until a younger guy climbed onto the bus wearing, of all things, a T-shirt with "The Beatles" emblazoned across the front.

"Lilac," I said, inclining my head to the boy. "Where did he get that?"

"Ah. Some human fashions are in style here," she said with a knowing smile. "We love your T-shirts. Humans rarely stumble here, and Fae rarely visit Terrin, but when they do, we get a wealth of new fashion ideas."

I mulled this over. "That's neat. Do you have any other things from Terrin?"

She nodded. "We have some novels. No films; we don't have electricity here." Obviously that meant no Wi-Fi either, which explained why my phone didn't have any service but my watch still worked.

The footman closed the door, and there was a rustling of fabric as everyone adjusted in their seats. Then I heard the driver urge the horses onward, and the carriage jolted into motion.

I struggled to get a glimpse of the carriage driver, but he looked fairly ordinary to me. He was wearing a long suit coat in a striking shade of green, had a bow tie around his neck (black this time), and wore a beanie hat pulled down low over his ears.

They were stunning horses, too, black and shiny despite the mud caked around their hooves. I had gone horseback riding a few times in my younger days, for my friends' birthday parties and things like that. I went through a phase when I was about ten where I was absolutely obsessed with horses. Grandma had the Black Stallion series, and she let me read all 20 books in the series. A lump formed in my throat just thinking about it. She had trusted me with her possessions, welcomed me into her home, and given me a wonderful childhood.

I sighed and shuffled closer to the window, leaning my head on the side of the carriage. Until now, I hadn't allowed myself to think about life without Grandma. But in this moment, the pain of losing her hit me hard. My eyes watered and my throat hurt, and I couldn't help sniffling.

Lilac put a hand on my shoulder, and I started.

"Nat, what's wrong?"

I hadn't told her about Grandma. It felt like if I admitted it here, of all places, I would never get her back. So many things in Feylinn were *impossible* in the human world… how could I admit my grandmother was gone? I wiped my eyes.

"I miss home," I told her. It was true. I wasn't referring to the false warmth of my mother or even Aunt Stephanie, nor was I talking about the "home" that awaited me in the future, independent and lonely. I meant Grandma, because she was the only person that made it feel like home.

She rubbed my shoulder. "I know it must be difficult." Her voice was soft.

"I don't think I'm ever going back," I said. It was something I had known deep down all along, from the moment I fell through the Well. There was no going back from this. Even if I made it through the ordeal, there was nothing waiting for me back home, and from what I'd seen, there was no place for me here either. Was I destined to always be cast out?

I found myself wanting to tell Lilac just a little bit of truth. "I lied to you," I said. "I'm not even supposed to be here. I'm just a human. My name isn't Nat; it's Cat, and I came here by mistake. I don't really belong anywhere."

She put a hand on my shoulder, eyes full of sympathy. "Maybe you think it's a mistake, but I think everything happens for a reason."

"But what good can I possibly do?" I whispered, alarmed to feel my eyes filling with tears. I blinked them away, embarrassed.

"I do not know how this will turn out," said Lilac. "But if I am still here, I will help you, Cat. Just as you have helped me."

"Thank you," I said, and I meant it. I had a total of two advocates in this world and Terrin combined, but two allies were far, far better than none.

Especially when both of them had powerful magic.

The carriage bumped along, carrying us to our fates. I didn't exactly look forward to getting to Windermere Castle and meeting this fabled Elide. Nerissa had been talking about her for ages; she had been so afraid to be late delivering her prisoner to Elide that she had forced us to cross a siren-infested river at dusk, knowing full well how dangerous it was. And we were going to walk in and just…demand to speak to her?

Yet it was the best plan we had. I leaned my head against the window and watched the town and forest flit by.

Chapter 35
Auri

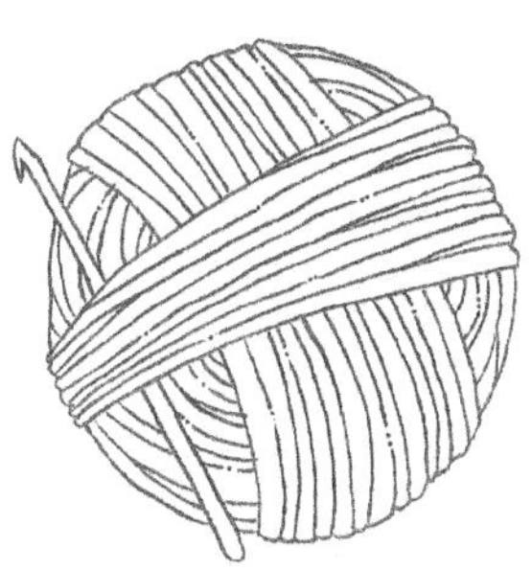

"Why would someone seek to attract the Fae sometimes and repel them other times? Much like people, there are good faeries and there are evil faeries, most of them falling somewhere in between. Wearing protective charms allows you to choose when you interact with them and gives you a way out should the situation turn dire."

- *The Modern Manual of Faeries by Eleanor Bishop*

"I NEED TO GO," I TOLD BASIL. HE WAS STANDING IN THE middle of the tower, fidgeting. "Thank you for helping me."

He watched me with his big blue eyes. "You cannot stay a little longer?" The loneliness in his voice went straight to my heart.

"I'm sorry," I said, feeling a pang in my chest, "but I'm a prisoner too." I went to the window, where I could see Nerissa and Hemlock standing below, waiting for me.

He didn't respond. When I turned my head, he was still staring out the window, the same view he'd probably had his whole life. How could I leave him to this?

"I thought you were going to rescue me," he said quietly.

I laughed on reflex. His face fell, hurt. "I'm sorry," I said, "I don't mean it like that. It's just…I'm no hero. I can't even rescue myself."

"That's not how the fairytale goes," he said, like he couldn't believe it. "I'm the proper age. You stumbled upon my tower…you are supposed to rescue me."

Nerissa had said that too—that I was entangled in the fairytale. If I walked away now, would I contribute to the slow but sure destruction of Feylinn? Based on Basil's story, failing to fulfill the curse would do just that. But being involved in two curses was too many.

"I'm sorry," I said again. "But maybe you don't have to be limited to your curse."

He blinked.

"You can escape," I said. "Even if I'm not the one to rescue you, that doesn't doom you to a life in this tower forever. You can escape on your own." His hair was certainly long enough to use as a rope.

"You mean leave…leave this tower, leave home?" He stood up from his chair, pushing it into the table neatly, and started to walk back and forth across the floor. It didn't look like he even realized he was doing it. How many laps had he paced in this tower, waiting for his mother to come and spend time with him, waiting for a shred of human companionship? How many boring afternoons had he passed, wondering if he would ever get out into the forest and explore the world? What kind of a life would I be leaving him to?

"I know it's scary," I said. "Believe me, I do. But you have to realize that nobody is guaranteed to come along to save you."

Basil stopped in his tracks. I knew it sounded terrible, but I had to make him realize that *he* was the only chance of escape.

"You don't have to rely on a prince or princess to come along and save you," I continued, sounding like every cheesy, generic empowerment speech I'd ever heard. But what else did I have?

He balled up his hands into fists, looking like he didn't know what to say.

"I just want to help you," I said, and I took a couple steps towards him. "But I can't if you don't let me."

Instinctively, I took his hands in mine, causing him to tense up even more. I gently coaxed his fingers free from their fists and laced our hands together, flashing for a moment to the memory of Cat's fingers threaded through mine. If I thought about her, I would break entirely.

Basil ducked his head, refusing to meet my eyes. "I want to help," I said gently.

"I don't know," he said. "I don't know what to do."

I squeezed his hands, marveling at how warm they were. He was still tense, never having had much human contact in his life. I hoped it might help convince him that this was the right thing to do. Truthfully, I didn't know exactly what to do, but this felt like the only right course of action. I didn't want to guide him astray, though; I didn't know what was best for him. Maybe someone really *would* come along to save him.

But I wanted him to know I was here for him, that I would help him if that was what he wanted.

"I'm scared," he said, so quietly I could barely hear it. He bowed his head lower so that his hair fell over his face, covering his eyes a little, but I guessed that there were tears in them. My heart broke for him.

"I know," I said. "I know exactly how you feel. My whole life changed a few weeks ago, too."

I slowly placed my hands on his shoulders, and when he didn't pull away, I enveloped him in a hug. "You're going to be okay. You will get through this. You just need to figure out what you want with your life."

"I don't know," he said, returning my hug awkwardly and hesitantly, but happily, it seemed. "I have never known what I wanted. It was all decided for me, long before I was born, with the…with the bloodline curse. And now…I have lived my whole life here, day after day, waiting, searching…" He broke off. Took a breath. "Searching for something. I do not know what."

"You'll find it," I said. "You can come with me now, if you want. But you don't want to go where I'm going."

He hovered near the middle of the tower, like he wanted to come with me but equally wanted to stay where he was. He was obviously torn, and I couldn't advise him. This was the biggest decision he would probably ever make, the biggest decision he had ever been faced with in his life. How did you decide to leave the only life you've ever known for something completely unfamiliar?

I glanced anxiously at the window. The sun was getting lower in the sky, and though I couldn't do anything fancy like tell what time it was based on the sun's position, I did know it was getting later and that Nerissa would be growing impatient. I needed to get going. I guessed I'd already been here for at least an hour. *How could I have left my bag with Nerissa?* I chided myself again.

Basil hurried to the window and expertly wrapped his hair around the hook, then let the long rope of golden hair slide down the side of the tower and to the ground.

I climbed up onto the ledge too, my insides torn in half between wanting to stay and needing to go. "Basil," I began.

He slid his hand into mine like I had done to him earlier, then pulled me gently off the ledge and back into the tower room. "I wish I could go with you," he said.

I felt the rough cobblestone beneath my feet, felt the ledge at my back, and knew I had to leave *right then* before it got any harder. But I couldn't force myself to, couldn't bring myself to pull away.

"I have never…well, I suppose, have never met *any* Fae before," said Basil. "So I suppose it does not mean much. But I have never met anyone like you, Auri." His gaze dropped to his toes, too shy to say anything more.

Of course I had made an impression on him; I was the only person he knew. But I tried to let him down gently. "Basil, you can leave. You'll be okay."

"I cannot," he said. "I cannot leave everything I have ever known on a whim. Not like this."

"I understand." I really did. I couldn't ask him to leave everything like this; it was completely unreasonable. "I just want you to be okay. For you to find a happy way to live."

"I don't know if I ever will," he said, "not like this. I…I've been thinking, for a while…I've had the feeling that nobody would be coming for me." He looked so dejected.

He made eye contact for a fleeting second and returned his gaze to his feet.

"I have to go," I said. "Are you sure you don't want…"

He tightened his grip on my hand for a second, then released it. My hand fell to my side. "I am sure. Go, Auri. Go home."

I wondered if I would ever see him again. There was no way we would just bump into each other. For the rest of my life I would forever be wondering what had happened to him. If he had found a way out or if he had chosen to stay in the tower forever. I would never know the conclusion to this version of the Rapunzel story.

I climbed onto the ledge and wrapped my hands around the hair-rope dangling from the top of the window.

"Wait," said Basil. He leapt nimbly onto the ledge next to me, brushed a strand of hair away from my face, and quickly leaned in and kissed me on the cheek. I nearly fell off the ledge right there and then.

He was sweet and it seemed like he had a good heart. It was easy to like him. But the only image that came to mind was Cat's freckled face.

I turned to smile at Basil. "Good luck," I told him. Then I summoned my courage and pushed my feet off the edge of the tower, gripping the hair tightly and beginning to slide down it. It shot through my hands, leaving them burning and tingling. I would have rope burn to add to my list of ever-growing injuries. I wrapped my legs around the rope as I slid for extra stability.

The forest floor approached quickly. Nerissa stepped out of my way, giving me a wide berth for my landing. I bent my knees as my feet slammed into the ground and stumbled away from the hair, dizzy.

"Where is the tower prisoner, then?" asked Nerissa. She was holding my bag. I had no way of knowing what condition the shawl was in.

"He's not coming," I said.

Hemlock handed me my sandals. I slipped them onto my feet with a nod of thanks.

Nerissa's expression was incredulous. "But the curse..."

"Curses are made to be ignored," I said, and walked away.

Chapter 36
Cat

"Wearing herbs near the heart is a particularly good way of self-protection. Pin a sachet of herbs under your clothing and over your heart. Bonus points if the pins are iron, which repels the Fae."

- *The Modern Manual of Faeries by Eleanor Bishop*

THERE WAS A CASTLE LOOMING ABOVE US.

A real, actual castle right in front of us. The kind you see in fantasy movies and books. I felt like I was about to stroll in for my first year at magic school. It was an enormous gray castle, turrets piercing the cloudy gray sky, deep green-blue moat circling the outside. There were guards stationed around it. We were perhaps twenty yards from the moat, and all around us were the castle grounds, sprawling and majestic. I would have happily spent hours exploring them; there were extravagant gardens with flowers of every hue, fountains with statues of beautiful faeries dancing about, and benches that looked so inviting to sit on, perched under sweeping willow trees.

But everything was graying; it looked like a picture

that had been taken and slightly distressed. Everything was gorgeous, no question about it, but everything looked diluted, like it was slowly dying. A pang of fear went through me—it was just like Lilac and Jack had talked about.

The world was dying because of an imbalance.

It was a hundred times worse than the Wasteland in the forest. That patch of forest had been tranquil and calm. Here it was like the life was being sucked from the palace.

"State your business," ordered the guard by the drawbridge.

"I am Lilac of the Fleurin bloodline, and I have returned to the curse."

"Royal business. Got it." The guard signaled to someone on the other side of the moat, and a drawbridge began creaking downward, sounding like nails on a chalkboard. I could hear Grandma's voice like she was there in front of me: *That needs some WD-40.* I missed her more than I thought it was possible to miss anyone.

The drawbridge thunked to the ground, held up by heavy chains. Beyond the drawbridge I could see into the castle courtyard, and I held my breath. There were dozens more guards in there; escape would be impossible.

There was no going back now.

"You just have to say it with confidence," whispered Lilac to me, "and they'll let you do just about anything." She winked. I knew she was trying to make me less nervous.

A second guard arrived to escort us across the drawbridge. The two guards exchanged a few words too quiet for me to hear. Then the first guard turned back to us. "Follow Rae. They'll show you where to go."

"Very well," said Lilac.

Rae was short and sturdily built with close-cropped red hair and a silver ring through one side of their nose. "Welcome to Windermere Castle," they said, voice soft but firm. "I understand you are here on royal business. Please follow me."

They led us across the drawbridge and into the courtyard, not leaving us much time to examine the castle around us, but I could see enough to know that there were doors going off in every direction. Maids, servants, and guards bustled around everywhere. This was sensory overload if I had ever seen it. Talk about being thrown into the deep end. I had never seen so many faeries in one place before. I wanted to look around and explore, to talk to the Fae and learn more about this new world.

There would likely be secret passageways around here, wouldn't there? If I was going to be kidnapped and dragged into a fantasy world, at least let me discover a secret passageway or tunnel. It would make an incredible story.

All of this would make an incredible story, actually. Too bad I wouldn't live to tell the tale.

We pushed through the throngs of people as we traversed the central courtyard. I didn't know anything about how castles were laid out. I would have to look it up if I ever made it home; I would be even more interested now that I had some personal experience. But it seemed fairly evident that we were going to a well-populated part of the palace. The throne room, maybe, if we were indeed going to see the queen.

The guard reached a tall door, framed with intricate stonework and carvings, and a servant opened it for us. "Thanks, Tara."

"Of course. I'll see you later for pastries, I hope?"

"Wouldn't miss it," said Tara with a laugh. "They're on you this time."

"If you insist." Rae waved us through the doorway.

As we passed, I met eyes with Tara, a pretty brown-haired girl with several piercings at the tips of her slender pointed ears. She stared at me with the same fascination I felt for her. It had to be an exciting day at work if you saw a few prisoners being escorted along. Or maybe that was an everyday occurrence. That was a sobering thought.

Rae led us along hallway after hallway, corridor after corridor, marching through so many entryways and exits that my head started spinning. I tripped my way up and down stone staircases, some of which spiraled around and around like a storybook picture, and nearly banged my head on low-hanging ceilings. I could have spent days exploring this castle; it was a feast for the imagination. There was no way I could keep track of where we were going. I didn't think Auri would be able to, either, even if she had a better sense of direction.

Would she trip over the uneven cobblestone without my hand to hold? The thought made my bottom lip tremble and I bit it hard.

"Nearly there," said Rae. "You should know that Queen Aurelia has a guest of honor at the moment."

I perked up. Information!

"Who is it?" I asked.

"Lady Elide." My heart dropped somewhere in the vicinity of my shoes. *Elide.*

"Why is she here?"

"She is merely residing here for an order of business. Business relating to the curse you spoke of." This was directed at Lilac.

"Does she have another castle?" I asked, nearly falling flat on my face as my foot caught on an uneven cobblestone stair.

"She has alternate lodgings when she is not here." Who wouldn't want to stay in a castle if they had the choice? On the other hand, maybe it got too busy sometimes. I understood the desire for solitude. "She is in the throne room now with the queen. She gave instructions not to be disturbed, as she has dealings with another subject, but this is a special circumstance."

Another subject?

Rae grew quiet, quickening their pace, which was really very unhelpful as I was struggling to keep up already. Castle cardio or what?

There was a even more dramatic door ahead of us, with two guards flanking it. They nodded when they saw us and pulled open the doors as we approached. And my mouth dropped open, because it *was* a throne room.

But I barely noticed anyone seated on the throne.

Immediately my eyes fell upon Auri.

She was standing in the middle of the room with Nerissa and Hemlock beside her. Relief flowed through me as I saw that Auri was unharmed, at least on the outside. I felt the butterflies return too. Auri's head turned as the door opened, and her eyes lit up when she saw me.

"Cat," said Nerissa. "I should have known you would show up."

Beside me, Rae descended into a profound bow. Remembering where I was, I dropped into a curtsy and saw Lilac doing the same, although hers was a dozen times more graceful than mine.

The queen was the most beautiful being I had ever seen. Second to Auri, that is. Her white-blonde cloud of hair formed a halo around her head that shone in the candlelight. She was a chubby woman with striking features, like they had been carved by a master artist, and her nose was delicate and pointed. She wore a turquoise dress with a sweetheart neckline that accentuated the soft curves of her figure, the skirt cascading down to the ground in flowing waves of fabric. It was a dress that befit an angel. The sleeves flowed down too; there was probably enough fabric in each one of those sleeves to make another dress, and her large hands peeked out from beneath them. She had a diadem on her head consisting of three garnet droplets positioned on her forehead and held together with a silver chain.

My heart turned over and did a few somersaults. My body considered passing out again.

"What is the meaning of this intrusion?" asked the queen.

"Forgive me, Your Majesty," said Lilac. "But I am involved in this curse, and I wished to see it through to completion." She bowed her head. It was a good cover story.

"Come forward," she said. "We were just beginning."

Lilac grabbed my arm and led me forward, so I was standing next to Auri. Her eyes were as wide as mine. Quickly, before I could say anything, she slid her hand into mine, and tingles bolted up my arm.

But I didn't have time to think about her affections. Nerissa shot me a look of pure disgust and then picked up from where she'd left off. "Queen Aurelia," she said, with more respect in her voice than I had ever heard from her before, "may I speak to Elide, please?"

"We are expecting her," said the queen. "You have done well. Is this the one?"

"This is the girl," said Nerissa, gesturing at Auri.

Yes. Auri was the reason; I was no more than a pesky fly to get rid of.

Queen Aurelia rose from her throne and descended the several steps to the ground, dress trailing behind her in a river of blue. She drew nearer to Auri, looking intently into her face.

"She looks just like her," the queen said.

I didn't even dare to speak. Nerissa would probably smite me where I stood if I accidentally disrespected the queen. I would probably say something totally offensive by accident.

Then a gust of cold air swept through the room. I would have wrapped my arms around myself if Auri wasn't holding my hand. I turned my head to see what was happening.

Through the door we had entered strode a woman about as different from the queen as you could get. Her skin was ghostly white, like she had never seen the sunlight in her life. Her hair was strikingly black and the contrast against her porcelain skin made her look sickly. She was wearing a dress of midnight black, long strips of fabric making up the overskirt, and it made her look like a ghost gliding along the ground. Her arms were exposed at the top and she wore long black gloves that shimmered ever so slightly. And she carried an intricately carved scepter with a stone set in the top, a stone that shimmered in shades of blue and red and purple, like the glass ball held an entire universe. Although she wore no crown, her hair was arranged in a braid that made it look like she wore a diadem like the queen.

She may not have been the queen, but she looked every bit as regal. And she walked like she owned the place, despite the fact that Rae had said this wasn't her home. I had absolutely no doubt in my mind that this was Elide, and I could see why Nerissa feared her, why she had done everything she could to meet the deadline set by this fearsome lady.

Nerissa dropped into a curtsy again, rising more quickly this time. "Lady Elide," she said.

Chapter 37
Auri

"Hagstones are stones that have a naturally created hole in them. They carry protective properties, and it's easy to put them on a chain and wear them around your neck. Look for them at the beach. They are only effective if the hole is naturally occurring, not if you drill a hole in a stone."

- The Modern Manual of Faeries by Eleanor Bishop

As ELIDE ENTERED, AN IMAGE OF THE SHAWL SWAM INTO my head, a stronger image than I had ever experienced before, taunting me with its lacy stitches and delicate thread. I absolutely had to continue crocheting it. All I could think about was the shawl and how badly I needed to have my crochet hook in hand, weaving it in and out of the stitches, catching the delicate thread in the neck of the hook, creating ornate lace and petals and making the shawl grow. I could almost feel it in my hands now, and my hands began to shake, trembling so hard that I had to place my hand on a nearby pillar for balance.

The feeling had come on so quickly, and now it was overpowering. Why did I need to work on the shawl so desperately *now*? Just like my magic, it had come out of the blue, a tidal wave of power. I had the sudden thought that Elide had somehow triggered this feeling. It was like a faint memory.

Cat tugged my hand. I snapped back to reality, feeling a flood of relief to have her next to me. I didn't know how she had escaped, but hopefully I would be able to ask her later. Cat was one of the most resilient people I had ever met.

A faerie with beautiful lilac hair was standing next to her, looking at Elide with scorn. Who was she?

Nerissa was talking, and I tuned back in to hear her say, "I have done the duty you assigned me."

"And done it well, I am sure of it," said Elide. Her voice was warm and rich but calculating. This was the kind of voice that could command an entire room, that could persuade people to do what she wanted in just a few simple words. "This is Auri, hmm? Will you not introduce me?"

The guard behind me pushed me forward at Nerissa's gesture to do so. "Of course, Lady Elide."

"Wait a moment," called the queen. "Elide, you will do well to remember that while you are in Windermere Castle, you answer to me."

Elide gave a perfunctory smile that said she was perfectly aware of this and she would absolutely comply, but only because it suited her. She was like a cat, I thought, a cat waiting to pounce on its prey. "I apologize, Queen Aurelia. I defer to you."

Queen Aurelia looked at me searchingly. "You are Auri?" she asked me.

"Yes, Your Majesty," I answered, finding my voice. I fidgeted with my hands behind my back.

"You look just like your great grandmother," she said wistfully.

I couldn't take my eyes from her. "You knew my great grandmother?" I asked, then quickly added, "Your Majesty."

"You are family, Auri. You do not need to address me with such formality," said Queen Aurelia. What did she mean? "I did not know your great grandmother. However, I am one of her descendants."

Time stopped for a minute. The whole room seemed to spin around and I had a hard time keeping myself upright. So I was related to this ethereal being somehow? I knew I had Fae lineage, but to be directly connected to Queen Aurelia, the most magical person I had ever encountered… "You mean we're related?" I breathed.

"Yes, my dear," she said. "That is why I had to bring you back here."

This was getting even more complicated than I had anticipated.

"Would you care to explain?" asked Elide, her voice sweet.

"That is, I think," said Queen Aurelia, turning her delicate face to Elide, "a job best suited for you, Elide."

Elide nodded. "Whatever you wish, My Queen. I would be happy to explain why we brought her here." It seemed that she had already anticipated Queen Aurelia's answer, though, like she knew the queen would pass the responsibility along to Elide.

She flicked her gaze over to me, dark eyes fixing on my face, and I saw so much pain in her eyes that it made my own stomach knot up in agony. Then it passed, but she continued to regard me as if she were looking at someone she knew. "It is a complicated story," she said, "and a long one, so you will do best to listen and not interrupt."

I nodded. It was long past time for some answers.

Elide paced in front of us, her shoes clicking on the floor. She held up her skirt so that she wouldn't step on it as she walked. "Now where do I begin?" she asked. "It goes back such a long, long time, and I was there from the very start."

"I know about the curses," said Cat. She sounded like she wanted Elide to get right to the point. "You need a balance of good and evil in the world, don't you?"

I looked at Cat. She bit her lip, like she wasn't sure if they would punish her or not for speaking. Well, if they tried to hurt Cat, they would have to get through me first…not that I was exactly much of a threat, but the sentiment was still there.

"And the bloodlines," I added. It looked like Cat and I were still on the same page.

"Very good," said Elide, sounding pleased. Her thin lips stretched into a smile. "So you have educated yourselves a little about Feylinn, I see. Good. I am pleased that you have made the effort, as it will make my job that much easier. I know that you have brought something very important here with you. In fact, it is the very reason that we are here, and I venture to say that you know this too." She was looking just a little to my right, unwilling or unable to meet my eyes. Whatever she saw there caused her that much discomfort. "Do you know the item I speak of?"

"The shawl." Of course. "But…"

"Did you bring it with you, my dear?" asked Elide, waiting for me to confirm. Dread shot through me as I looked to Nerissa, absolutely certain she had unraveled it.

"Yes, I think Nerissa has it…" I looked toward the faerie for confirmation. Nerissa produced my drawstring bag as I watched. It was muddy and dirty from being dragged through the forest, but I saw a little pink thread poking out of it, and my heart leapt at the sight. I couldn't bear to think of all my hard work in a pile of tangled thread at the bottom of the bag. Unraveled. Gone.

"Indeed. So you say this is cursed, do you not?" asked Elide. She began walking in slow paths in front of us, skirt gliding along the polished floor, shoes clicking rhythmically. I nodded. "You have experienced it. The dreams, the all-encompassing thoughts, the tunnel vision, I believe it has been called. You can think of nothing except this shawl, am I right?"

"Yes." She was not surprised. Of course not. She had described all the symptoms perfectly; now was she going to tell me *why* these things happened?

"Disconcerting, I am sure." She flicked her hair off her shoulder. "Fear not. It is all normal, perfectly commonplace. In Feylinn, in any case."

"Get to the point," said Queen Aurelia in her musical voice. "We haven't got all day." She took a seat in her throne, propping her hands on the carved wooden arms. I could see what she must look like to her people, regal and imposing, looking out over the crowd of her populace.

"I apologize. I have simply waited so long for this moment," said Elide. "But Auri, I know you have waited a long time too. You have waited a long time to know what is happening to you. You are afraid. I see it." She stretched out a long, white finger and touched my cheek, fingernail scraping along my skin. "So time for answers. We have to go back to the beginning, a hundred years ago, long before you, or your mother, were born…"

"We get it," said Cat. All eyes snapped to her, the only person with the audacity to interrupt Elide. "It was a long time ago. You cursed Auri's great grandmother, didn't you?"

Elide paused. The whole room held its breath.

Then Elide let out a surprised laugh. "The little human grows tired of my monologuing, I see."

"Don't call me that," snapped Cat. "I might be a human, but I'm not any less than the lot of you. And my name—"

Nerissa slapped her across the face. I gasped, lunging forward, but a guard caught me around the arms before I could get any further. Cat cried out and her head snapped to the side with the force of Nerissa's strike. "Do not address Her Majesty in that tone of voice," said Nerissa.

Cat's hand rose to her face, trembling, and I saw a handprint splashed across her freckled cheek.

Chapter 38
Cat

"Pixies are what most people think of when they think of faeries. Don't confuse the two. Pixies are the equivalent of mosquitoes in the human realm; they are small, quick, fairly simplistic, and are usually viewed as a nuisance. Faeries, on the other hand, are the size of humans and much more intelligent."

- The Modern Manual of Faeries by Eleanor Bishop

MY CHEEK BURNED, AND I PRESSED MY HAND TO IT, MY EYES watering. I had expected no less from Nerissa.

"That was unnecessary, Nerissa," said Elide, watching her with mild interest. "The human girl was merely voicing her opinion. Is that not encouraged in Windermere Castle?"

I regarded Elide with narrowed eyes. Nerissa hadn't deterred me by the slap; I knew very well what they thought of me here. "I know what you're planning to do with me," I said. "I know humans are disposable for you. But my name is Cat. At least have the decency to call me by it."

Catherine was the name my mom had given me. Cat was the nickname from Grandma. I had traded one in for the other, and I was proud of it. I held my head high, waiting for recognition from Nerissa. The faerie didn't move, waiting for some sign from Elide. And Elide? She gave a small, firm nod.

"I can admire that," she said. "Cat. We will do well to remember that."

I looked at her, stunned. Auri wore the same expression. This was not the response I had anticipated. Obviously Elide had some level of respect for courage. "Why do you need Auri here?" I blurted out. I realized I had no idea.

"You, Auri," said Elide, "I have big plans for you. *You* are going to save the world." She laughed, and I couldn't tell whether or not she was joking.

"And Cat?" Auri asked, before anyone could cut her off. "You'll let her go free? If you only need me..."

I squeezed her hand, trying to urge her not to do whatever it was she had planned. I wouldn't allow her to bargain for my life with hers hanging in the balance.

"Oh, I am not sure yet," Elide said. "Perhaps you have an idea?"

We looked at each other, both filled with the same terror. I didn't want to die, but better me than Auri. *I'll get to see Grandma again.* "Just leave her alone," Auri said. "Please. I'll..."

"Perhaps if you do everything I require," said Elide, "then I will do just that. Leave your girlfriend in peace." My face heated up. Did she know what that word meant to us in the human world? "You blush. Adorable. I will not deny you two *are* quite sweet together."

Auri couldn't meet my eyes. My shoulders slumped. After everything we'd been through, it was clear that she still didn't think of me as more than a friend. I had read her emotional state after the siren attack as interest, when now it was obvious she was just terrified.

"We're not..." I mumbled, trying to spare her the embarrassment.

"Ah? I am not sure you really feel that way, deep down," said Elide. *Now* she looked into my eyes, and I could see her pain reflected from deep within. I doubted that she intended for me to see, but it was glaringly obvious. I had felt that pain twice in my life, and I didn't wish it on anyone else, not even an evil faerie. It was the pain I had felt when my dad died in a horrible car crash when I was a child—the pain I'd felt when I found Grandma limp on the floor. The pain you only understood once you'd lost someone forever.

At that moment, I felt what Elide must have felt sometime in her life, and I found myself feeling sorry for her. I didn't envy anyone experiencing that kind of pain. It brought up feelings that I had been trying to suppress. It was painful to keep my distance from Auri; it had been painful to hide my feelings for her for over a year. But now I knew the truth, and it hurt.

I would never get a chance to open up to her and tell her how I really felt about her—just like I had missed the chance to open up to Grandma.

"Never mind that," I said. I didn't want to brush this off, wanted *so badly* to pull Auri aside right there and level with her, or even just kiss her in front of this entire room of people. I didn't care who was watching. But instead I had to keep going, had to find out what Elide was going on about. We could still turn this around. "Just tell the story, please. What happened?"

"Very well," said Elide. "Long, long ago, there was a princess who lived a luxurious life. She had everything she could desire—a loving family, a beautiful castle, dresses in every color and fabric and style, servants to wait on her every need, and the future of being the perfect queen for all of Feylinn." Her voice changed while she told the story, becoming more lilting and melodious, like she was truly taking us on the journey with her. She sure could spin a yarn. "But Princess Azalea was not content. She wanted more out of life than to be the future queen. She wanted freedom. Freedom, however, is one of the things that a future queen cannot have. She must stay reliable, must stay by her people's side. Her sixteenth birthday grew nearer and with it the day of her coronation as queen of Feylinn.

"A very different story was taking place on the other side of Feylinn at this same time," she continued, voice dropping a little. "Fifteen years earlier, a young faerie was learning *her* place in the world. Only hers was not so glamorous as Azalea's. While Azalea lived in her castle of light, bringing happiness and prosperity to all who were around her, this faerie's job was to bring darkness to the world. There can be no good without evil," she said.

Queen Aurelia joined her as she said the last sentence,

lips moving nearly soundlessly. I didn't even think the queen noticed she was doing it.

"The faerie had been taught this from a young age. She knew it was her responsibility to uphold the night so that others could enjoy the day. She was happy to serve her kingdom, happy to uphold the balance in Feylinn, for without a balance of good and evil, the world will crumble."

Exactly like Jack had said.

"She came from the Pryderi bloodline, this young faerie," said Elide, and her voice was full of pride. "She was proud of this, more than anything, and sought to bring her bloodline glory and honor. Now, the bloodlines of the night, or the *evil ones*, I believe you would say…they, too, have traditions. You will be familiar with this, as I know there are many traditions in Terrin as well."

Traditions? I guessed there were some silly ones, like kissing a random person on New Year's Eve, or decorating trees every year on Christmas, or bringing people chocolate on Valentine's Day. I had dreamed of getting flowers for Auri and asking her to be my Valentine. Grandma and I even had traditions of our own, like making a birthday treasure hunt for each other, and always eating dessert first on Saturdays. Who would carry those on now?

"The bloodlines tend to gravitate toward similar curses, you might say," continued Elide. "I hesitate to use the word curse, for it sounds so negative, and it is completely essential to the well-being of Feylinn. However, *curse* it must be. And there are similar curses for different bloodlines. There is one bloodline, for example, that creates curses that are inspired by hair. One, in particular, delights in tempting people into stealing from their garden—the scent of the rapunzel is intoxicating, I am told. Then, they come to collect the newborn child as payment—you are familiar with this one?" she asked, seeing Auri's face light up with recognition.

"They're raised in a tower," I answered. "The Rapunzel story. That's where it came from?"

"Yes, the humans do get some of our stories from time to time," said Elide. "Interesting indeed. That is the curse of the Tressa bloodline. It goes back as far as I can remember."

Auri's eyes widened at the mention of the Tressa bloodline. What did she know about it?

"I met someone from the Tressa bloodline," she said, seeing my confusion. "His name was Basil. He told me a little about it." My stomach filled with jealousy; had she met someone else? She didn't look at me, which made me feel worse. But I knew I was being ridiculous.

"The Pryderi bloodline is one of the most well known," continued Elide, adopting her authoritative storyteller tone again. I vowed not to interrupt this time. "They specialized in fiber curses. Knitting, spinning, weaving, things of that nature." Auri and I exchanged a look. *Crochet.*

"Hundreds and hundreds of years ago," Elide went on, "one particularly intrepid young faerie cast the fabled curse of the spinning wheel. It was an especially creative one. She cursed the spinning wheel so that the Princess Azalea would prick her finger and fall into an enchanted sleep, only to be woken by true love's kiss. And that is what happened. For the Pryderi faerie, Mal, was merciful, and she did not wish to kill Azalea. She merely wanted to maintain the balance. That is all. With a sleep of a hundred years, she punished Azalea without killing her, and Azalea lived a happy life after her extra long beauty sleep. And so it continues to this day. The Pryderi bloodline curses the princesses of Windermere Castle, the Windermere bloodline."

"And this shawl is one of those curses," I confirmed. The shawl really was cursed just like Auri and I had suspected.

"That is correct," she said. "A bit of a twist on the classic curse, I suppose. A little creativity keeps things interesting." She smirked. "It was supposed to lull the person who made it into a trance, except this time, there was a difference."

Dread started forming in my stomach. I thought I knew what the difference might be.

"What was the difference?" Auri asked.

Elide looked right into her eyes this time and said: "The difference is, this curse had no countercurse."

Chapter 39
Auri

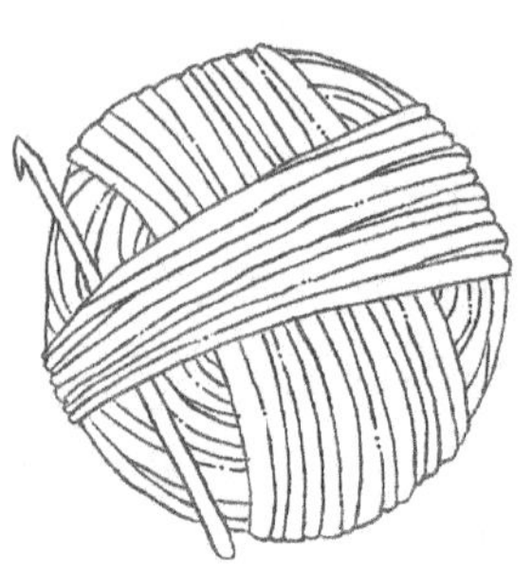

"The most important thing I've learned about magic in all of my research is that it exists everywhere. It doesn't have to be big, flashy, or noticeable magic to be important. The small things are magic. Love is a kind of magic. So, you see, it really is everywhere."

- The Modern Manual of Faeries by Eleanor Bishop

No countercurse. That meant that I was surely going to die from this shawl. The last crochet project I would ever work on.

All this time I had thought for sure that there *had* to be a cure for the Briars and Roses Shawl…that if we just walked long enough, searched the forest, interviewed the Fae, did *something*, then I could have my life back.

But there was no way around it. My life really was over—there was no avoiding the truth.

Cat's jaw had dropped slightly, leaving her agape like a goldfish, as she processed this news. "No," she protested. "That can't be true, there has to be some way…"

"This curse is one of the strongest in the land," said Elide, dropping all storyteller pretenses now and speaking directly to us. "When Azalea escaped, it threw our world into a terrible imbalance. It is *her* fault that our world is dying. Our world is dying, and the only way to save it is to strike the perfect balance again. We need good and evil, and the evil has been lacking ever since Azalea escaped into the human world."

I remembered the dead patches in the forest, marring the verdant beauty of the endless trees. I remembered how much stronger it was near the palace…it must have been because the curse took place here. So the palace was the first thing affected.

"That darkness is spreading. Wherever we do not strike a balance, it grows. When there is no push and pull, it is only emptiness, and it is entirely the fault of the Pryderi."

"You cannot blame them entirely," said Nerissa. "Lady Elide, you know that it is not entirely their fault." Nerissa sticking up for us? A bit late for that, but I welcomed it nonetheless.

"I know it started when the Pryderi faerie failed to uphold her duty," Elide said.

"What do you mean?" Cat asked. "Who failed to uphold her duty?"

"The Pryderi faerie came to Windermere Castle ready to fulfill her duty," Elide explained. "She had the curse prepared. Nerissa, hold it up for us." Nerissa obligingly held up the shawl. "Very good. Mal was ready to present this gift to Princess Azalea on her sixteenth birthday. The kingdom would be plunged into a panic, and the stillness would stop spreading. Good and evil, light and dark, perfectly balanced.

"Only this faerie grew distracted and forgot why she had come. She grew…attached to the princess. She befriended her, grew fond of her, forgot her mission." Elide turned away from us for a minute, and I could see her mood darkening. She clearly did not relish reliving these memories. "She decided the princess was more important than her people. She decided that one life was more important than the lives of all the Fae in the kingdom, than the future of Feylinn. She chose to spare the princess, and in doing so, she condemned the future of everyone."

"She let her go," I whispered.

"She asked a faerie to warn her," said Elide. "The faerie told Azalea that someone was trying to kill her and she needed to flee the palace. She gave her directions to the Well, the one that you came through. Go to Terrin, she told her. You will be safe there. You will have to live your life among the humans, but you will *live*, and if you stay here you will be killed. She justified this to herself, the Pryderi faerie, by saying that she was still cursing Azalea. She was still cursing her; what did it matter if Azalea fled the curse first?"

The faerie by Cat's side stepped forward. "I don't regret what I did."

Cat gasped. "Lilac?"

Lilac said to Cat, "I told you I've never believed in the 'Land of Curses' philosophy. So I was happy to go along with it. I didn't know it would result in the destruction of Feylinn and my imprisonment."

"Mal valued Azalea's life more than anything else. She would do anything to save that one princess." Elide sighed. "This is why emotion has no place in dark magic. How few Fae realize that. Azalea escaped as planned, and with her, the original Briar Rose bloodline, because she had no siblings. Azalea's parents never had any more children. Your beautiful Queen Aurelia here is a distant cousin of yours, Auri."

I nodded in slowly dawning comprehension.

There was no countercurse. There was no cure to the shawl. I was truly cursed and truly screwed. This kept repeating through my head, filling me with dread. I was really truly going to die here. Now. Today.

No way out.

"When the faerie knew what she had done, she was filled with remorse," said Elide. "If this were your typical fairytale, as you call it, she would have made amends right there and then and lived happily ever after. But there were no happily ever afters for this faerie. There was nothing she could do. She could not go after Azalea or she would face splintering the world even more. For when Azalea left, the world started dying—dying for real this time."

Cat was listening just as intently as I was.

"She knew that the only way to break the cycle was to retrieve Azalea and finish the curse for real. However, I am sure you have noticed, you are not Azalea. You are her great granddaughter."

"If you were there from the very start…" I stared at her. "You must be ancient." She didn't look a day over twenty-one.

"I am immortal," she said. "Cursed myself, you see. There is an interesting thing about the Land of Curses. Once a curse is made, the faerie cannot die until the curse is fulfilled. By failing my curse, I doomed myself to immortality." She gestured to herself, resignation in her face.

"You!" gasped Cat. "Of course. You're the Pryderi faerie!"

Elide regarded her with a mildly pleased expression. "Yes. You figured it out. It was me. I am paying for my mistakes. If I had cursed her properly, I would not still be alive now. I am cursed with immortality until I see this curse through to the end. And Auri is the next best thing to Azalea. She is the perfect living descendant."

What if she had picked Aidyn instead? I shivered at the thought. I couldn't bear the thought of Aidyn going through this; I would much rather it be me. Of course, Aidyn couldn't crochet, either, so maybe that had something to do with it… plus, I was a girl and I was the exact age of Azalea in the original legend. "You're going to kill me," I said, and I felt the weight of the words.

"No," said Cat.

"Yes," said Elide.

I had known it was coming, but I still felt sick to my stomach.

"Well, technically, *I* am not going to kill you," said Elide. "You are going to continue crocheting the shawl. I have no idea why you were able to get so far on it; you are obviously stronger than I anticipated. I will admit that. However, I can see you weakening, and Nerissa has told me as much."

Nerissa stepped forward holding the bag that contained the shawl. I took it with trembling fingers. Opening it up, I looked inside with my breath held, and then I gasped: the shawl was still in one piece. Not a single stitch had been unraveled.

I looked up at Nerissa sharply. "Why…"

It must have been Elide's orders. In that case, something far worse was probably about to happen to me now when I started crocheting it. I was going to die, and it would be a stupid crochet shawl that killed me. If only Genevieve could hear about it. This would have gotten Yarn Emporium so much publicity.

"Wait!" gasped Cat. "Queen Aurelia, are you going to stand by and let this happen?"

The queen was sitting in the throne with her head bowed, hands clasped in front of her as if in prayer.

She looked up at Cat's proclamation. "I am so sorry," she said, "but there is no other way to save my kingdom." She looked at me with sympathy and guilt in her eyes. "I truly did not want to do this, Auri, my dear, but I have to do what is right for all of Feylinn."

"But this isn't right!" exclaimed Cat. A guard came to restrain her as she grew more upset. "You can't honestly believe that killing Auri is the right thing to do!" She was starting to cry. "Do you really have to do this?"

"The curse should have happened a hundred years ago," said Queen Aurelia, her voice quiet and resigned. "The only way to save the world is to finish what we started all that time ago."

"That's why she's in your castle," said Cat. "That's why Elide is here. Nerissa said she was here on a matter of royal business…" She reeled back. "Royal business is arranging the murder of an innocent girl!" She looked at me, panic all over her face, and tears streaming down her cheeks.

I knew all of her protesting wouldn't make any difference, although I did appreciate her trying. Maybe it would be okay, even if I wasn't around to see it. Maybe my death would balance out the Fae world. Maybe something good would come of this. Maybe I *had* known from the very start that I would never make it out of Feylinn alive. Falling down that Well really *had* killed me, it had just taken a little bit of time to catch up with me.

I was going to die here today. Really and truly. Although I didn't expect to live to a hundred, I always figured, perhaps naïvely, that I would make it past the age of eighteen. There was so much I would never get to do. I would never get married, never see Yarn Emporium become the most successful yarn store in the state, never watch Aidyn graduate from high school, never get to know Cat better and maybe even be her girlfriend. This was really it. This was the end.

Chapter 40
Cat

"Have you ever wondered where the last plastic lid went, or where your sock disappeared? This happens when you displease the Fae that live in your house. By leaving offerings to them and treating them with the same respect you show your human neighbors, they will begin to leave you alone. Sometimes the Fae simply want to be noticed."

- The Modern Manual of Faeries by Eleanor Bishop

No. This couldn't be happening again. I could not lose someone else I loved. Hadn't the universe taken enough from me lately?

"Cat," Auri said, and something in her voice made me stop. There were tears in her eyes and anguish was written all over her body. "It's going to be okay."

"No," I said. "No, this is not going to happen."

"It's the only way," she said.

"No!" I exclaimed. "I'm not going to stand by and let you be killed by this stupid curse!" I turned to Elide. "If you just need to kill someone, take me instead. But let Auri live."

Auri was gripping my hand so tightly, I could hardly feel my fingers. "Don't you dare."

"Even if I wanted to, I couldn't," said Elide, watching us with detached interest. "She does not bear the curse."

"Just give me a minute," Auri said. "Please. I want to say goodbye."

Something changed in Elide's expression, almost like she felt the tiniest bit of sympathy. Not guilt, but like she understood, like this was awakening long-dormant feelings in her too. Despite everything, she, too, had been in love once.

"Very well," she said, turning aside. Auri ran to me and I pulled her into my arms. The floodgates opened and I couldn't hold back my tears. It should've been Auri who was crying, facing her death, but instead it was me. Selfishly, I couldn't bear the thought of losing her. Not someone else. I would rather have died a hundred times over than experience this.

Auri held me while I sobbed. She smoothed down my hair. "Shh," she said, trying to soothe me. She stroked my shoulder gently with her hand. "I'm so sorry, Cat," she whispered, her breath tickling my ear. "I don't want to leave you."

There were so many things unsaid between us. I hiccuped, trying to get myself under control. "You're not going to die here today," I told her.

"I am," she said, "and I need to tell you something. I need you to listen to me." Her voice was determined, and she pushed me back so she could look me in the eyes. "I am so sorry, Cat. There's something I've been needing to tell you." She slowly reached into her pocket and pulled out a sheet of paper. She pressed it into my hand. "Please don't hate me for keeping this from you. I couldn't bear to cause you more pain. But you deserve to know."

I opened the paper. It was crinkled from being submerged in the Aethelney, but the words were still legible although blurred. As I caught a glimpse of the handwriting, the world changed into slow motion. I would recognize the loops of that cursive handwriting anywhere. It was a letter from Grandma…to me.

It was a suicide note.

I made a sound of disbelief.

"I'm so sorry," whispered Auri.

I felt a pang of anger at her for keeping the note from me. But at the same time, I knew my anger wasn't really directed at her. I was angry at *Grandma*. Angry at her for leaving me. Didn't I deserve *someone* who stuck around? Was I really that horrible of a person? And at the same time, what kind of granddaughter was I for not noticing how miserable she was?

Tears were running down my cheeks again. Perhaps they had never really stopped.

"She loved you, Cat," whispered Auri. "It was depression. Not her."

Deep down I knew that, but it didn't stop the pain. It felt like it would never go away.

"I thought it was the curse," I choked out. "I thought it made her…"

"Maybe it pushed her over the edge," said Auri. "You can't really know. But you do know that she loved you."

Regret burned inside me, regret that I had never opened up to her. This was my last chance to avoid repeating the same mistake. "Auri," I said, "if you're going to die today, you need to know something." *Deep breath. Just say it.* "I think I'm in love with you. I've been falling in love with you for a long time now."

Her eyes widened. She looked speechless.

"You don't have to say anything," I said, "but I just wanted to tell you. That's all."

Her eyes were filling with tears. She rose on her tiptoes to kiss me. When she pulled back, she whispered, "I think I'm falling in love with you, too."

I had imagined her saying those words so many times under radically different circumstances. Wasn't fate cunning that I would hear it right before she died?

I heard the footsteps of a guard starting toward us, no doubt to pull us apart. My tears wouldn't let up. Auri's own chin was starting to tremble.

"Promise me something," she said, and I nodded frantically. "When I die, I want you to help the people here. The Fae. Promise me you'll watch over them. Free Basil."

"I promise," I said, anything to make her feel better, still trying to think of a way out.

Then a guard was ripping her away from me, and her warmth was gone, and they had to forcibly restrain me. "Please," she said, and I didn't know who she was talking to.

Auri pulled the shawl out of the bag. The ethereal pink thread seemed to mock us. How could something so exquisite be so lethal? It was hard to believe that her fate—our fate—was contained in this tiny steel crochet hook and hank of thread.

"Elide," Auri said, "if I do this, you must *promise me* that Cat lives." Auri looked her right in the eyes, and that flicker of pain passed through them again. It suddenly hit me. That was the same pain had I felt in my own eyes when I had thought Auri would never love me back. Elide had been in love once, too…and Auri looked just like Azalea. Elide had spared Azalea's life because she was in love with her!

"The human girl? Why should I listen to you?"

"Because," Auri said, "You cannot *make me crochet.*"

Auri stared her down. She knew it was true. And there was the flaw in the curse: you could drag someone's finger to a spindle and prick it, you could lock someone in a tower against their will, but when it came down to it, you really could not force someone to crochet.

"You must promise me that Cat will be returned to Terrin alive and well," she said, with more authority in her voice than it had ever carried before. She looked regal, princess-like, just like her ancestor Princess Azalea. "I want you to swear to it in front of all these Fae, and I want Queen Aurelia's word as well. I need to know that Cat will be safe."

Elide looked at me. I glared right back. If Auri could be brave, so could I.

Auri and Elide stared at each other for what felt like an eternity. Then Elide said, "I will make a binding oath with you. The human girl means nothing to me. Not if we can restore balance to Feylinn."

Auri exhaled a breath of relief, trying not to show the extent of how afraid she had been. "Make the oath, then. I want everyone here to be a witness."

I wiped my cheeks, watching her. I started to make my way to the side of the room, trying to look like I was breaking down and just needed somewhere to lean against.

Elide crossed the dais and descended the steps along with Queen Aurelia. "Here is how a magical oath works, Auri," said Queen Aurelia. "Tell Elide exactly what you want her to agree to, and she will repeat the words. You are familiar with marriage vows?" Auri nodded. "This is similar."

I sidled up next to a guard.

Elide placed one hand on her scepter and held the other one out to Auri. Auri took her hand, recoiling a little at her icy fingers, probably the same temperature as her heart. "Um," she said, likely trying to think of the right words. If I knew anything about magic, it was that there could be no loopholes. Everything had to be perfectly closed up, leaving no room for interpretation. Grandma said it was like a legal contract.

"Do you swear," she said, "to provide Cat with an escort to safely travel through Feylinn to the Well?"

"I swear it," Elide said calmly. A little vine curled around her hand where Auri was holding it, and warmth flooded through me at the sight of her magic, comforting despite everything.

"Do you swear to safely provide her with transport through the Well to Terrin?"

"I swear it."

The leaf continued its journey along her hand, twining their hands together, weaving them and binding them to each other.

"And do you swear that no harm will befall anyone in her family or my family?"

"I swear it."

The vine lit up where their hands were tied together, and Auri jerked her hand away as if she'd been burned. Elide met her eyes, unyielding. "I swear all of this, Auri. You have my word. You have the witnesses of all the Fae in the Royal Court of Windermere."

She let the vine release and Auri pulled her hand away from Elide's. The light in the room flickered back on, all the candles in the chandelier overhead swaying back and forth.

"Now it is time to uphold your end of the bargain," Elide said firmly. "Have a seat, Auri. Right now you are the queen."

I looked in horror to see that Queen Aurelia had descended from her throne and was gesturing for Auri to walk up there. Auri opened her mouth to protest, but Elide said: "Princess Azalea was going to die on the day of her coronation. It is only fitting that you meet your fate while seated where she would have been."

Ceremony. Of course.

Auri nodded obligingly. She ascended the steps, sandals and jean shorts looking completely out of place amidst all the splendor of the throne room. Yet despite the filthy clothes, she still looked beautiful. Regal, even. There were five steps up to the platform that held the throne, and there was another large throne to the side, presumably for the king. The queen's, however, was the bigger and more intricate one, with a plush pink cushion and gilded sides. She turned and sat down, the throne room sprawled out in front of her, Fae watching her intently, but her gaze narrowed in on me.

And she saw what I was planning to do.

Her mouth opened in surprise.

I yanked the sword from the guard's sheath next to me and sprinted for Elide. I never thought I would be in the position to kill anyone, but if this was what it took to save Auri, there was no choice at all. I would deal with the aftermath later. The sword was on its way down when it froze in the air.

I struggled, but I couldn't break free. My arms felt like they were paralyzed.

Elide plucked the sword from my hand like it weighed nothing. Then she waved her hand and sent me crashing to the floor. Before I could figure out how to move again, two guards came rushing over to tie me up.

"Turn her to face the thrones," instructed Elide, and I was yanked around to face them.

I had a front-row seat for Auri's execution.

No matter how much I kicked and thrashed, the guards

were stronger. I knew there was no hope of getting free, but I didn't stop struggling as I watched.

Auri put her hook into the loop where she had left off the shawl. It was so small, only a few rows completed, but I could see the beautiful flowers and petals and loops looking exquisite in the pink lace. Maybe they would bury it with her. I knew, just knew, that when she started crocheting, it would take effect quickly. She had gotten this far on the shawl, but Elide couldn't be wrong—something about Feylinn was having an effect on her.

This was the moment.

She looked at Elide, who was watching her with bated breath, and to Queen Aurelia, who looked like she was near tears. She met my eyes again.

I'm sorry, I mouthed.

Me too, she replied.

Then she stuck the hook into the shawl and made the next stitch.

Chapter 41
Auri

"Faeries have a longer life span than humans; they can regularly live to 150 years old and sometimes as long as 200. But they are not immortal; not unless they are caught in a curse themselves."

- *The Modern Manual of Faeries by Eleanor Bishop*

THE HOOK IMMEDIATELY CAUGHT THE TIP OF MY LEFT pointer finger, and it plunged into the skin. I gasped, watching it sink into the flesh and a drop of blood come to the surface. My finger had been extremely sore and sensitive after so much crocheting, and it took almost no effort for the hook to pierce the skin. A single moment of pain raced up my finger, and then I was left watching the blood well up. I held out my finger so Elide could see what was happening.

I waited for death to come and carry me away. I realized I had no idea what came next—would the Grim Reaper come and invite me along? Would I black out and wake up in the afterlife? Would everything turn to oblivion? And how soon was it going to happen? It was scarier waiting for it to happen than having it actually happen, like waiting for a vaccine at the doctor. *Just take me already.*

Nothing was happening.

With this much drama surrounding a crochet stitch, I really should have died by now.

I pricked my finger with the crochet hook again, wincing again at the pain. The blood increased. It dripped down my finger in a river of red, and I wiped it on my shirt, staining the fabric. Just add it to all the other grass and mud stains I had acquired. A little blood made me look badass. "I swear, I don't know what's happening," I said. What if she thought I was using my magic or something? "Elide, why am I not dead?"

She looked absolutely dumbfounded.

"You should be dead," she hissed. "That curse…it is foolproof! All this ceremony, all this preparation, all for nothing…" She turned to Nerissa. "How? How is this happening? Did you bring me the wrong—"

"I brought you the right girl!" exclaimed Nerissa. "She is Azalea's descendant, she is Aurora Davis, I have done everything right, my lady!"

"Then why is this not working?" roared Elide. Half the candles in the chandelier flickered off. The room was plunged into a state of partial darkness, providing truly dramatic mood lighting. I sat there, unsure of how to proceed. I was prepared to die; I had even welcomed it, now that I knew my death would save Cat. What was I supposed to do now that I *wasn't* dead? Somehow I had lived; I had defied the odds. But what was I supposed to do now?

I rose from the throne, feeling very unsure of myself. "I don't..." I said.

Elide turned to me, eyes filled with anger and something I couldn't quite place. "How could you," she said. "This was my plan...I was going to make things right."

"I haven't done anything!" I said. "I did what you asked, I kept crocheting the shawl, I..."

Elide flung out her hand and a wave of dark magic swept out, a tide of what looked like black dust. It charged directly toward Cat and struck her in the chest, flinging her to the ground.

"No!" I screamed, running down the steps to her side, but Elide stopped me with another wave of magic. Instinctively I threw up my hand to protect myself, and a wall of vines erupted in front of me, stopping the dust before it could reach me. They wilted almost instantly when the dust hit it.

"*You promised!*" I hollered, screaming so loud the words tore at my throat. "*You swore you wouldn't hurt her!*"

"*And you promised you would die!*"

I was crying, tears streaming down my face, half of rage and half of anguish about Cat. I flung out a vine at Elide, and she countered it with a wall of black flame. It burned up my poor little plant before it could reach her at all. I couldn't defeat her, and she couldn't kill me, and Cat was probably dying as we spoke. I couldn't lose her. I couldn't go on without her, not when all this was my fault, not when *I* was the one who should have died.

Not her. Me.

"You're horrible," I said. "I just wanted to save Cat. That's all I wanted. I would have done *anything*."

"Except die yourself," spat Elide. "What good are you?"

"I tried!" I wailed. "I was willing to give up my life for her! I made you swear, I made all of you watch…I would have died to save her."

Elide and I circled each other. If this was going to be a fight, it was going to be one hell of a fight, and I sure wasn't going to be the one who came out the winner.

"I made the same mistake," she said. A cloud of dust rose up around us and gathered us together, shielding us from the rest of the room. It was just me and Elide now. "I chose her over everything. I chose Azalea."

The pain in her eyes was so clear. When she looked at me, she was filled with regret, filled with memories from all those years ago. She had lived with that pain ever since. "You loved her," I breathed.

"But she never loved me," said Elide. "I would have given up everything for her. *Everything*. Just like you and Cat. I see how you look at each other. I know how that feels. But you are just like me, Auri. You chose her over everything else; you chose her over Feylinn."

I was standing on a mossy patch of grass now; it had sprung out from beneath my feet and was spreading out to the edge of the dust, light and dark, good and evil warring with each other.

"I did choose her," I said. "Because I care about her. Can't you understand that?"

My finger was throbbing, pain traveling up my entire arm. It hurt more than a simple finger prick should have hurt. And suddenly it struck me. Everything suddenly became clear, the biggest light-bulb moment I had ever had hitting me like a cannonball in a still pool of water. I knew what I had to do.

First, that I *was* dying as we spoke.

Second, that it was taking longer than Elide had anticipated because she had grossly underestimated me… and my magic. There was even more life within me; my blood was teeming with the ability to make plants grow, to call flowers into being. That very magic was sustaining me. It was helping me keep going long past what I should have been able to do.

Third, that Feylinn had started dying about a hundred years ago…when Azalea had escaped into the human world. The world wasn't dying because of a lack of curses; it was dying because Azalea wasn't there. The world was dying because her descendants had grown up in Terrin instead of here. Azalea's descendants helped keep Feylinn thriving due to their ability to control the plants, their ability to make the forest flourish.

I could turn all this around. All I had to do was survive the day…which meant that I had to break the curse.

So I looked Elide in the eye and said, "You're right. I know what I have to do, I just…don't want to die." It was true, even if not in the way she had expected. By my feet, a single rose bloomed, springing into existence at a single flick of my fingers. Nobody deserved to have this much power. I *had* to put it to good use; I had a responsibility to Feylinn to help this beautiful land thrive again. And to do that, I had to finish crocheting the shawl.

The shawl that had haunted me for weeks. The shawl that made my fingers bleed. The shawl that consumed my being, that followed me into my dreams, that had caused Eleanor's death and now Cat's. *Don't think that, Cat's not going to die, she's not.* It couldn't be too late.

"You must do it," hissed Elide. "You must do it for the good of Feylinn."

I held back tears, feeling the gravity of the moment. "You cannot interrupt me while I do it," I said. "This is going to be the last thing I do…I don't know, I…"

She looked at me, and then a path cleared through the fog and dust, leading to the throne. I ascended the stairs slowly and picked up the shawl. My finger throbbed, and the blood wouldn't stop flowing from my fingertip. I knew for certain that I would not be able to finish crocheting the shawl; my time was running out. Even now, I could see the world getting blurry around the edges, like Elide's magic was crowding in from every corner, filling my vision with dust.

I couldn't crochet it.

But there was something that could.

I gently twirled the fingers of my right hand, coaxing a vine to start blooming. It spiraled up from my palm shyly and accepted the crochet hook I pressed into it. I urged another vine to come up from the ground and gently gave it the shawl. Then I showed them how to make the stitches, letting the hook go in and out of the shawl gracefully, beautifully, magically.

Rose petals bloomed along the vine and wove themselves into the shawl as the vines worked. More of them joined, working rows and rows of stitches faster than I could see, building tall trellises of stitches and creating lacy fabric quickly and expertly. I breathed shallowly, knowing my time was running out. The thread spiraled out from the hank inch by inch. My vision was beginning to close in on itself. *Please,* I silently begged my magic. *Please help me.*

And then the final thread was pulled through and my hands were falling to my sides and the vines were draping the shawl around my shoulders. It was light and impossibly silky and cradled my shoulders like it had been designed just for me. The vines stuck the crochet hook behind my pointed ear as a finishing touch.

I felt a rush of cold run through my body, and my vision cleared. Finally, *finally,* the shawl vanished from my subconscious, like a bad dream that disappears upon waking. The cloud of dust fell to the ground, and moss grew over it instead, filling the entire throne room with green.

Elide stood there looking incredulous, like she couldn't believe what she was seeing. Neither could I. "The curse is broken," I said, my voice ringing through the room. "I'm free. You are all free. There is no need for curses; all you need is the Briar Rose bloodline here in Feylinn."

"Healed," said Elide, her voice no more than a whisper

on the wind. Then she wasn't there at all, she was dissolving like ash in the wind, like the hundred-year-old faerie she was, and the vines had enveloped her.

———————

I ran to Cat, skidding to a stop by her side. She was breathing shallowly, lying flat on her face where Elide's spell had knocked her. I rolled her over onto her back and pulled her head onto my knees. "No, no," I said, "you're going to be okay, Cat, you're going to be fine."

"Auri," she said, gazing up at me, lips slightly parted. "You did amazing."

"You're going to be fine," I exclaimed. I couldn't even tell exactly what was wrong, only that Elide's magic had done terrible damage deep with Cat, and it hadn't faded when she did. "Please. Please do something!" I begged anyone who was listening.

"You were so ready to die a minute ago," she breathed. "Now it's my turn."

"No!" This couldn't be happening. This was supposed to be a happy ending. I couldn't lose her. Not after all this.

"You're so beautiful," she said, "you're a real queen." Her eyes fluttered closed, long lashes settling like a butterfly on her perfect freckled cheeks. She sighed out a long breath, chest shuddering. Her skin was starting to look like dust had settled on it, like Elide's magic was covering her.

My chest hitched. *Please! This can't be happening!*

Then instinctively I whipped the shawl off my shoulders and wrapped it around Cat instead of me. I tucked the shawl ends into each other and pulled her into my arms, praying that something would happen, that the magic would do the trick. Because this shawl was full of life itself. It had been woven from enchanted yarn by magical vines, imbued with the power of Feylinn, and I had defeated all the odds to finish it. I focused all my energy on the shawl, filling it with good vibes and prayers and every ounce of hope that I possessed, forcing it to realize that Cat was meant to live.

She was meant to live.

Damn it all, Cat was *going to live*!

Chapter 42
Cat

Even the Fae don't know what happens after death. It is a mystery to them just as it is to us. And when they die, nobody knows where they go, either. It's perhaps the biggest thing that humans and faeries have in common: they don't know where they go after this realm.

- The Modern Manual of Faeries by Eleanor Bishop

DARKNESS. AURI'S FACE FADED INTO THE FOG THAT WAS closing in around me. It was like dusk approaching and with it, the uneasy feeling of descending into the dark.

I couldn't feel anything, which was good because the last thing I remembered feeling was pain. But now all I felt was numb. Then came a spark of light, like a match striking in the dark. I turned toward it, because when there's dark that's what you do—turn to the light.

It felt like I walked for seconds and hours at the same time, but when I got to the light, I squinted in disbelief. Everything was dark except for a small glass table with a candle atop it. And sitting by the candle, the only thing visible in the flickering light, was Grandma. She looked just like she had the last time I saw her alive: white-and-red hair puffed around her head, big round glasses, smile lines etched upon her oval face. "Grandma." It came out half sob.

"Cat," she said warmly, rising from her seat. "I've missed you."

What was happening? Was I dead? I didn't even care, because Grandma was there and I wasn't going to lose this moment with her. I hurled myself into her arms, and for a moment there was complete bliss.

"Am I dead?" I asked finally, my voice muffled by her shoulder.

"What do you think?" asked Grandma.

"I have to be, if I'm seeing you." Right? She tried to let go of me, but I clung more desperately to her, unwilling to let the hug be over.

"That's one way of looking at it." She never did give me a straight answer even when she was alive.

"I missed you so much," I said, and then the events of the past week crashed down on me and I started to cry. I'd been holding it together these past few days, trying to be strong for Auri, but I couldn't do it anymore. Now Grandma would see how broken I truly was inside. I cried so hard I could barely breathe, and she just hugged me through it. "I'm never going to let you go again."

"But then how will you get back to Auri?" she asked gently.

I stiffened. She knew about Auri? If she could see Auri, did that mean she knew I was gay? And here she was, hugging me anyway? Even if she already knew, I wanted to tell her myself because I owed her that much. "Grandma," I started, but she cut me off.

"I know you, Cat."

"Are you reading my mind?"

"You think I can do that?" She stroked my hair gently. "I saw what happened just before you entered this place. And I know she's there now, panicking, trying to bring you back to life. Would you leave her there like that?"

"You left me like that," I whispered, my lip trembling. "I tried so hard to save you."

"Sometimes you can't save a person. And that's not your fault."

"But I should've seen that you were depressed. I should have *known*."

"Cat, sweetheart. You of all people should understand this. You can't know what's going on inside somebody else's mind."

Of course I knew. "But I should've seen that you were in pain. I wanted to be there for you like you were there for me."

"You have *always* been there for me."

Being in her arms was like being home. How could I leave this? How had I lived without it? It hurt to be here with her when I wasn't sure I could stay. I *knew* she was dead, but here she was, in my arms. Just being here hurt so much because I knew it would hurt all the more when it came time to let her go.

"Do you love her?" asked Grandma softly.

I stepped back so I could look her in the eyes. "Yeah. I do." I paused. "I wanted to tell you, Grandma. I was just scared."

"You thought I would stop loving you because you're gay? You think there's anything you could tell me that would make me stop loving you?"

Of course I had known that. But my brain just made it hard to believe. "It just felt so scary…I couldn't do it."

"You're perfect just the way you are. If you find somebody who treats you like a princess, then I'm happy."

I sniffled, then giggled. "But Auri actually is a princess, Grandma."

"Well, she'd better treat you like a princess, too. Nobody is good enough for my granddaughter." The corners of her mouth lifted in a smile. "She's a good crocheter. Ask her to make you a blanket, keep you warm."

"I'm glad you got to meet her." Me, Grandma, and Auri had spent hours together already, crocheting at Yarn Emporium.

"You think I didn't see you blushing when she was around?" This, of course, made me blush. "I know you, Cat. I know you aren't interested enough in crochet to sacrifice an hour every Saturday night unless you had an ulterior motive."

She had known all along. Or if she hadn't known, then she had suspected. "Why didn't you say anything?"

"I knew you would tell me when you were ready."

But I had never been ready. "What if this is all in my head, and I never got the chance to tell you in real life?"

"Maybe that's true," she said with a shrug. "But maybe it's not. Can you live with not knowing?"

It always came back to that. Could I live with the uncertainty? "There's so many things I wish I had told you."

"That's life, Cat. You just have to learn to live with those regrets and do better the next time."

What did I regret? So many things. But it warmed my soul to know that Grandma approved of my girlfriend. Could I call her that? All those years of longing for someone, and now I had Auri in my life—a girl who was the human equivalent of sunshine and flowers. Auri, who was left alone in an unfamiliar land, burdened with the weight of her new responsibilities as princess. Auri, who would be left to cope with my death and the guilt that accompanied it. I knew what it felt like to not be able to save someone. How could I do that to her?

"You really love her," said Grandma.

I nodded.

"Then go back to her."

"But I love *you*."

"I know you do. So show me that you love me by living your own life."

"I want *you* back. Please. It hurts all the time, Grandma. I think of you every day, and it hurts so much."

She didn't say anything, just let me cry it out.

"I feel so empty without you, and now that you're gone, it feels like there's this cavern inside me. Like I'm hollow, and everybody sees a whole person, but they don't know I'm actually broken inside. And it physically hurts. Because I know I can't reach you." I gulped down a breath of air. "I don't want to say goodbye. I don't know how." She stroked my hair, and I closed my eyes at the touch of her slender fingers. "You don't have to know how. You just have to do it anyway."

"I don't want to."

"Everything has to end someday, Cat. The important thing is that it happened at all. The fact that I'm leaving you now doesn't discount the time we spent together."

The tears spilled out of my eyes even though they were squeezed shut. "I want more time with you."

"That's how you know the time we had together was meaningful."

"It's not fair."

"Cat, you know better than anybody that life isn't fair." She pushed me back from her so she could look into my eyes. "You just do your best with the shitty hand of cards you're dealt. And it looks to me like you're doing a pretty damn good job."

"I'm doing a horrible job," I sobbed.

"I don't think so. And neither does Auri."

"I'm not good like you. Not deep down, not really."

"Do you really think that, sweetie?"

"You're the one who made me a better person. You changed my life. You changed *me*, made me who I am, made me a kinder and more compassionate person. And I can never repay you for that."

"I just helped you become the person you were meant to be all along. You always had that good heart inside you. Always."

"I want you back," I whispered.

"You want me. But you don't need me."

I held onto her for what felt like forever as the words sank in. There were so many things I wanted to say to her, so many things we had never gotten to experience together. But I'd already had such a good life with her. She had plucked me out of my home when things got so bad and raised me with all her love. And now, maybe she was right. Maybe I could keep going.

I didn't want to. But I could do it anyway.

Slowly, I pulled away from her. The moment when I let go of her hand was the hardest of my life because I knew it was the last time we would ever touch. "You think I can do this?" I asked.

"It doesn't matter what I think," she said gently. "Do *you* think you can?"

I nodded. "I can do it."

I knew that Grandma wouldn't be the one to step away. I had to make that choice myself. Stay here, with her? Or go back to the world of the living and make the most of my life?

I didn't even know if this was real or made-up. But I could choose to believe it was real, and that was good enough for me. You never knew for sure in this world, but love was real. And maybe that could be good enough.

So I took a deep breath and tried to imprint this image of Grandma into my mind forever. "I love you," I said, because those were the words I wanted to leave her with. And then I turned around and walked away.

The first few steps were so difficult that I didn't think I could keep going; the ache of leaving Grandma was so strong that I could barely keep putting one foot in front of the other. But you don't have to feel like you can do it. You just have to do it anyway. I forced myself to keep going, and then the next step didn't hurt as much. It still ached like someone had thrust a dagger into my heart, but I put one foot in front of the other and in a few more minutes the darkness around me had begun to lighten.

Grandma had been right, as usual: the dusk will always brighten to dawn if you hold on long enough.

I squinted into the brightening fog, and then my heart skipped a beat. I could just barely discern the silhouette of a person. An enemy? No, it was Auri, and when I saw what she was doing I couldn't breathe. She was rocking my limp body back and forth, crying into my shoulder. The Briars and Roses shawl was completely finished and wrapped around my body, and she was whispering pleas into it, begging for me to come back to life.

And I knew I had made the right decision, coming back.

I slid back into my body and felt all of the pain from my injuries crash back into me. For a minute, I didn't remember how to breathe, and I panicked, but then my chest rose and fell on its own and I opened my eyes.

Auri stared down at me in disbelief, her own eyes red from crying and fluid running from her nose.

"Auri," I croaked.

"You're alive," she said in disbelief.

"So are you." I blinked the last wisp of fog from my eyes and sat up, the shawl falling off my left shoulder.

She sniffled, wiping her nose unceremoniously on the Briars and Roses Shawl. "I was so scared. I thought…"

"I know." I wiped a tear from her cheek. "I'm here. I'm okay."

"You're okay," she breathed. Then she pulled me into a hug, burying her face in my shoulder the same way I had clung to Grandma earlier, like she couldn't believe her eyes but maybe she could believe her other senses. She held me like she was drowning and I had saved her. I pulled back, tucked a strand of hair behind her perfectly pointed ear, and gently kissed her.

Because now we had all the time in the world.

Epilogue
Cat

Three Months Later

I FINISH PACKING THE BOX OF CHINA AND TAPE IT CLOSED. Auri picks it up to carry it to the car. "Is that the last of it?" she asks me.

"That's it," I say. It's taken the better part of a week to get all of Grandma's possessions properly packed away, but with Auri's help, we finally finished. "Just bring it on out to the car, will you?"

I get to my feet, stiff from sitting on the floor for so long, and survey the house one last time. There are so many memories here. The chip on the kitchen counter where we dropped a full pan of cookies; the corner where we managed to wedge a pine tree for Winter Solstice every year; the armchair where Grandma crocheted every night. I feel a pang in my chest at the thought of leaving.

But, I remind myself, this is only a place. The memories will always be with me.

I blow my nose and head to the car, picking up Simon the sloth on the way. I give the door one last pat goodbye.

Auri has managed to cram the box in the back of the car, but it's a tight fit. She gives me a wide smile as I exit the front door. "Ready to go?" she asks.

"More than ready," I say, checking one last time that the door is locked behind me.

I drive. She navigates. My anxiety isn't so bad when she's patiently giving me directions, being quiet when I'm concentrating, and never judging me when I need to pull into a parking lot (or even the side of the highway) and take a few deep breaths. I think back to when I thought she would leave me if she found out about my mental illness. That couldn't have been further from the truth. Love will never cure OCD, but having someone by your side is invaluable.

I finally pull into Auri's driveway. She was so happy to be able to provide her family with money simply by using her portion of the royal treasury. Her new house is small but charming, with a Volkswagen beetle in the driveway and her younger brother waiting on the porch. "Auri!" he cries when he spots us, leaping up from his perch to run to the car. I park and get out. Auri is hugging Aidyn.

"Say hi to Cat!" she says.

"Hi, Cat," says Aidyn. He gives Auri a knowing smirk.

Auri shoves him playfully. "Go get your suitcase," she says. To me: "He's been teasing me mercilessly ever since we started dating. Says it's about time I found somebody." She rolls her eyes.

My smile threatens to split my face in two. "I agree," I say, sliding my hand into hers. "It's about time."

Aidyn emerges carrying a suitcase that's almost as big as him. Auri shakes her head at the sight. "What are you *bringing*?" she asks.

"Books." He gives me a fist-bump as he walks past. "Can I put this in the backseat, Cat?"

I help him wedge the suitcase in with mine and Auri's.

Ms. Davis joins us by the car. "It's always lovely to see you, Cat," she says, and gives me a hug. I return it, feeling more welcome than ever before. "Thank you for taking Aidyn along with you. He's been looking forward to this for weeks."

"I'm going to visit Fairyland," he crows.

"Just mind your manners," implores Ms. Davis.

"He'll be fine," Auri says, and ruffles his hair. "Worst thing that happens, he gets turned into a tree."

"Auri!" exclaims Ms. Davis, just as Aidyn says, "Cool!"

We get into the car, and Auri gears up the GPS for our drive to Mount Rainier. I'm still getting used to the changing altitude and my ears pop every couple miles, but other than the painful pressure from time to time, the drive to Feylinn is incredibly beautiful. "We'll see you in a week," Auri says to her mom.

"Drive safely," Ms. Davis says to us. She winks at me.

I smile back.

I tap the wheel three times with my right hand before we set off. Auri reads the directions to me, Aidyn passes me snacks from the backseat, and the two of them fight over the aux cord. One of Grandma's blankets is folded in the backseat, destined for my room in the palace and for cuddling with Auri, which is my new favorite hobby.

Aidyn reads aloud to us from Grandma's recently published book, which her publisher and I worked on together after her death. It's the modern manual of faeries based on her blog. After all the years she spent working so diligently on it, I knew it had to see the light of day. "Did you know that pigeons are actually faeries?"

"No shit," exclaims Auri. "You're making that up."

"I am not!" He passes the book to her in indignation. And I melt a little when I see them interacting with Grandma's words. How she would have loved to see this.

It feels like I have two homes now. One is in Feylinn, where Auri and I are familiarizing ourselves with Fae culture. She's required to spend most of her time there to keep the world thriving, and I'm not complaining about staying there. I never thought I'd be dating a princess. We're changing the world together: now that Feylinn is the Land of Spells rather than the Land of Curses, we can finally help people like Jack and Basil. Nobody has to be the victim of a curse anymore.

My other home is with Auri. I never dreamed of being welcomed in by her family, but Ms. Davis has taken me under her wing.

I only wish Grandma were here to see Feylinn.

A truck honking startles me out of my daze. Even magical faerie princesses and their girlfriends are, unfortunately, not immune to traffic jams.

Author's Note

Although this book is fiction, some parts of it are all too real. Cat's OCD is based on my own experience with the disorder. OCD stands for Obsessive-Compulsive Disorder and is an anxiety disorder that often coexists with other mental illnesses like Generalized Anxiety Disorder (GAD) and Panic Disorder. If you're suffering from OCD, know that there are resources out there to help (see the end of this note).

I was diagnosed with GAD when I was 6, but I was 19 before I got the OCD diagnosis–13 years after my symptoms started. This is, unfortunately, super common for people with OCD. The average length of time between onset of symptoms and diagnosis is 11-14 years. The main reason for this is that people don't understand what OCD actually is—they only know what they've seen in media, which are usually just stereotypes. That's not to say that stereotypes aren't true sometimes. But they weren't true for me, and I suffered from lack of diagnosis, as do many other people.   So it's not only hurtful but dangerous to see it used flippantly: people describing themselves as "so OCD" because they like sorting their pencils by color, or sweaters that say "Obsessive Christmas Disorder" on them. This would never be done with a physical disease like cancer or diabetes, and it shouldn't be done with a mental illness either.

OCD is a noun, not an adjective. It's a serious disorder, not a personality trait. In fact, the World Health Organization ranks OCD as one of the 10 most disabling conditions. It is the hardest thing I have ever experienced. But it can be manageable. Therapy and medication have helped improve my quality of life.

During the worst of my OCD as a teenager, I used books as escapism. But I never saw a character just like me, who was fighting her own brain. If I'd read about somebody with OCD, I might have gotten diagnosed sooner. Most of all, I would've felt less alone. So I wrote the book I wish I'd had when I was younger.

In the rare cases where a character has OCD, the story usually focuses on their mental illness. They don't usually get to be the hero in speculative fiction. I wanted to change that. In this story, Cat has severe OCD, but it doesn't define her. It's a huge part of her life and limits what she can do, but she's much more than just her illness. It's part of her, but not all of her. Her romance with Auri doesn't cure her because she doesn't need to be "fixed." Auri loves Cat for who she is, mental illness and all.

If you have a mental illness, please know that it gets better and that you are worthy of all the love in the world. You are not less than, or a burden, or a bad person, or any of the thoughts your mind throws your way. There is hope, and you are worth it.

Resources to learn more about OCD:
International OCD Foundation: iocdf.org
NOCD: treatmyocd.com
Get to Know OCD Podcast (on the NOCD YouTube channel)
Psych Central OCD Resource Directory: psychcentral.com/ocd/ocd-resources
National Alliance on Mental Health: nami.org
OCD From A to Z free blog series: claireoliviagolden.com/mental-health
Turtles All the Way Down book by John Green, and movie adaptation (YA fiction)
The Man Who Couldn't Stop: OCD and the True Story of a Life Lost in Thought by David Adam (nonfiction)

The Unraveled Shawl
Crochet Pattern
Crochet your very own Briars and Roses shawl!

After the events of *Unraveled*, Cat and Auri had a hard time knowing what to do with themselves now that nobody's life was on the line. So Auri started teaching Cat to crochet, and she designed this pattern for her. It's a non-cursed alternative to the Briars and Roses Shawl and is perfect for beginners. Crochet has been an excellent way for me to cope with my anxiety, so here's hoping that Cat finds it beneficial, too.

Of course, your mileage may vary when it comes to curses, so always make sure to keep your eyes out for vengeful faeries. *The Modern Manual of Faeries* by Eleanor Bishop contains some helpful tips and tricks.

Materials

You will need yarn, a crochet hook, and a yarn needle to weave in your ends. You can make this shawl with any weight yarn and the appropriately-sized hook. Gauge is unimportant for this project as long as you're happy with the resulting fabric. If your chains are too tight, go up a hook size; if they're too loose, go down a hook size. I've made several versions of this shawl and will share the details below, but I encourage you to pick a yarn you like and make your own version in the spirit of this book!

For the original version of this design (the one in the pictures), I used approximately 600 yards of a mystery worsted-weight (size 4) yarn that did not have a label and an H (5.00mm) hook.

For the shawl in the photo tutorial, I used two skeins of Red Heart Bambootiful and a G (4.00mm) hook. The yarn is classified as a bulky (size 5) yarn but works up more like a worsted, and it's delightfully silky.

For a super fuzzy and cozy version (not pictured), I used two 8-ounce skeins of Red Heart Hygge in "Powder," which totaled 500 yards. This is a bulky (size 5) yarn and I used a K (6.50mm) hook.

Terminology & Special Stitches

US crochet terms are used in this pattern. Abbreviations used are ch (chain stitch), sl st (slip stitch), and sc (single crochet).

Flower Fringe: This is always worked at the end of a row. Please refer to photo tutorial for clarification.

Ch 8, sl st in 4th ch from hook, forming a small chain loop that you'll work into while making the petals (Photo 1). Ch 4, turn so that you can begin working into the chain loop you just created (Photo 2), sc in chain loop (Photo 3). *Ch 4, sc in chain loop* 4 times - 5 petals made (Photo 4). Ch 4, continue to next row of shawl (Photo 5).

Photo 6 shows a closeup of the flower fringe. You can change the number of petals in your flowers to mix things up a bit. (It's a great exposure therapy exercise for me and Cat, who both like having things in perfect order and symmetry.)

Unraveled Shawl

Row 1: Ch 4, sl st to first ch to form a ring. *Make Flower Fringe, sc in ring* 3 times. *Ch 4, sc in ring* 2 times, ch 2, dc in ring (counts as last ch-4 space) - 3 chain spaces.

Row 2: Make Flower Fringe, turn, sc in first chain space. Ch 4, sc in same chain space. *Ch 4, sc in next chain space* across. When you reach the last chain space, work ch 2, dc into same chain space. Your shawl will increase by 2 chain spaces each row.

Repeat Row 2 until the shawl is as long as you wish it to be, reserving enough yarn for the last row.

Ending Row: Make Flower Fringe, turn, sc in first chain space. Make a second Flower Fringe, sc in same chain space. *Ch 2, sc in next chain space* across, ending with 1 sc in last chain space. Make Flower Fringe, sc in same chain space. Make a second Flower Fringe, sl st in same chain space.

Fasten off and weave in ends. Block if desired.

You are free to do whatever you wish with the things you create from this pattern, but please credit the designer.

Acknowledgements

It is surreal to be writing acknowledgements for my book. From the earliest version of Unraveled back in 2015, to the first edition in 2020, to the version that you are holding in your hands right now, I am forever grateful for all the support I've received along the way.

Thank you a thousand times over to Fractured Mirror Publishing for giving *Unraveled* a home: Emily, Allison, Alex, Carol, and Patterson. And to Ivy for such a beautiful book cover.

To my online friends who offered valuable feedback and encouragement: River, Cloud, filliefanatic (and Sarah), Astri, Mrs. Micawber, Lydia Redwine, Tessonja Odette, and so many more. I may have never met you in person, but I'm grateful to call you my friends.

To the teachers who encouraged me: Deborah Mueller, Travis Grail, Megan Savage, Mary Bartholomew, Jimena Alvarado, Chrystèle Luneau, Kimberly Mukobi, and Christopher Broderick.

I'll always be grateful to my first publisher, Gurt Dog Press, for their support of *Unraveled* back in 2019: Nem, April-Jane, and Linn.

To all the staff at Annie Bloom's Books for their contagious love of books and for an amazing seasonal job while I was in college, with a special shoutout to bookstore cat Molly Bloom. And to the staff at Grand Gesture Books, especially Katherine Morgan, for proving once again that indie bookstores are the best place in the world and for being such positive and joyful people.

To Danielle, Dori, and Dr. Black for the OCD treatment that helped me get my life back.

To my family and friends for your love and support. Nana, thank you for spreading the word to the entire state of Michigan, with an honorable mention to Uncle Jeffrey for buying enough copies to entertain a small city. A special thanks to Anna and Emma for welcoming me into your life for the entirety of Covid lockdown and making me feel at home. Thanks to Grandpa Golden for reading *Unraveled* even though it was totally not your jam; I'm proud to be a third-generation Golden writer. Thank you David and Jeanne for adding it to your bookshelf.

Shimaira, thank you for being my friend in books, cats, yarn, and all the important things in life. I'm so glad that our books brought us together.

Keaton, your texts equally terrify me and delight me. Thank you for being my bestie ever since we sat next to each other that fateful day in our J.R.R. Tolkien class. I think of you every time I see something filled with beans that shouldn't be filled with beans.

Special shoutout to my critique partner and book bestie Julie for the coffee-fueled writing sessions, the unhinged fangirling over our shared favorite books, and the illuminating conversations about how many girls it would take to lift a man's dead body. May we never be arrested for our Internet search history.

To the animals that helped with the writing process, especially: Ruby, Maisie, Daphne, Blanche, Pearl, Clementine, Ginny, Kody, Cow Pigeon, and Bubba. Special thanks to Harriet, my pet chicken who perched on my foot while I wrote and whined her opinion from time to time, and whom I miss every day. And to my emotional support cat Persephone who filled the empty spot in my heart that Harriet left. Thank you for sitting like a gargoyle on the arm of my chair and silently judging what I write.

To my mom, for her unconditional love and support no matter what, for the peanut butter toast when my stomach was upset, for the endless supply of hugs and pep talks, for the handmade blankets that kept me warm during late nights of writing, and for always believing in me.

To my dad, for teaching me the difference between "its" and "it's," for the matching purple sweatshirts, for the stuffed pandas (particularly Bob and Rick), for reading my favorite books so we would have something in common, and for being an idiot with me in the grocery store.

To Audrey, for the late-night conversations, for putting up with me (and the Yarn Blob) as a roommate, for always having my back, for helping me reorganize my bookshelf, and for the beautiful art in this book. I'm lucky to call you not only my sister but my friend.

To Lewis, who gave me the kind of love I thought only existed in books but turned out to be so much better in real life. When *Unraveled* first released, you were my boyfriend, and now I have the honor of calling you my husband. You are a dream come true, and I love you 5ever.

To you, if you're reading this. I hope you see yourself in these characters and that it helped you escape from the real world if only for a little bit. Thank you for reading. Cat and Auri are rooting for you, and so am I.

To God, or the universe, or whatever saw fit to give me so many blessings in my life. I don't take it for granted.

And to Little Claire. I wrote this book for you.

About the Author

CLAIRE OLIVIA GOLDEN likes books, yarn, and the Oxford comma. She graduated summa cum laude from Portland State University with a B.A. in French and English and is an author and fiber artist. Claire lives in Portland, Oregon with her husband and cat.

Visit her online at:
claireoliviagolden.com
IG: @claireoliviagolden